TASK X

TASK X

A PROJECT MOLKA Novel
Fredrick L. Stafford

This is a work of fiction. Names, characters, businesses, places, events, and incidents are either the products of the author's imagination or used in a fictitious manner. Any resemblance to actual persons, living or dead, or to actual events is purely coincidental.

Copyright © 2022 Fredrick L. Stafford
All rights reserved.

No part of this publication may be reproduced, stored in a retrieval system, copied in any form or by any means, electronic, mechanical, photocopying, recording, or otherwise transmitted without written permission from the publisher.

To My Wonderful Readers

Thank you, once again, for your continuing and amazing support of this series!

This will wrap up volume one of the PROJECT MOLKA Series, but she will back at some point in the future.

Until then, please join her as she helps Kang in Book 1 of my new [PENTAD Series!](#)

Please leave me an Amazon review!

Ok, here we go with Task X for our Molka!

Best Regards,
Fredrick

P.S. Please Follow Me on [Facebook!](#)

Visitation Room
County Jail
South Florida
Sixteen Months Prior

"I was in the military," Molka said to Nadia. "A helicopter pilot serving with special forces. My unit was sent to eliminate the leadership of an extremist group—I won't say which group or in which country—who kidnapped and executed two of our soldiers. The mission was successful. At least, we thought it was. On the way out, we took ground fire from surviving members of this group. My helicopter was hit several times. One of the hits—a lucky shot—caused a sudden hydraulics failure. No chance I could get us back into friendly territory. I brought us down with a controlled crash. Everyone survived."

"While we waited for another helicopter to extract us, we we're assaulted by at least twenty-five militants. We engaged them in a firefight. Two members of our team were wounded. The rescue helicopter arrived. The enemy closed to within twelve meters of our perimeter. One of our team members, Sergeant Weizmann, removed a door gun from the helicopter and charged them. They ran. The rest of us got on board. Sergeant Weizmann ran to join us and got hit. We saw him go down. It looked fatal. They were right behind him and started firing at us again. We barely got out. Another team returned for Sergeant Weizmann's remains later, but his body was gone. We thought locals buried him."

Molka continued. "We found out later the leadership of the extremist group wasn't there during our mission. But some of their family members were. An explosive charge used to open a reinforced door killed an eight-year-old boy, the son of one of the leaders. We took this hard. We were told there would be no non-combatants present."

"We also learned Sergeant Weizmann didn't die that night. The extremist group carried him off, got him medical care, and saved his life. When he was well enough to talk, they tortured him. Sergeant Weizmann was strong and brave and stood up to it for days, but he broke in the end, like everyone under professional torture. They videoed parts of his torture and his execution. They sent our government the tape. I heard it's unwatchable."

"A year to the day after that mission, six simultaneous explosions went off in my country. Each one killed a family member from my team that night. It was later revealed that Sergeant Weizmann had given the extremists some of our names while under torture."

A single tear escaped each of Molka's eyes and crawled down her cheeks, but her voice remained strong. "One of the explosions, a car bomb, killed my eleven-year-old sister Janetta. It also killed the foster parents she lived with at the time. I never got to meet them. They were taking her to the first day at her new school. I should have been there for that. She sent me a picture of herself in the outfit she would wear. It was a white dress with pink flowers on it. She wore a pink bow in her hair. She was smiling. She had just got braces put on her teeth. I still have the picture. It's on my desk in my office. I eat lunch with her every day."

"So, you asked why did I take this job? The person, the monster, the one who took away my little Janetta, still lives. And so do I. And I can't live with that."

CHAPTER ONE

**California
Northwest of Lake Tahoe
Sunday, July 17th
3:47 PM**

"And that's the real story of my very first kill, 14 years ago next month."

Molka didn't offer any verbal or physical reactions during the storyteller's disgusting, horrifying, gory, blood-drenched recounting of his very first kill.

Because her mind fixated on how not to be his latest kill.

And at that point, she gave herself one chance in 1000.

She occupied the passenger seat in a moving semi-trailer truck with no trailer attached, still outfitted in her all-black tactical ensemble from the previous night's Project Kaelee extraction op.

Since she awoke minutes before, her focus remained out the front windshield and on the two-lane-wide, gravel road they traveled, which bisected large, remote, pine forest-covered hills, and she considered opening her door and leaping out.

However, her front-cuffed hands and a modified seat belt restraint system pinning her to the seat at the waist, chest, and neck prevented her surprise exit and escape from the tale-telling truck driver to her left.

The late 30s white male, presented as plain-spoken, plain-faced, medium built with brown eyes and hair, and dressed plainly in work boots, blue jeans, and a white pocket t-shirt. And if you passed him on the street, if you even noticed him, you would think him a plain, non-threatening-type guy, which probably was exactly how he wanted it.

He added a disturbing remembrance to his story's ending. "And I just remembered, my first kill was a real corn-fed and hand-spanked Nebraska girl, I'm here to tell you."

Molka glared over at him. "What was her name?"

He grinned, ecstatic. "Debra Ann. My Debra Ann for eternity. And soon, you'll be my Molka for eternity."

Molka returned her gaze to the windshield and a subject change. "What is this road, anyway?"

"It's actually a firebreak. Lots of wildfires in this area."

"It's very well maintained for a firebreak," she said.

"Yeah, they also use it to move firefighting equipment on, which makes it very convenient for me to move my rig on to drive to my graveyards."

"You said graveyards, as in plural."

He gave a proud nod. "That's right. I run coast to coast and border to border, so I have graveyards all over the place."

"How long was I out?"

"Over eight hours." He time-checked a digital clock on the truck's instrument panel. "Closer to nine hours now."

She glanced at him again. "Are you the one who hit me from behind?"

"Yeah."

"What did you hit me with?"

He reached his left hand next to his seat and held up a short, black leather-covered truncheon. "This handy brute."

"Thanks for at least not splitting my head open with it."

"Oh, I have lots of practice with Little Thumper here. That's what I call this. I just use him to put them to sleep so they can wake up and play." He placed it back where he got it. "You'll see what I mean by that in a bit."

She ignored the sick taunt and viewed her purse and luggage case on the floorboard next to her tac-boots. "Nice of you to grab my stuff for me."

"That was Raziela's request. She said everything you brought to Arizona needs to go with you where you're going."

"You mean to a grave in your graveyard?"

He offered another ecstatic grin. "Comfortable?"

She raised sarcastic eyebrows. "Very. Nice of you to cuff my hands in front. Much easier on my poor little sore shoulders."

"Raziela told me to do that too. She said you were her favorite whore she used as a sweet little honey pot, and she had some affection for you for that. So, not to make you suffer any more than necessary. Unfortunately for you, I can't promise you that will actually happen."

"Are my friends she shot dead?"

"Honestly, I don't know. Right after I hit you, Raziela helped me haul your ass out to the truck, and then we both hauled ass."

Molka said, "You're obviously one of Raziela's contractors. So it's hard for me to believe she didn't tell you why she shot them."

"I'm not a contractor. I'm a self-employed, owner-operator, long haul trucker."

"That's your public persona because you're a disgusting disgrace to all real truckers everywhere. But what's your dark side hustle with Raziela?"

He laughed. "Dark side hustle. You're a funny one, Molka. Maybe the funniest one yet. I'll just say Raziela throws me a girl once in a while that needs to vanish."

Molka studied his face closer. "I think I've seen you before. Where do I know you from?"

He smiled. "Funny and smart, a quality victim. You've made my day. You saw me at Grammy and Grampy's Family Restaurant, main street Miracle City. I watched you eat breakfast there every morning since I arrived in that town a week ago."

"Yes. I remember seeing you there. You seemed like a plain, non-threatening-type guy."

"That's what they all say. Right up until I'm not. Now, we'll be there in just a bit, and I have some thinking to do. So, keep quiet while I do my thinking, and then I'll let you have your final words."

He placed both hands atop the big steering wheel and stared straight ahead with calm, pitiless eyes.

Molka took the time to replay the events from the past 12 hours. From getting Kaelee out of Pirro's compound, the wild pursuit and shootout with his men literally into the river, the handsome hero Chase Stephenson rescuing them from a watery death, hearing Kaelee and Chase being shot in the lake house's living room, seeing the smiling shooter Raziela on the couch telling her she was next, to waking up under a serial killer truck driver's sickening control.

Bringing her to the long odds of seeing another 12 hours.
Time to employ critical thinking and try to survive.
Study your surroundings.
See what you can use to your advantage.
One thing leaped into her mind.
The truck's interior looked immaculate.
He obviously took pride in its appearance.
It served as his business and business office.
He wouldn't want to trash it with his hobby's activities.
And shooting or stabbing her inside it would be messy.
Of course, he could always strangle her.
But that risked her soiling herself and his pristine interior.
Maybe a worse clean up job than blood and tissue.
So he would take her out of the truck.
To inflict his torture, rape, and killing fun.
Perfect.

A few minutes later, he brought the truck to a stop on the desolate firebreak road shrouded by the pine covered hills. "We're here." He pointed past Molka out her side window at the tree line. "Your final resting place is already dug about 10 yards that way. I chose the spot well. You'll never be found. Now have your say. Start the begging and hysterics and screaming. The louder and more desperate, the better for me. No one can hear you way out here, and I love it."

She offered a slight grin. "I think you're the one who better start the begging and hysterics and screaming."

He smiled. "Why should I?"

"Because I'm not going into that grave. You probably are."

"Ok, funny, smart girl, I'll play your little, stalling the inevitable, game before we play my inflicting the unbearable game. How do I end up in that grave?"

"The people I call to get rid of your body will likely use it since you chose the spot so well."

He kept up his smile. "And what will these people you're going to call do with my pride and joy here?"

"Not sure. They might take it to another location and torch it. Or keep it to use on another job."

"Is that right? And before you call these people to bury my body and steal my truck, how am I going to end up dead?"

Molka locked a confident stare on him. "I'm going to slash open your carotid artery."

"Oh, really?" He chuckled.

She added a confident nod to her stare. "Yes. And then your last moments will be the most terrifying you've ever experienced, just like many of your victims. Think of them as you die."

He chuckled, arrogant again. "You're a real piece of work, Molka. But considering all my skinning knives are locked up tight in the exterior storage compartment under the sleeper and me, and Raziela gave you a deep weapon's pat down, including me getting my hands deep inside your panties—"

Molka interrupted. "I'll remember you told me that when I cut you."

He grinned and continued. "The only thing you have to cut me with is your smart-ass tongue. Until I remove it, or I could just gag your mouth with something you may not like."

"I'll remember you said that too."

He laughed. "I must say, of all my victims, you're the calmest, bravest, most defiant of them all. Of course, when I go to work on you with the pliers and hammer, your attitude will adjust a bit."

"If you're putting me in that grave, shouldn't we get out now?"

"Yeah, but first, I've got to put you out again." He reached beside his seat, retrieved, held up Little Thumper, and smiled. "I'll be right over there."

She grinned. "I can't wait."

TASK X

After he jumped out and closed the door, Molka used all her strength to pull her cuffed wrists toward her shirt's neckline.

The restraining belts dug into and scraped her forearms.

Her finger's reached for the neck cord of Loto's good luck necklace.

They found it.

Flipped the necklace's flower pendant from under her shirt.

Grabbed the flower's bottom.

Pulled out the small, razor-sharp dagger.

Closed her hands over it.

And held them chest level in a praying position.

Her door opened. He climbed onto the fiberglass boarding steps under it and poked his plain-faced, smiling head inside. "Guess who?" He viewed her hands. "Oh, you want to pray now. Too late for that. But go ahead and pray and plead." He smiled again. "I want to watch."

A second's fraction later, her hands fired forward blade first, and she slashed open his left carotid artery.

His face transfigured into vivid terror.

His warm blood spewed on her right cheek.

She leaned her face away.

He opened his mouth to scream.

Nothing came out.

He collapsed backward and dropped onto the dirt road.

It took Molka about five struggling minutes to position the blades to cut through the three belts.

Freed, she wiped the blood from her cheek on her shirt's hem, raised the blade to an attacking position in front of her, jumped to the dirt next to the splayed on his back serial killer, and prepared to cut him some more.

But his open-mouthed, terror-filled face had become a death mask.

Molka suppressed an urge to kick his face in anyway. "Picked the wrong victim this time, didn't you, you sick bastard?"

She bent and wiped the blood on the blade on his pants leg and placed the blade back into the necklace.

Thank you, Loto. Again!

She knelt beside the trucker, found the handcuff key in his right front pocket, and spent another five minutes struggling to position the key to unlock her left wrist.

Left wrist free, she quickly uncuffed her right wrist, tossed the key and cuffs atop his body, climbed back into the truck's passenger side, retrieved her purse, dropped back down, removed her phone, dialed 911, and put the phone to her ear. "I want to report a double shooting... The address is 5204 Lake Terrace Drive, Miracle City, Arizona... Oh, can you connect me to the 911 operator there... Yes, I can hold... Hello, yes, a double shooting... The address is 5204 Lake Terrace Drive... A 28-year-old female and mid-30s male... About eight hours ago... Yes, I can hold...."

While she waited, she used the map app to identify her current location because she had no idea where she was.

The 911 operator came back on and gave Molka updated info. "Oh. They have?... Any word on the victim's condition?... I understand. Yes, I'll contact the Miracle City Police now. Thank you."

She ended the call and made a video call to Azzur.

His face—as tired and haggard as you would expect for being awoke at about 2 AM local time—appeared on screen. "Are you on the way home?"

"No," she said. "Can you get a GPS lock on this phone?"

"I have had one on it since it was issued to you."

"Ok. Send a cleanup team to this location."

He said, "A cleanup team or a cleaning team?"

"Cleanup. I've already done the cleaning." She faced the screen toward the trucker's blood-drenched face and shirt.

Azzur sighed. "So, I see. Stand by."

His face left the screen.

Molka sat on the truck's boarding step and used her breathing exercises to shut down her still-pumping adrenaline pump.

A few minutes later, Azzur appeared back on screen. "The closest location to you where I can dispatch a cleanup team from is San Francisco, about three hours away."

"Ok. I'll wait right here for them. I don't think I'll be disturbed by anyone unless there's a sudden wildfire. And, um, this dead bastard admitted to me he murdered a girl from the state of Nebraska named Debra Ann 14 years ago. Maybe get word to the authorities there so her family can get some closure and comfort."

"Understood. Stand by." His face left the screen again. A few moments later, it came back. "The cleanup team is on the way. Give me a full incident report."

"That can wait. I have something more important to talk to you about now."

"You just killed someone. What could possibly be more important?"

Molka's face assumed a serious demeanor. "I have something I need you to do for me. And if you refuse, I'll come and kill you next."

CHAPTER TWO

Private Jet Leased by the Counsel
Flying Over Central Idaho
11:44 PM

"Chase Stephenson Bail Bonds, Chase Stephenson speaking."

"Hello, Molka speaking."

"Molka! Thank goodness! You, ok? Where are you?"

"Yes. On my way home."

She sat with her phone to her ear, relaxed in a butter-soft, cream-colored, leather luxury cabin seat inside a Gulfstream private jet chartered in San Francisco to bring her home as ordered by the Counsel director when he learned about the bizarre and traumatic ending to Project Molka's ninth task.

She also dressed travel-comfortable in a cute, new, white with black stripes tracksuit and new white cross-trainer sneakers she purchased at the airport after the contractor cleanup team Azzur dispatched dropped her off there. Her hair was ponytailed, and she wore her black-framed glasses.

Chase continued: "Deputy Chief DeLuca's been burning up my phone all day asking if I knew what happened to you, where you were, and if I knew the shooter."

"What did you tell him?"

"The truth. A woman I'd never seen before shot me. I went down, knocked my head on the coffee table, and passed out. When I woke up, the shooter and you were gone."

"And you're back at work already."

"Of course. Super sore, though."

She smiled, impressed. "You're all man, Chase Stephenson."

Chase: "Fortunately for my bills, criminal behavior never stops."

"And fortunately for your life, the Level IIIA vest you smartly wore under your shirt, stops nine-millimeter."

"How did you know about that? Oh, never mind, your family has resources. Did you talk to Kaelee yet?"

"No," Molka said. "She's still in the ICU, heavily sedated."

"They told me she's going to make it. Is that true?"

"Yes. They think so. The round glanced off her sternum and then glanced off a rib before it lodged in her right lung."

Chase: "Ballistic trajectory is a funny thing sometimes."

"It definitely is. I've seen some crazy ricochets and bounces that have spared lives and taken lives with no regard to intent."

Chase: "After I was shot first, she must have flinched slightly to her right before being hit. Which saved her from being hit in the heart."

"And I understand you saved her life by calling emergency medical and giving her first aid."

"Those paramedics saved her. Do you know the shooter?"

Molka's jaw tightened. "Yes. I. Do."

"Care to tell me who and why it happened?"

"Not at the moment. Sorry."

Chase: "I think it wasn't personal against me and I just got caught up in some of your family's business."

She grinned. "Intelligent and handsome, my two weaknesses."

Chase: "I'm just glad you're ok."

"I'm glad you're ok too. And glad you'll get to take your son to that Dodgers game for his birthday tomorrow."

"That's all I could think about on the way to the hospital. Any big plans when you get home?"

Molka gave a slow, determined nod. "Yes. The biggest plans I've ever made."

FREDRICK L. STAFFORD

WEDNESDAY
JULY 20TH

CHAPTER THREE

Fitness Center
Azorei Hen Neighborhood
Tel Aviv
4:37 AM

Nice to be back in her old routine, even if just for a few days. And in the pre-program era, her predawn workouts—with no one else there to stare at her tall, lean, muscular body, ask questions about her intense routine, or make lame propositions—always set the tone for a positive, productive day in her veterinary office.

Of course, she would have preferred to have met with Azzur as soon as she got home. She even demanded it. But Raziela's outrageous actions against her, Kaelee, and Chase in Arizona made Azzur unavailable.

He was summoned, along with the department chief, to Jerusalem to personally brief the prime minister and then held over for another day of meetings with the prime minister's staff.

So her meeting with him got pushed back until 9 AM that morning.

Wearing a black tank top over black shorts and white cross-trainers, she sipped from her water bottle, leaned against the

TASK X

Smith Machine after a final set of heavy squats, and planned some cardio to finish the workout.

Something high intensity to build up stamina for the upcoming events she looked forward to. So would it be the battle ropes or the assault bike? Or…15 high-intensity seconds on the assault bike, jump off, and go straight into 15 high-intensity seconds with the battle ropes, followed by 15 seconds' rest. Then repeat for 10 cycles.

As she considered the challenging choice, the nostalgic sadness of her old neighborhood 24-hour fitness center made her grin.

Same old squeaky pec deck. Same old all-sports channel on the old wall-mounted monitors. The same old upbeat dance mix music on the sound system. And the same old bleach, ammonia, sweat smell. How do you even get such a combination to be permanent?

The only thing that wasn't the same old thing was another vehicle other than hers in the parking lot: a white SUV arriving about five minutes after she did.

She noticed it, glancing out the large front windows as she sat on the floor stretching between sets. But instead of parking next to her car in the many available front-row spaces outside the entrance, the SUV backed into the parking lot's far side directly across from the entrance, which seemed somewhat odd.

And even odder, an hour later, the driver still hadn't exited to come inside to do their work out. And since all the other businesses in the little strip mall around the fitness center didn't open for hours, the SUV driver must have come to work out, right?

Wrong.

Years of being peeped on gave her another reason.

The driver wasn't even a gym member.

And they were early.

Attractive young girls from the nearby university would arrive soon for their pre-class workouts. Molka passed them coming in as she left many times over the years.

And the peeper's early arrival earned a little bonus show in her.

Ugh. What a sleazy, skeezy week. First, the serial killer trucker and now a serial peeper.

Maybe walk across the parking lot and confront the degenerate? Tell them to get control of their sickness and their life before things spiral out of control, and they end up with their carotid artery slashed open and buried by strangers in a remote grave, never to be found.

But she wanted to get her cardio in and get home as soon as possible for a shower and a good breakfast before fighting traffic for an hour on her drive across the city for her most important meeting with Azzur ever.

Fifteen minutes later, Molka peeled her drenched body from the floor near the battle ropes. She pushed herself through 11 high-intensity cycles: ten for the workout and the eleventh for her little Janetta.

She put her water bottle and towel in her gym bag on the floor, zipped it up, slung it over her left shoulder, exited the building, ignored the peeper, got into her loyal little white Toyota, started it, and headed for her apartment.

And a block away from the fitness center, a rearview mirror glance showed the peeper became a follower, maintaining about a 15-car length distance.

She sighed, disgusted. "Unbelievable."

What to do?

Obviously, the safe and sensible thing to do would be not to allow them to trail her to her apartment.

The safe and sensible thing to do would be to pull over in a well-lit public area and stop.

And if the follower followed her to this spot, the safe and sensible thing to do would be to call the police and report the suspicious activity. And give them a description of the vehicle and the driver and license plate number, if possible.

TASK X

And then the safe and sensible thing to do would be to listen to the police's advice which would likely be to stay where she was secured in her car, and hopefully, the follower would leave.

And if they didn't leave, the safe and sensible thing to do, they would tell her, is drive to the nearest police station, which would undoubtedly scare the follower off, and then the police would perhaps conduct a cursory investigation.

But the safe and sensible things to do wouldn't send the message she wished to convey to the follower, now to be considered a stalker in her mind, which was:

You picked the wrong girl to stalk this morning!

Instead, she would give them the scare of their lives and put it in their head for life that not all their victims will be victimized.

Molka reached into her purse on the passenger seat, removed her faithful Beretta 96A1, and laid it in her lap. And since she and the stalker were the only vehicles in sight at that hour, there would be no time like the present for the intervention.

She slammed on the brakes, screeched to a stop, put the car in reverse, sped backward toward the stalker—who had stopped in their lane—and when she was about 10-meters from collision, she jerked the wheel hard right and spun around 180 degrees, executing a perfect J-turn, to face the white SUV at a five-meter distance.

Before the stalker could react, Molka burst from her car with her weapon, assumed a combat shooting stance, aimed at the driver through the front windshield, where she found out the male driver had a male passenger.

Peeping/stalking in pairs?

She yelled: "Driver! You and your peep-stalk partner step out slowly and hold your hands very high!"

Both doors opened and the stocky, bearded, dark-haired driver and the boney, clean-shaven, fair-haired passenger complied with her slow and hands high demand while offering her nervous grins

Grins from behind which revealed familiar faces:

The stocky man being Dov, and the boney one Jaron.

Two of Azzur's men from the pre-Traitor days who she engaged in a one-sided, violent encounter one night in her office parking lot prior to her second task.

Molka smirked at their grins. "Ha. Look who it is. And stalking me in another dark parking lot, no less. Come back for round two, guys. Even though you both didn't make it through round one last time."

A black t-shirt and jeans wearing Dov said, "Easy, Molka. We don't want any more trouble with you."

A blue polo and jeans-wearing Jaron said, "That goes double for me, Molka."

She lowered the weapon but stayed on alert. "Then why were you watching me? And yes, I know, Azzur told you to do it."

Jaron said, "He ordered us to keep eyes on you around the clock starting today."

Her face became perplexed. "Tell me why? No. Wait. Let's get out of the middle of the street first." She pointed to a closed pharmacy half a block behind them. "Meet me over there."

Two minutes later, with the two vehicles parked driver window to driver window, Molka leaned out hers and asked driver Dov: "Why does Azzur want you to keep your eyes on me?"

"Jaron misspoke," Dov said. "He meant Azzur wants us to keep eyes out for you. For your safety."

Her face became perplexed again. "My safety? What do I have to worry about in my own neighborhood?"

Dov said, "Azzur didn't tell us. You'll have to ask him."

"Ok. I'll go ask him right now."

Jaron said, "You mean at your 9 AM meeting?"

"No. I mean now. Right now. And you two will take me to him."

During Azzur's younger days serving as a Counsel covert operative and assassin, he got his name placed on more than a few kill lists. And once, in a rare glib moment, without divulging the targets, he told Molka who held a few of the kill lists he appeared on. Then it wasn't hard for her to match notable assassinations with those holders and be surprised he still lived.

It probably surprised him too. Which is why he carried a not unreasonable paranoia and caused him to keep several apartments around the city and never spend more than two nights in any one. And instead of her trying to follow Dov and Jaron through the city to Azzur's hideout choice that night, it would be easier to have them take her straight to Azzur and afterward bring her back to her car left in the pharmacy parking lot less than two blocks from her home.

She rode in their SUV's backseat, racking her mind for why Azzur wanted 24-hour protection assigned to her in her home country. Part of an elaborate cover story he was building as a pretext to deny her request at the meeting? She wouldn't put it past him. But she wouldn't let him get away with it either.

After a few silent moments, Dov spoke up. "Molka, we never got to explain why we treated you the way we did when we first met. But please understand we were under Azzur's orders to do all we did. He wanted to toughen you up for the tough tasks ahead."

Jaron said, "But we discovered you were more than tough enough. We've both been on indefinite medical leave since we got out of the hospital from what you did to us that night."

Dov said, "I still only have about 60 percent use of my left hand after the butchering wrist lock you put on me. They think that's all I'll ever have."

Jaron said, "And I still get dizzy spells from the fractures your knee and kicks put on my jaw and skull."

Based on their threats that night, was her brutal preemptive surprise attack on them warranted? Yes.

But then, did she let her emotions get away from her and overdo the follow-up beatings she inflicted on them? Yes.

She sighed and said, "Ok. I shouldn't apologize because your injuries were all Azzur's fault for him sending you to harass me like that. But...I'm sorry."

Dov said, "No apologies necessary, Molka. We know what we signed up for. Just glad you didn't kill us that night."

Jaron said, "That goes double for me, Molka."

She sighed again. "I'm glad I didn't kill you both too."

But it was closer than you'll ever know.

CHAPTER FOUR

Azzur's safehouse for the night was located 15 kilometers and 15 minutes south from their starting point in Jaffe: a beige stucco with a red-tiled roof, two-story townhouse sitting a block from the beach in a nicer neighborhood.

Dov parked in a short driveway fronting a closed, white metal gate in a tall, white privacy fence. A security camera atop the fence monitored the gate, and a stainless-steel intercom speaker was mounted to the gate's right.

"Ok," Molka said. "Let's all go ring the buzzer and wake him up."

Dov and Jaron exchanged nervous glances, and Jaron said, "Are you sure you don't want to call him and tell him we're here? That intercom makes a very loud, annoying alert sound inside the house, and he hates it when we've used it."

She opened her door. "And I hate it when he has two of his minions following me around without telling me. So…." She stepped out with her purse slung across her body and moved toward the front gate.

Dov and Jaron followed her.

She reached the gate, pushed the black call button below the intercom speaker, and looked up at the security camera.

After a long beat, Azzur's voice answered from the intercom speaker: "Good morning, Molka."

Molka answered. "Time for us to talk again."

"Yes, it is. And we shall, in my office at our 9 AM appointment time."

Dov leaned forward and spoke toward the speaker. "Sorry, she spotted us and insisted we bring her here now."

Azzur: "Molka, I will discuss this at our meeting in a few hours."

She shook her head. "No. I'm wide awake and fighting mad. So I'm rescheduling our meeting for right now, right here. Are you coming out, or am I coming in?"

Pause.

Azzur: "Dov, Jaron, wait in your vehicle. Molka, come in."

A moment later, a metallic click sounded, and the gate auto-opened to the left.

Molka entered and walked up the driveway past a dark metallic gray BMW toward the front door. Before she reached it, it opened to Azzur wearing a white t-shirt over gray sweatpants and bare feet.

She walked past him, entered onto a beautiful parquet floor, and into a nicely decorated living room somewhat spoiled with a smoker's reek.

He closed the door behind them. "We will talk in the kitchen."

She followed him into an all-stainless-steel appliances kitchen and helped herself to a wooden chair at a large wooden dining table.

He moved to a coffee maker on the counter. "Would you like some?"

"No thanks. I'll take a bottled water, though. I dehydrated myself with some crazy cardio this morning."

"All I have to drink is coffee and energy drinks."

"Coffee, energy drinks, and cigarettes. You know, one of these days, high nicotine and caffeine consumption will cause your heart to say, you win. I quit."

He leaned his back against the kitchen counter and faced her. "Yes, and until that day, I get to enjoy high nicotine and caffeine consumption."

Molka raised her eyebrows, sarcastic. "There is that, I guess. Now before I ask you if your meetings in Jerusalem told you why Raziela shot Kaelee and my friend Chase and tried to have me killed, why did you send your guys to spy on me?"

He turned away, opened a cabinet door, removed a white mug and glass ashtray, placed them on the counter, and watched the coffeemaker work. "By the way, through our friends in the NIB, I got word to the Nebraska authorities about the truck drivers' confession of the murdered girl. They have his name and asked you to give them an affidavit detailing what he told you. They promised to keep your name redacted until a potential trial. Of course, there will never be a trial because he will never be found. And you are under no obligation to provide them with an affidavit."

"I'll do it," she said. "If they agree to share it with the girl's family. Maybe give them a little closure through comfort, as I said."

"I will pass that along."

"Thank you. Now, why did you send your guys to spy on me?"

Azzur poured a cup of coffee, picked up the ashtray, sat opposite her, and placed the mug and ashtray before him. "Not to spy on you, to protect you."

She sat back and folded her arms across her chest. "Ha. And then who's going to protect them?"

"Your encounter with them notwithstanding, they are quite capable."

"I'll have to take your word for it. Why do you think I need protection."

He sipped his coffee. "From Raziela, of course."

Molka uncrossed her arms and leaned forward. "She's the one who needs protection from me when I find her. She's back here? Where exactly is she?"

"This country us the only place we are certain she is not. It is her co-conspirators that she can send after you that you need protection from."

A sly smile crossed her lips. "Well, I already took care of one of them."

"He was not one of her co-conspirators." Azzur reached into his sweatpants pocket, removed a cigarette pack and a silver lighter, lit up, and blew smoke. "Prepare yourself for a shock."

Molka said, "That's psychologically not possible for humans. So just say it straight out."

"Raziela was part of the Traitors."

A shockwave crossed Molka's face. "I would say you're joking. But you never joke. Are you starting now?"

Azzur's face remained unamused.

She shook her head, still stunned. "I thought she might have snapped when she got fired and came to kill her co-workers, Kaelee and me. But I would never have imagined her betraying our country in such a devastating way."

"No one could, which is why she is the last to be uncovered. When she was dismissed from the Counsel, she knew her contacts with our enemies—her co-conspirators—would have no more reason to shield her identity and would offer to sell her out to us for an exorbitant sum and that we would be happy to pay it. Which we did."

He sipped his coffee again and continued. "She correctly deduced you would be the one we would send to eliminate her. And obviously, she came back to Arizona to kill you first and decided to contract the job out to the serial killer truck driver. After his failure at your hands, she will undoubtably try to have you killed again, anywhere, anytime. Which is why I assigned you protection."

"Ok. I can appreciate that now." Molka's eyes drifted past Azzur in thought. "But that's not actually what happened in Arizona. It's all hitting me just this instant. Kaelee and Chase were only inconvenient witnesses who showed up with me at the lake house that Raziela wanted to get rid of. But she didn't want me to die there too. And so she used her serial killer trucker friend to take me for a long ride and keep me occupied for a few hours to give her a head start to disappear."

Azzur paused his mug at the lips. "Explain why you think that to be the case."

Molka continued. "She didn't tell the trucker about my capabilities. She told him I was a prostitute she used to honey pot people. And she told him to cuff me in front and ensure I was comfortable on my last ride. And she made him take my purse and all my stuff with me so I could access my encrypted phone to get myself extracted."

He flicked ash. "So, you are saying she was reasonably sure you would be able to neutralize your captor and escape?"

Molka nodded. "Yes."

"Why would she want to put you in such a position?"

"Maybe she thought it would give me one last test. And if I passed it, it would prove me worthy."

"Worthy of what?"

Her eyes refocused on Azzur. "To come after her and try to kill her. This is now a sick game for her. She's gone crazy."

"If all that is true, or regardless, you will indeed go after and try to kill her." He puffed and blew smoke again. "Your final task is to call the final Traitor, Raziela, into account."

Molka shook her head. "I don't need a task to do that. That's now a personal matter."

"All the better." Azzur stood. "Report to me in my office at the previously scheduled time, and we will discuss the task in detail."

"Apparently," she said, "the demand I made right before I left the US was something you didn't take seriously."

"You did not make a demand. You made a threat to kill me. And I let it pass as merely adrenaline-fueled rhetoric after a highly traumatizing event not to be taken seriously."

She flashed him a serious stare. "I was serious."

"Therefore, if I do not modify our agreement and give you the identity and current location of the one who killed your younger sister immediately so you can go get your vengeance before you complete your tenth task, you will kill me."

"Yes. So will you meet my demand?"

"I will not."

Molka reached into her purse with her right hand, removed the Beretta, placed it on the table with her hand resting on the grip, and kept her serious stare on Azzur's face.

Azzur locked his eyes on the weapon, and he sat back down, removed a fresh cigarette from the pack, lit it, inhaled, blew smoke, brought his gaze back to Molka's stare, and said, "I know the real reason you are making this threat."

"Is your no, final?"

His eyes remained locked on the weapon. "The real reason you are making this threat is that you are scared. Scared that Raziela may kill you before you can kill her. And if so, your younger sister's death will never be avenged. Correct?"

She gripped the pistol. "Last chance. Is your no, final?"

He gave an unafraid nod. "It is. Kill me if you must."

Molka smirked and sighed, and placed her weapon back in her purse. "Ok. You were right. My threat to kill you was merely adrenaline-fueled rhetoric after a highly traumatizing event. But the underlying demand remains. So I'll have to use my other option."

He inhaled and blew smoke. "You have planned a contingency for my denial?"

"One of the many things I've learned from you these past few years is that no plan is complete until you have contingencies for it."

He cocked his head to the right. "Did I indeed teach you that?"

"Yes. So this will be your own fault."

"And what is your contingency?"

"I'm going over your head and cashing in some of my popularity with the Counsel's upper management."

He sipped more coffee. "Please elaborate."

She said, "The department chief is very impressed by me and a big fan. He told me so in a beautifully written letter I received from him in the hospital after Australia. He also said to feel free to ask if there was anything he could ever do for me. I thought he was just being nice. But I'm going to call him on it. And I think he'll choose me over you." She grinned. "Nothing personal."

Azzur waved a dismissive hand. "Of course not. And do not take it personally when your request is denied again. I enjoyed dinner with the chief and his lovely wife, Hannah, last night. You were his main topic of discussion. He was ecstatically enthusiastic about his most admired Project Molka delivering the *coup de grâce* on the last living Traitor, Raziela, and finally closing this dark chapter for the Counsel and the country. He even mentioned he is already preparing his report to the director."

Molka shrugged. "Ok. Then I'll go over the department chief's head and talk to the director."

He inhaled and blew smoke. "And when will you do this?"

"Today."

A slight, smug smile crossed his lips. "You will request a meeting with the director today and expect him to see you?"

"Yes. I've met him before. He's a big fan of mine too. And I think he'll also choose me over you." She smiled smug at Azzur. "Nothing personal."

He stubbed out his half-smoked cigarette and stood again. "Project Molka, will you never learn?"

"Learn what?"

"That arrogance is where confidence goes to die."

# CHAPTER FIVE

**Counsel Headquarters
Office of the Deputy Director
Tel Aviv
3:59 PM**

The all-business female secretary in the outer office spoke into her headset. "Yes, sir. I'll send her right in." She turned her attention to Molka, seated in a waiting area across the room, and said, "The deputy director will see you now. First door on the left."

Molka rose, styling her black, slim-cut Prada pants suit over black leather flats. Her hair was ponytailed, she wore her black-framed glasses and carried a small black purse. An ensemble she kept from her second task's "costumes." And the last time she wore it was her first meeting with Raziela, which could be a bad omen. But it was the only thing in her current closet to give the professional look she wished to convey.

She crossed the room to the hallway on the secretary's left, moved to the first door on the left, opened it, and entered a large conference room.

A long, high-polished, dark wood conference table featuring 20 high-backed, black leather seats anchored the room. The three near walls mounted over a dozen large monitors tuned to various world news channels, and a movie theater-style screen comprised the far wall displaying a blue background and the official, white-colored crest of the Counsel.

How many life-changing, nation-changing, world-changing decisions came from briefings given in that room?

And Molka's turn had come.

Beside the table's far end seat stood a tall, fit man in his 50s with a gray military-style haircut over striking blue eyes and a tanned face with a prominent nose. He wore a white, long-sleeved dress shirt rolled to the elbows and a blue tie over dark blue dress pants.

Molka knew of the man by his esteem and legend.

He offered her a slight smile. "Good afternoon, Molka. I'm David Shiloah, Counsel deputy director."

She reflexively came to semi-attention. "Yes, sir. Your reputation proceeds you. And may I say, sir, your previous service with the Unit was very inspirational to me."

He nodded, humble. "And your current service with the Counsel is very inspirational to me. Bringing in Gazi Sago and Aden Luck back-to-back will be studied and admired by this organization after we are both long gone."

"Thank you, sir."

He folded his dark-haired arms across his chest. "Don't thank me yet. Because I'm about to temper the good news you just received in your meeting with the director."

"Sir?"

"In other words, putting realism on the expectations emitting from the director's office is my job."

"I see," she said.

"However, first, as promised, the current location of your target. He gestured to the seat to his right. "Please sit down."

Molka moved into the swivel leather seat and sat.

The deputy director sat in the end seat beside her and swiveled to face the theater-style screen. His right hand held a small black remote, which he pointed at the screen and brought up a satellite photo showing a large body of water marked South China Sea with a black-lettered white label.

TASK X

He viewed the screen and spoke. "The South China Sea encompasses 1.4 million square miles, making it almost one and a half times bigger than the Mediterranean. It's a key commercial gateway that sees one-third of the world's shipping pass through it each year, accounting for multiple trillions in trade. It also holds 12 percent of the world's fish catch and vast reserves of crude oil and natural gas beneath it."

"For decades, China and neighboring Southeast Asian nations have disputed territorial claims in the South China Sea largely centering around this small group of islands, the Spratly Islands." He zoomed the satellite image in to show a group of small islands.

"In the more recent years, China—obviously the dominant power in the region, and claiming national security concerns—began building artificial islands atop reefs in the Spratly Islands and then constructed military bases on them."

Molka spoke up. "I've heard something about this. Those militarized islands are China's way of telling the US Navy to stay out of the South China Sea, right?"

He answered with a diplomatic face. "That conflict with our American friends is not within the purview of the Counsel to comment on, officially."

"Yes, sir. I understand."

He continued. "However, some feel that if a confrontation between the US and China were to occur, the South China Sea would be a very likely flashpoint."

"Needless to say, US intelligence keeps a close watch on these artificial island bases. Some of which are quite large and feature aircraft landing strips, harbors, missile defense systems, troop garrisons, and perhaps most importantly, highly advanced radar systems."

"Many of these islands are known by the name of the reefs they were built upon, such as Johnson, Hughes, and Mischief. However…" He zoomed in on a small island hosting several structures. "…this small artificial island located approximately 225 kilometers east of the Philippines was built atop an unnamed reef and is referred to by American intelligence as simply Base X."

She leaned toward the screen for a closer view. "And is that where my target is hiding?"

"Yes, for at least the past few years." He switched off the map, the screen returned to the Counsel crest, and he swiveled his chair to face Molka. "And now for the realistic tempering. Your target is considered by the Counsel and the prime minister as officially untouchable. Which is why we have done nothing to the target since he was located, even though the target assisted in many attacks on our nation."

Molka said, "This is something I've never understood, sir. I was only told the reason is national security related."

The deputy director continued. "The official reason falls under national diplomatic relations because your target's sanctuary on that Chinese military island has been directly authorized by the Chinese Communist Party, or much more likely, in my view, authorized by a friendly associate of the target in Chinese Intelligence. In either case, it's been determined by our leadership the international blowback we would have received for eliminating the target outweighs the past crimes the target has committed against our nation."

Molka nodded, frustrated. "The nuance of global stratagems."

He offered a suppressed grin. "That sounds like Azzur talking. But yes, that is the case. Regrettably, the world authority must be appeased."

She frowned. "The world authority is a term Azzur also just started talking about. He said it was the new nomenclature of the same old world order. I'm not even sure what any of that all means or who it is, but it always seems to be on the wrong side of what's right."

"Off the record," he said, "I am not necessarily in agreement with the policies of the world authority, and I am more inclined to sympathize with your position."

"I appreciate that, sir."

He continued. "In any case, the approval the director gave you to go after your target only means you will be given an indeterminant leave of absence from the project's program to attend to a personal matter. We cannot provide you with any personnel, support, equipment, or financing. And we can only offer you access to limited intelligence that cannot be traced back to us."

She nodded. "I understand, sir."

"I know that makes your op theoretically impossible, and for that, I am truly sorry, Molka."

"With respect, sir. Theoretically impossible or not, I'm still going to attempt it."

"I know you will. Which is why I must add, that should you be apprehended and-or charged with the violation of any laws in any foreign nation, we will unequivocally disavow all knowledge of your operation and of you and aggressively assist and-or initiate your prosecution and punishment."

"I understand, sir."

He focused his striking blue eyes on her large oval blue ones. "I knew you would."

Molka took a deep breath, exhaled slowly, and squeezed her purse tight. "And the identity of my target?"

"For plausible deniability reasons, I won't be the one to tell you that. Azzur will take over the briefing from this point. The intelligence report on Base X that we can share with you and a bio on your target has been sent to him. I just spoke to him before our meeting. He's waiting for you in his office now. That's all I have for you, and we never spoke."

"Yes, sir. Thank you, sir."

She stood and moved toward the door.

He called after her: "Molka?"

She paused and turned to face him. "Yes, sir?"

"Send the son of a bitch to the deepest pit in hell."

"Yes. Sir."

As soon as Molka's car exited the Counsel headquarters' super-secure compound and its vast array of electronic eavesdropping systems, she pulled over into a shopping center parking lot, removed her phone from her purse, and dialed.

Kaelee's pleasant but weaker sounding, feminine voice answered. "Hello, Molka, AKA The Legend."

Molka smiled. "Delighted or disappointed?"

"Delighted. Calling me two days in a row is amazing. To what do I owe the honor?"

"First, how are you feeling on your first day back home?"

Kaelee: "Better. A little better each hour. My mom and dad have been babying me, and I love it."

"Good. I'm happy to hear that. I talked to Chase. He shook it off like it was nothing and went right back to work."

"I talked to him too. I'd like to go to Vegas and talk to him some more when I'm better, but I know he has the hots for you."

"Hey, I make no claims on him. But isn't he a little too clean and decent for you? I thought your type was dirty, downlow bikers?"

Kaelee giggled. "Ha, ha, ha. Very funny. But I know you have something else to tell me. Your voice has that determined edge again."

"You're right. Remember the promise you made me that night on the river?"

Kaelee: "Of course."

"I want to talk to you about that."

"Great. Give me like…a few more weeks or maybe a month, and I'll be strong enough to travel, and I'll come see you, and we'll plan it, the biggest and best animal shelter and rescue in the country."

"No. Not about that yet."

Kaelee: "What then?"

"I just met with the Counsel director and deputy director."

"Nice. What did they want to see you for? I mean, I know you're the AKA Legend, but…."

"I actually wanted to see them."

Kaelee: "You requested the meeting? Why did…oh, wait a second. I know why. I know what you're going to do. That's awesome."

"I could really use your help."

"You've got it. I'm 100 percent behind you. Just tell me what I can do for you."

CHAPTER SIX

**Office Building
Downtown Tel Aviv
6:03 PM**

The lobby directory in the plain, gray 10-story downtown office building listed the fourth floor as occupied by ICM Business Solutions: A subsidiary of ICM Electronics of Lowell, Massachusetts.

Both titles represented fictional entities created by the Counsel, and the fourth floor actually housed several Counsel offices, including Azzur's.

Molka entered the building's elevator—still styling her Prada outfit and carrying her purse—and pushed the button for the fourth floor.

The elevator opened out onto a reception area containing several chairs fronted by a receptionist desk and a seated, young, attractive female receptionist. A large ICM Business Solutions logo dominated the wall behind her.

She looked up at Molka.

"Good evening," Molka said. "I have an appointment with Azzur."

As Molka knew she would, as all receptionists in that Counsel front business always did, the woman pointed without comment to a closed door on the room's opposite side with a security camera mounted above.

Molka moved to the door, stood before it, and looked up at the camera.

The door unlocked and opened, as Molka knew it would, to the struggling new beard of a college-aged male slinging a UZI. He stepped aside, and Molka entered a long hallway with several closed doors on each side, all with a security camera mounted above them.

She moved to the last door on the right and waited. A buzzer sounded, an auto-lock clicked, Azzur's office door opened, and she stepped inside.

Raziela's bright, airy redecoration had undergone a total restoration to Azzur's original dark paneling, a huge world map on the right-side wall, Azzur's dark metal desk in the back, a single metal chair fronting the desk, and a permanent cigarette smoke haze.

Azzur sat behind his desk wearing a light brown, short-sleeved dress shirt. A cigarette smoked in a glass ashtray at his right elbow, and a cigarette pack and a silver lighter lay aside it.

Two standard briefing tablets waited at his left elbow.

Molka took the seat fronting the desk as she had done many times before.

He offered a forced smile. "And so, ego lives to be arrogant another day. I stand corrected."

She nodded, serious. "I appreciate your concession. I know that's a rare and hard thing for you to give. So I decided I wouldn't say I told you so. Then I changed my mind." She grinned. "I told you so."

His face returned to unamused, and he passed her one of the tablets. "That is the limited intelligence report the deputy director ordered me to give you."

"What's on the other tablet?"

Azzur puffed and blew smoke. "What you've waited over 10 years for. A full and up-to-date briefing on the one who killed your little sister Janetta."

Molka focused on the tablet's blackened glass screen.

TASK X

Her eyes burned, then reddened, then moistened.

Her heart broke loose from its moorings.

And then lodged in her throat.

She told her arms to raise, her hands to pick up the tablet, and her fingers to turn the tablet on so she could finally view the monster who murdered her little Janetta.

But nothing happened except her trying to keep from bursting out into uncontrollable weeping.

After a few moments, Azzur said, "Are you not going to look at the face I am about to brief you on?"

She stomped down emotions to allow critical thinking to rise and said, "Yes. But before you do, I want some advice from you, and then I need two favors."

He flicked ash in his ashtray. "What advice do you want?"

"If this were your op, how would you handle it?"

He rested his cigarette in the ashtray, opened his top desk drawer, removed a gray-colored remote control, pointed it at the wall-mounted monitor on the left, and powered it up to show a Philippine Islands map.

Molka grinned. "Ha. You knew I would ask."

He zoomed the view to the southeast to a large oblong land mass. "That is Palawan. Which is a 280-mile-long by 31-mile-wide island archipelagic province of the Philippines bordered by the South China Sea to the west and the Sulu Sea to the east.

"If this were my op, I would base in Palawan's biggest city, Puerto Princesa," He zoomed in on the view of a large city located on the island's east coast. "As that is where the international airport is located. However…" He shifted the view across the island. "I would stage the op from across the island on the South China Sea coast. And the ideal place for that would be an hour north of Puerto Princesa here, on Ulugan Bay." He zoomed in on a larger-sized bay. "From there, the target location would be approximately 225 kilometers, or 120 nautical miles, due west."

Molka said, "So you would prefer to make this an amphibious operation?"

"No. However, the robust Chinese military air-threat radar coverage in the Spratly Islands necessitates it. I would use a commercial-type fishing vessel similar to the ones used in those waters as your transport. Then I would make a night landing with two assault teams. One to neutralize the Chinese garrison stationed on the island and the other to eliminate the target. Then extract the teams back to the transport vessel. And as an added precaution, right after extraction, I would employ a diversion by destroying the island's power station and long-range comms antenna with timed high explosives to cut communications with their command base and focus their attention inward as you make your withdrawal back to Palawan."

"That's a fairly simple plan," she said.

"Most successful plans are. The more complex the plan, the more that can go wrong."

Her eyebrows rose with sarcasm. "And we should know, right?"

He laid the remote aside and picked up his cigarette. "Now, I assume one of the two favors you need to ask is if I can provide you with any personnel to assist. Off the record, of course."

She said, "I actually wasn't going to ask you for that, but if you're offering...."

"The best I can do is assign you Dov and Jaron."

She smirked. "The best or the worst?"

"Do not base your opinion on them from one brief and violent encounter in a darkened parking lot in which you held the one-time advantage of surprise. I trained those men, and you would find them very competent and useful professionals."

She shrugged. "Again, I'll have to take your word on that."

"Would you like them or not?"

"I'll take them. I'm desperate."

"What is the first favor." He puffed his cigarette.

"Weapons and equipment. I know you have a black-market guy in the Philippines because you have them everywhere. You do, right?"

"Correct."

"Then I need you to put me in contact with them and give me your best referral."

"I can do that. He goes by the name Bennie Berlin. He is an American once based in Berlin whom we did a lot of business with back in the old days when he was known as the *Baron of Berlin*. Now he is based in Manila. He can get whatever you need, all high-quality merchandise. However, you cannot trust anything he says until you verify it and after you verify it, you should still not trust it. He plays a dirty game."

Molka said, "Umm…you know anyone a bit more honest?"

"Not in the Philippines. And his services also cost a considerable sum. Much more than you could make in several years in your little private practice."

She flashed a prideful face. "My little private practice pays me in ways money never could. But I already have the financing of this op covered."

He flashed a perplexed face. "By what means?"

"Don't concern yourself with that." She unzipped her purse, removed a folded sheet of white paper, and held it out for Azzur. "Concern yourself with this. That's my second favor."

He gave the paper a quizzical glance. "What is this?"

"The rest of my team that I would like you to gather for me."

He took and unfolded the paper, read silently from a list of printed names, and said, "One of these individuals is awaiting trial by an international war crimes tribunal and is being held in maximum security detention."

Molka said, "Then get them out."

"Another one has not been seen since you last saw him two years ago."

"Then find them."

"Yet another one is already scheduled for another task later this month."

"Then replace them."

He glowered over the page at Molka. "You seriously expect me to locate all these individuals?"

She glowered back. "I expect you to locate them within 24 hours. Because you're the best in the nation at doing that, which likely makes you the very best in the world."

Azzur stubbed out his cigarette butt in the ashtray, lit a fresh one, and said, "Your cleverly placed compliment puts me in the position of having to back it up."

"And I know you will. Just tell them I need their help and give them my encrypted number to contact me for more details. I'll handle it from there."

He placed the list in his shirt's top pocket. "It will be done as you asked."

"Thank you." She took in a deep breath and expelled a slow exhale. "Ok. I'm ready for the briefing on the target. I'll look at the face now." She snatched the other tablet, powered it up, opened the desktop's only folder, viewed the photo of the face she imagined a million times, and said…nothing.

After a moment, Azzur said, "You have no opening comment?"

She continued to stare at the photo. "It's just that… It's just that he doesn't look like a monster."

Azzur inhaled his cigarette and blew smoke. "Real monsters seldom do."

CHAPTER SEVEN

7:34 PM

In Azzur's office building's underground parking structure, Molka walked past her car and approached Dov and Jaron in their SUV several spaces away.

Driver Dov rolled down his window. "Hello again, Molka."

She stopped beside the window. "Azzur assigned you to me."

"We know," Dov said. "He just told us. For an operation. He didn't say what it was, though."

"I'm canceling your protective services as of this moment. Go home now and pack for two weeks duty in a tropical climate. Then I suggest you go straight to bed."

Jaron said, "Where are we going and when?"

"I booked you both on a flight to Puerto Princesa in the Philippines that departs at 11 AM tomorrow. It's a 14-hour trip, and the Philippines are six hours ahead of us, so you'll get there early morning local time. I'll arrive one week from today and the rest of our team the following day."

Jaron said, "Who's the rest of our team?"

"I'll let you know when I get them all confirmed."

Dov said, "What do you want us to do when we get to the Philippines?"

She said, "Pick up the rental vehicle at the airport I also got for you, check into a local hotel, and wait for me to contact you. I'll reimburse you for the hotel and give you some cash now for meals and other expenses. You'll have to exchange our currency for Philippine currency when you get there."

"We know," Jaron said. "We've been all over the world many times."

Dov smiled giddy, "Including the Philippines. It's beautiful and relaxing there. Can't wait to get back."

Jaron smiled giddy, "And they have great food and pretty women. I'm excited to get back there too."

Molka thrust her head into the driver's window—causing both men to flinch away from her—and seethed. "Let me explain something to you two morons. This op is not a vacation to enjoy good food and pretty girls. It might look a lot like a vacation where we're heading, but it's far from it. This op is the most important thing I've ever done or will ever do in my entire messed up life. It will make all my tasks seem like insignificant wastes of time. So if you're not ready for a full-on, heads down, hyper-focused, no-nonsense commitment to the op, I want nothing to do with you."

Dov offered a humbled expression. "We understand what you've been through in your life. Azzur's told us. And I promise, if you allow us on your team, you'll get everything I have and as much more as I can scrape up to give you. I want to help you complete this op, even if it kills me."

Jaron offered a humbled expression, "That goes double for me, Molka."

Molka exhaled heavily. "Alright." She pulled her head from the window, opened the left rear passenger door, and got into the backseat. "I'm sorry I called you morons. Now take me to a cash machine. On the way, I'll explain the op."

CHAPTER EIGHT

Molka's Apartment
Azorei Hen Neighborhood
9:36 PM

After consuming a take-out dinner of delicious hummus and pita bread from her favorite little neighborhood restaurant while watching mindless drivel on TV, Molka showered, put on a clean, white, sleeping t-shirt over clean blue panties, double checked the door and window locks—in case Azzur's concerns about Raziela co-conspirators proved true—carried her purse to her bedroom, placed it on the nightstand, removed her Beretta from it, put it aside the purse, set her nightstand alarm clock to 5 AM, crawled into bed, and pulled the sheet over her.

Day over.
Countdown started.
One week to wait.
Then she would be in a position to strike.
And a few days later, she would strike.
Then it would be done.
Then it would be over.
Then all would be right.
Right?

Go to sleep.
Go to sleep.
I need all the rest I can get.
Go to sleep.
Ugh.
Why can't I sleep?
She sat up.
Trying to sleep became pointless.
Restless.
Frustrated.
Anxious.
Can't just lay here.
Must talk to someone.
Like who, though?
She knew who.
She threw off the sheet and rose from her bed.
Pulled on sweatpants and running shoes.
Gathered her purse and weapon.
Trotted downstairs.
Grabbed her keys from the kitchen counter.
And headed out into the night.

Tel Aviv Cemetery
11:09 PM

Molka knelt in the dark before her little sister Janetta's headstone holding the tablet containing the briefing on her target.

"Hey, silly."

"Sorry for coming so late. But I had to talk to you about something important."

"Yes, I know I look like a bum. I was already in bed and just jumped in the car the way I was."

"Anyway, I want to talk to you about this person."

She swiped the tablet to the target's photo, then swiped to and read from the intel bio.

"His name is Alberto Ramirez."

"He was born to an affluent family in Guatemala. They sent him to Europe to be educated. He got a master's degree in engineering and intended to return to his home country and help modernize the power grid. What a noble and worthwhile endeavor. If only he would have followed through with that."

"But instead, he fell under the spell of his radicalized uncle who radicalized him and took him to the Middle East where he learned bomb-making."

"They found out he was a natural, genius bomb maker and became highly sought-after by his uncle's preferred terrorist organization. But he discovered he was more interested in getting rich than revolutions and became a contract bomb maker for hire."

"He did lots of bloody work for several of our country's enemies. And maybe even several of our country's friends. Who can tell. The world is so confused and conflicted, yet connected in the worst ways now. Anything is possible and probable. That's one thing you're lucky you don't have to deal with anymore."

"But he was embedded with one of our country's enemies the night I flew with the Unit when they tried to eliminate him."

"We missed him, and he went into hiding."

"Then the Counsel found him a few years ago."

"He's being sheltered on a remote Chinese military base in the South China Sea. Exactly why, or even if, the Chinese government is protecting him or if it's someone within the Chinese government or intelligence doing so rogue, no one in our intelligence or even the Americans are quite sure about."

"Or maybe they are and don't want to divulge it due to the nuances of global stratagems. Yes, I know that sounds like Azzur talking."

"But back to this person. He's—"

Molka's eyes filled with tears.

"But he's the one."

"He's the reason you're not here with me."

"He's the one I've lived to kill."

"And in a few days, I'm leaving to kill him."

"For you."

"And for us."

"And then we can both finally rest in peace."

**WEDNESDAY
JULY 27TH**

CHAPTER NINE

Puerto Princesa International Airport
Puerto Princesa, Palawan
Philippines
7:17 AM

Dov waited alone for Molka in a section of blue plastic seats in the waiting area for the arriving flights.

He dressed casually in a red t-shirt over baggy blue shorts and rubber sandals. His right hand held a phone, and his head held sunglasses perched atop it.

Along with about two dozen other passengers from her connecting flight from Manila, Molka deplaned from exterior airstairs into the muggy morning air and entered the terminal. She spotted Dov and approached him in a travel-comfortable, sleeveless, yellow summer dress and white sneakers. She styled her hair in a French braid ponytail and wore her black-framed glasses.

Dov rose when she came close. "Welcome to Puerto Princesa. How was your flight?"

She frowned. "How was yours last week?"

"Long, tiring, uncomfortable, frustrating, and bad mood inducing."

"I have nothing to add to that." She gestured to his garb. "I guess you're going with the laid-back tourist legend."

"No legend necessary. This is a t-shirt, shorts, and sandals-type of island. It's gut punch hot and humid."

She frowned again. "From extreme wet heat to extreme dry heat back to extreme wet heat, welcome to the summer of Molka."

He flashed a perplexed face. "What's that mean?"

"Nothing. Let's get my bag."

They crossed the small—but modern—terminal toward the baggage retrieval area.

Molka said, "Did you guys check out of the hotel here and move to the new base?"

"Yesterday," he said. "And may I say that was a great choice you made. Azzur would have never done anything like that."

"Well, I just thought combining the operations base with the staging area would be more convenient since we'll only need to use the airport twice more: when the VIPs arrive and when we all leave."

"All true, and also a great choice. But I actually meant your choice of location. It's incredible."

They arrived at the baggage carousel where her black, hardside, rolling luggage case rode. She retrieved it, and they exited the building back into the humid morning air, crossed four lanes used for arrivals and departures—hosting a few yellow taxis and blue, three-wheeled, motorcycle-powered cabs—and entered the half-full, outdoor, public parking area.

Dov pointed about a dozen spaces down to a coral-pink-colored mini-bus. "That's us."

Molka's face cast confusion on the large vehicle. "What's that? Where's the SUV I rented for you guys?"

"Jaron is using it today to scout for boats, as you ordered. This is the resort's courtesy shuttle. They use it to do what we're doing, take guests from and to the airport. And I thought it would be better to transport our VIPs. It seats 18 passengers and will be much more comfortable than cramming everyone in the SUV."

Her eyebrows rose, impressed. "That's actually a very good idea."

Dov used a key fob to auto-open the bus's twin glass folding entrance doors, and they climbed two steps inside a clean and clean-smelling interior.

Dov moved into the left-side driver seat and buckled up.

Behind him, a center aisle separated four rows of double, black vinyl, high-back seats. A black vinyl bench seat ran across the bus's back end with seating for two more.

Molka chose the double seats in the first row, right side as you faced forward, putting her diagonal from Dov for easy communication. She placed her case on the window seat and sat on the aisle.

Dov started the quiet motor, and a moment later, they exited the airport and joined the traffic on Puerto Princesa Drive North for the 55-minute drive northeast across the island to the South China Sea coast and their base on Ulugan Bay.

She opened her case and removed and powered up a new, secure laptop to which she uploaded the data on the briefing tablets given to her by Azzur containing the Base X intelligence report and her targets bio. In the past week, she used the supplied info to build a slideshow presentation to brief the VIPs. It still lacked a few more slides, and she worked to create them on the ride.

After over 30 minutes of silent driving, Dov spoke up. "Molka, is it ok if I discuss something with you not related to this op?"

She raised a wary eyebrow while still working on the laptop. "As long as it's not something profane."

He glanced over at her, perplexed. "What? Oh, yes, you mean the profane, obscene things Jaron and I said to you when we first met. No, it's nothing like that. All that stuff was from a script Azzur wrote for us."

She kept working. "I didn't know Azzur had such a profane, obscene side to him."

He smirked. "You have no idea. But I wanted to say that I know you don't think much of Jaron and me, but we both think a lot of you. Azzur let us read your task's final reports, and they read like great action-adventure, suspense-mystery, dark comedy-tragedy movies. We've both become huge fans of you. And we're both very honored you brought us on the team."

His kind words and praise caused the guilt pangs of her beatdown on them to pang again, and she went for a subject changer. "Give me a report on our new base. Was Kaelee able to secure us 11 rooms and exclusive use of the hotel's conference room for as long as we're there?"

His face beamed. "She did WAY better than that for you. She secured you exclusive use of the ENTIRE resort for as long as we're there."

Molka's eyes popped off the laptop onto him. "Wait. What? No."

His face held its beam. "Oh, yes."

"Wow. How is that even possible?"

"She made a deal with the owner to tell all the guests a nearby gas leak made the property unsafe, and they were relocated with upgrades to other resorts on the island, all at Kaelee's expense."

Molka shook an awestruck head. "Wow and wow."

He continued. "And she arranged to have the staff sent home at full salary until we leave. Except for the kitchen staff, she paid a bonus for them to prepare our meals daily and two housekeepers to clean our rooms and do our laundry."

Molka remained awestruck. "Wow and wow and wow. That's way beyond what I asked her for."

"She really admires you. She told me so several times when we talked."

Molka said, "I never even looked. What's the name of this resort?"

"Club Utopia."

CHAPTER 10

Club Utopia Palawan is a luxury, 19-hectare, all-inclusive resort strategically located on magnificent Ulugan Bay.

It is a tropical paradise with breathtaking landscapes and seascapes, natural tourist attractions, and exhilarating dive sites.

Standing gloriously on azure waters and an expansive 700-meter pristine beach that is unmatched in Palawan, the resort offers plenty of lounging options and a myriad of activities such as kayaking, parwa sailing, diving, and hiking.

Sixty-two rooms include beachfront villas with private balconies exuding elegant simplicity affording the most indulgent stay.

If you're looking for wellness, our spa is a must-try for in-house guests.

Discover the island life and experience the best of world-renowned Filipino hospitality here at Club Utopia.

    Molka lowered her phone from which she had been viewing the resort's website while the drive to it continued.

TASK X

Place sounds amazing.

And...

Ha. How ironic it is that Alberto Ramirez's final hell on earth will come from a place called Utopia.

About 20 minutes later, Dov exited the main highway they used to travel northeast to cross the island and onto a single-lane, hillside road cutting through dense, jungle-like terrain.

After about two kilometers, they came to a clearing in the growth, and to the left and below them, the azure blue and tranquil turquoise gorgeousness of Ulugan Bay came into view along with the resort.

The reality justified the online hype.

A large, main building sat terraced into the hillside overlooking a pristine white sand beach. The structure displayed Polynesian-style architecture featuring a high-peaked, faux thatched roof and dark, native wood siding. The same style carried to the other buildings on the sprawling property, including those clustered around an exceptionally large swimming pool and over a dozen beachfront villas.

They reached the resort's closed entrance featuring a large, coral-pink sign with turquoise letters welcoming you to: Club Utopia. A single metal bar gate restricted entrance and displayed a white sign with black letters informing: Club Utopia Resort Temporarily Closed.

Dov stopped the bus outside the gate, exited, swung it open, got back into the bus, drove it through, stopped, got back out, closed the gate behind them, and drove on.

They traveled a gently winding road for about half a kilometer through a beautiful botanical garden and emerged at the main building's covered, half-moon-shaped entrance.

Dov parked outside the building's large, double glass entrance doors and behind a line of three coral-pink, white-canopied electric carts.

They exited the bus—Molka with her rolling case—and entered into the air-conditioned cool main hotel lobby, beautifully appointed with Polynesian-style décor, polished wood floor, and a round, centrally located check-in desk. On the space's far side, six floor-to-ceiling windows offered a picture-like view of the resort's main beach and the bay.

Dov pointed to a large hallway opening to the left. "That leads to a big bar-lounge-nightclub-type venue."

He pointed to a large hallway opening to the right. "That leads to the regular hotel suites on two floors."

He pointed to closed, wooden, double doors to the right of the big windows. "And that leads to a large conference room we converted into the briefing room you asked for and your office."

Her face puzzled. "My office?"

"Yes, I'll show you."

He headed toward the doors.

Molka left her case beside the check-in counter and followed.

Dov opened the double doors, and they walked into a spacious, red-carpeted, wood-paneled, corporate-quality conference room.

Along the walls in the room's rear sat multiple stacks of chairs. The room's front hosted a large, polished, dark wood conference table with four high-backed, tan leather chairs on each side and one at the far end. Beyond the table, a wooden podium stood to the left, and the wall behind it mounted a huge monitor.

They stopped in the room's center, and Dov said, "Will this setup be ok for your needs?"

She nodded. "Yes. This will be just fine."

"I can also configure the monitor in here to sync with your laptop for your briefings."

"Perfect. Thanks. Can you also configure the team's briefing tablets I sent you to do the same?"

"It's already done. I also put the name labels on them you asked for. They're waiting inside the credenza behind your desk. And their encrypted phones you sent are also ready to go."

She nodded, impressed. "Great."

"Your office is right over there." He walked, and she followed across the room to a closed door on the right side, and he opened it. "We figured you wouldn't want to intrude on the resort manager's private office, so we cleared out and equipped this conveniently located storage room for you."

Molka peeked in to see a brown wooden desk holding a resort phone, a brown leather office chair, a brown wooden credenza behind the desk hosting a printer-copier, and in the far corner, a mini-refrigerator and two chairs that matched the ones stacked in the conference room.

She said, "Where did all this stuff come from?"

"Various backroom areas in the resort. I put a 12-pack of bottled water in that fridge. Not sure yet what snacks you like. Will this do?"

She offered another impressed nod. "Since I didn't expect to have an office, yes. This will do beyond great. Thanks."

"Thank Kaelee. Ready for a tour of the rest of the resort?"

CHAPTER 11

Molka rode as front passenger in one of the coral-pink, white-canopied electric carts parked outside the main lobby entrance with her luggage case in the backseat.

Driver Dov swung around the building and onto a wide, asphalt path that curved downhill under a cooling tree canopy.

The path emerged aside the large, sparkling clean swimming pool surrounded by a slate-type rock pool deck and white-cushioned lounge chairs and tables covered by brightly colored umbrellas. And clustered around the pool sat the Polynesian-style buildings Molka viewed from the road on the way in.

Dov stopped the cart and pointed to the largest structure to the pool's left. "That's the restaurant where the kitchen staff will work from. They'll prepare anything on the regular menu and also take off the menu requests and prepare them, if possible. We're welcome to eat in the big dining room, take it out, or order room service from menus in every room. They'll be here every day from 5 AM until 8 PM."

Molka said, "That's all very generous of them."

"Well, Kaelee's paying them very generously." He pointed at the second-largest structure to the pool's right. "That's the spa." He pointed at the row of smaller buildings fronting the pool. "From left to right are the fitness center, gift and apparel shop, dive shop, and another bar-lounge."

Dov drove on, and the path paralleled the immaculate white sand beach for its entire 700-meter length until they came upon an artificial channel cutting through the beach connecting the bay to a large, artificial lagoon and marina where he stopped.

The lagoon measured about 50 meters wide and about 200 meters long. The end nearest the channel featured a big, wide, main dock large enough to host a mega-yacht on one side and another smaller, but not small, dock on the other side. The lagoon's inland portion moored a few rental fishing boats, sailboats, and catamarans.

Molka viewed the marina layout. "It's perfect for the op. This is why Kaelee picked this particular resort. Ok. Let's keep going."

The path turned right, headed back up the hill, then curved left to go around the lagoon.

Dov pointed to the right, farther up the hill toward the resort property's far side. "Over there are the tennis courts, a running course, a rope course, and a greenhouse."

They reached the lagoon's opposite side, and the path curved left and downhill again and ended at another pristine white beach hosting a line of 20 villa suites setback about 30 meters from the water.

Each villa sat atop pilings and continued the resort's Polynesian-style architecture but featured subtle design differences to make them all unique and give them a residential neighborhood feel.

Dov swept his right hand down the beach. "And the tour ends here at our accommodations."

Molka's eyebrows rose, surprised. "Really?"

"The resort owner himself told me since Kaelee leased the entire resort, she wanted her guests to have the best rooms."

"What does the resort owner know about us?"

"Only that we're guests of a rich American woman. And what she paid him, stopped any other questions he might have."

Molka smiled, satisfied. "Very nice work, Kaelee."

"Yes, she's good. How do you want to assign the villas; Jaron and I are already using villa 20 down there at the far end."

She flashed him a curious glance. "Why are you two sharing a— Oh. Never mind."

"No, that's not it. We always room together on an op so we can watch each other's backs when we sleep. Old habit for security reasons. We've made a lot of enemies over the years."

She glanced down the beach at the last villa. "I see…. And that works out well for us in a way."

"How so?"

She continued. "When the weapons and equipment arrive, we can store them in your villa, and that would make me feel better to have a double guard on it at night. We can break a couple of the Glocks out of the order for you to use."

"That's not necessary." He lifted his t-shirt to reveal a Glock tucked into his front waistband. "The first thing Jaron and I do when we arrive in a new place is get armed up. As I said, we've made a lot of enemies over the years."

"Ok. I'll take villa number one and assign the VIPs villas two through nine in alphabetical order so I can better remember who is where."

"Understood," he said.

"And from now on, keep all exterior doors in every building locked at all times. Starting with the hotel lobby front doors. We don't know the neighborhood. And we don't want any curious neighbors wondering why this place is closed and wandering in here to investigate and wandering into our business."

"Understood. I'll do that right away. Which reminds me." He removed a coral-pink keycard from his short's front pocket and handed it to her. "Your master keycard."

She unzipped her purse, placed the card inside, removed her phone, and checked the messages. "Alright. As of now, all the VIPs are still confirmed to arrive here by noon tomorrow. I want you to greet each one, give them a quick tour, explain the kitchen policy, take them to their villa, and tell them to report to the briefing room at 1 PM. I won't have time to see them until then."

"Understood. I'll handle it, Molka."

"Did you get the binoculars for the recon?"

"Yes, military-grade Steiners, as you requested."

"Good. Dov, I'm appointing you as the base commander. Which is a different position from a team leader in that—"

TASK X

He interrupted. "I know what it is. It means you want me to oversee the daily operations here so you can be free to focus 100 percent on the op. No problem. I've done that job before and will take care of it."

"Ok. Sounds good." She exited the cart and grabbed her case from the backseat. "I'll get out here and go to my villa. Keep an eye on your phone. I'll check in later."

"Yes, Molka."

He drove off, and she walked across the sand to villa one, climbed four stone steps to a wooden veranda—slinging a comfy-looking hammock—used the keycard to open the door, and entered.

The spacious suite's main room emitted a clean, lemony aroma and featured a high ceiling with a ceiling fan and off-white walls over polished wood floors accented with off-white rugs.

The furniture was of a contemporary style done in blue cloth and looked newer, as did a wooden desk holding a phone and a large wall-mounted monitor. And as Dov said, a restaurant menu lay atop the desk.

A king-size bed with a white linen canopy dominated the room's rear. She crossed to the bed, laid her purse and case atop it, and then walked into the attached bathroom to find an immaculate, sleek, frosted glass and gray stone shower and a white commode and sink.

Hunger moved her back into the living area, the desk, and the restaurant menu. She scanned it, made a selection, picked up the phone, and speed-dialed the restaurant.

A man answered in polite Filipino-accented English, and she ordered an early lunch of grilled shrimp salad with a double portion of shrimp and a bottled water he said would be delivered in only about 10 minutes.

Nice.

Premium resort.

Premium service.

She turned toward the large front windows, viewed the gorgeous beach and the bay, and planned her day. After eating, a shower, change into working clothes, and head to her office to finish preparing her first briefing for the VIPs.

Part of her would have loved to slip into a bikini and hit the beach or the pool.

But that part of her was the selfish-distracted part.

A part of her from the past.

A part of her she needed to suppress.

Because a serious job needed to be done.

And serious people were coming to do that serious job.

And she had serious work to do before that could happen.

**THURSDAY
JULY 28TH**

CHAPTER 12

Molka time checked her phone again: 12:56 PM.

She sat at the desk in her makeshift office dressed in what she decided would be her standard duty uniform for the non-tactical or training portions of the op: a black polo shirt tucked into khaki tactical pants over black tactical boots.

Her choice, she hoped, would project a more professional and serious presence than t-shirts and shorts during her first time commanding a real special operation.

She also high-ponytailed her hair and put in her contacts.

The door opened, and Dov and Jaron entered in what would become their usual t-shirts, shorts, and sandals and closed the door behind them.

Molka addressed her assistants. "Everyone here?"

Dov said, "Yes, all seated and waiting for you."

"How do they look?"

Jaron said, "Like a mensch convention on steroids."

"I mean, what are their attitudes like, loose, confident, ready for action?" She grinned. "I'm sure they're already swapping war stories and engaged in cute male bonding."

Dov and Jaron exchanged nervous glances.

Molka flashed a curious face. "What's wrong?"

TASK X

Dov said, "None of them have said a word yet. They're all just sitting there kind of eyeing each other."

Her inquisitive face held. "What do you mean kind of eying each other?"

Jaron said, "It's like they're throwing some serious suspicion at each other."

She nodded, knowingly. "Oh, ok. I know the two men you mean. They have an adversarial history but they're on the same side now and it's all good. It will just be a little awkward for them at first, I guess."

Dov said, "It's not just those two throwing some serious suspicion at each other."

Molka's burrow furrowed. "Well…that's natural for that group. Because of their particular and unique professions, they would naturally be predisposed not to trust strangers at face value. After I do the introductions, they'll loosen up, I'm sure." She addressed Jaron. "Check in with the kitchen to ensure the lunch buffet will be ready to serve in about 20 minutes."

"Ok, Molka," Jaron said and left the office.

Molka stood and addressed Dov. "Stay close out there in case I have any technical troubles."

"I just tested everything again. Your laptop is waiting for you on the podium. Swipe it, and your first slide will appear on the big screen."

"Thank you." She took a deep breath.

He offered her a respectful nod. "You got this, Molka."

Molka exited the office and approached the conference table from the rear.

All eight men seated at it rose and smiled at her, and some started to speak.

She held up a stop sign right hand. "Gentlemen, please hold all personal greetings and be seated."

All eight men complied.

Molka moved behind the podium to the table's front left, and Dov stood against the wall to her right.

She took another deep breath and addressed the men. "Thank you for coming, gentlemen. This week, I limited our previous communications to brief non-verbal messages for security reasons. However, I'll meet with each of you individually after this short introductory briefing, and we'll exchange pleasantries and get caught up."

She turned toward the large wall monitor, swiped her laptop, and a satellite image of the Spratly Islands appeared. "The target is located approximately 225 kilometers—120 nautical miles—due west in the South China Sea from our base here on a Chinese artificial island military installation that US intelligence has named Base X."

She swiped again and brought up a satellite image of Base X. "The target lives in a guarded residential compound on the island's north side." She used the cursor arrow to point at it. "Here on the island's south side," she used the cursor arrow to point to it, "is a Chinese military early-warning air radar installation with a garrison estimated to be of no more than 20."

"To circumvent the robust Chinese military air-threat radar coverage in this area—including the installation on the island itself—we will affect a nighttime, covert, amphibious interdiction, neutralize the garrison, breach the compound, eliminate the target, and make an amphibious extraction."

"And right after extraction, we will employ a diversion by destroying the island's power station and long-range comms antenna with timed high explosives to cut communications with their command base and focus their attention inward as we make our withdrawal back to Palawan."

Molka faced the men again. "That's just a very basic outline of the op. Tomorrow morning, we will all conduct an aerial recon in a leased aircraft posing as legitimate media on a pre-registered civilian flight. Then we will reconvene and make our tactical plan to execute the op."

"One other thing, Dov and Jaron will issue you briefing tablets with the information I just presented and will update you with the new information we gather and the tactical plan when it's ready. Also, please give your phones to Dov and Jaron before you leave this room to be secured in the hotel safe. They will issue you an encrypted phone to use until we leave."

She moved from behind the podium and sat in the end seat. "Now I'll make the introductions of your teammates."

She turned to the first chair to her right, seating a late-30s white male around six feet three, with an amateur bodybuilder-type physique, brown hair cut military style, deep-set brown eyes, and strong jawline, and wearing a navy-blue polo and tan pants.

She made the introduction: "This is Warren. He served in the US Army Special Forces. Currently a top tier operative with the Corporation. Warren will act as my XO. XO, meaning executive officer, or second in command, for our non-military teammate. If something should happen to me, he will take over leadership and complete the op."

She pointed to Warren's right, seating a mid-60s white male, stoutly built with steel-gray-hair, adamant blue eyes, a rock-like jawed—softened a bit, but just a bit by late middle age—with an oversized nose to smell an enemy's fear and thin, serious lips that gave away few secrets and wearing a red, short-sleeved, button up shirt and green pants.

She made the introduction: "This is Colonel Nikolai Vasilyevich Krasnov—the famous Red Wolf. He served with high distinction in the Russian Army special forces. Widely considered a tactical genius in special actions. The colonel will plan and oversee the ground operation of the op."

She pointed to the colonel's right, seating a mid-40s white male, sinewy-framed with wavy, shoulder-length dark-brown hair parted on the side and featuring a perfect bang flip, hazel eyes, and beard stubble covering an angular face, split by a slightly crooked, roguish smile and wearing an open-collared, white silk dress shirt and white dress pants. A gold hoop earring shined from his left ear.

She made the introduction: "This is Captain LJ Savanna. Former modern-day pirate and scourge of the Caribbean and an expert seaman. Captain Savanna will be in charge of amphibious operations for the op."

She pointed to Savanna's right, seating a mid-30s Asian male, very fit and tall, sporting a fresh haircut styled hip in a sleek side-parted pompadour with devilishly pointed sideburns and wearing a charcoal-colored designer V-neck t-shirt over stone-colored slim-fit pants.

She made the introduction: "This is Kang. Formerly of the North Korean GBR. Now with Pentad. Another top tier operative and very familiar with the Chinese military. Kang will act as our intelligence specialist and interpreter, as he speaks fluent Chinese and some Filipino."

She turned to the first chair to her left, seating an early 40s white male exhibiting a lean muscular fitness with short, side-parted, ash blonde hair, attentive blue eyes, and a pointed nose jutting over a close-cropped ash-blonde beard and wearing a tan sports coat over a white dress shirt and brown pants.

She made the introduction. "This is Reinhold Jager. He prefers just Jager. Formerly with German Army special forces, combat veteran, and expert human hunter. He will act as our scout and acquire our target on site."

She pointed to Jager's left, seating an early 30s, white male, diminutive but fit, blonde-highlighted dark hair sporting sleek, designer titanium-framed eyeglasses matching large titanium-hoop earrings hanging from each earlobe and dressed Tel Aviv hipster-style in a lavender slim-fit long-sleeved dress shirt tucked into slim-fit, yellow dress pants.

She made the introduction. "This is Nathan. He's a combat photographer, videographer, cartographer, and surveillance drone expert. He will prepare up-to-date operational maps after the recon."

She pointed to Nathan's left, seating a late-30s white male, athletes build, sporting side-parted brown hair topping a broad forehead, an angular face with blue-green eyes, and full lips under a sharp nose and over a handsomely clefted chin and wearing a tight, dark blue, open collar, pressed dress shirt—with the sleeves rolled to the elbows exposing muscular forearms—and mauve-colored, pressed, slim-fit pants.

She made the introduction. "This is Luc Durand. World-class free solo climber and locks expert. Luc will get into the target compound undetected and open any door for us from the inside."

She pointed to Luc's left, seating a late-30s Asian male, shorter, in-shape body with thick, combed back black hair, and a clean-shaven face with an angular jawline and wearing a bright orange, surf shop logo t-shirt and blue jeans.

She made the introduction. "This is Shizi. He served in a Taiwan Marines anti-terrorist unit. He's an explosives specialist and will act in the same capacity on the op."

She gestured to Dov. "And you've already met my assistant, Dov, and my other assistant Jaron will be serving a buffet lunch in here shortly."

On cue, Jaron arrived with two kitchen personnel all pushing rolling food service carts stacked with covered serving dishes.

Molka continued. "During lunch, I'll summon each of you into my office for a short individual meeting I spoke of earlier. And after you have lunch and our meeting, please feel free to relax for the rest of today. We leave for the airport at 4 AM tomorrow for the recon flight."

Warren raised his hand.

Molka recognized him. "Yes, Warren."

"May I address the team for a moment?"

"Of course."

He stood and glared at Kang. "I would just like to point out that our intelligence specialist *of* the GBR—and I say *of* the GBR because I believe once in, never out—is the same man who incapacitated me in Australia with a powerful stun gun, then abducted me and kept me shackled and under heavy sedation for almost three days. So, please forgive me if I say I don't trust anything our intelligence specialist says. And I can't work with someone I can't trust."

Kang stood and glared at Warren and spoke in slightly Korean-accented English. "If I may retort. An employee of the Corporation is hardly a credible spokesperson for trustworthiness. And I can name a few dozen Central and South American and Middle East countries who would back me up on that."

Molka addressed the two men. "Warren, Pentad thinks very highly of Kang. And Kang, Warren is honest to a fault and—"

Jager raised his hand and interrupted in German-accented English. "Request permission to speak."

Molka recognized him. "Yes, Jager."

He stood and glared at Colonel Krasnov. "I don't like serving with a disgraced, notorious war criminal. Or Russians, in general, for that matter."

The colonel stood, glared at Jager, and spoke in Russian-accented English. "Never yet convicted of a war crime. And perhaps your dislike of Russians stems from your fascist criminal ancestor's humiliation by us?"

Molka addressed the two men. "Ok. Let's not bring politics into our—"

Captain Savanna raised his hand and interrupted. "Pardon me, Lady Molka. May I interject here?"

Molka recognized him. "Yes, captain."

He stood and glared at Luc. "I know of this Luc Durand, international playboy, and master criminal, or so he fancies himself. But there's only room for one charming rogue pillager on this crew, and that man is me. Naturally."

Luc stood, glared at the captain, and spoke in French-accented English. "I have heard of you and your exploits too, captain. And as it turns out, we have even plied our trades on some of the same wealthy people. However, I stand second to no one in our profession, most particularly a pirate."

Molka addressed the two men. "Luc, captain, this is pointless and silly. I think you two will actually become—"

Nathan interrupted and raised his hand. "Excuse me, Molka."

Molka recognized him. "Yes, Nathan."

He spoke in Hebrew-accented English. "May I say something I think will save us all?"

"Please do."

Thank goodness for levelheaded Nathan to calm things!

Nathan stood and glared at Shizi. "Laili told me about Mr. Shizi there. She said he has the guts of a lion, but he's a raging alcoholic, predictably unpredictable, and reliably unreliable. Which also describes my father. And I wouldn't want to be near my father if he had explosives, and the same goes for him."

Shizi stood, glared at Nathan, and spoke in Taiwanese-accented English. "I haven't had a drink in months. And I don't know you, so who in the hell are you to judge me, anyway?"

Simultaneously, all eight men resumed their bickering battles with increasing decibel levels to speak over the others.

Molka called out:

"Gentlemen."

They ignored her and bickered louder.

She called out again:

"Gentlemen."

They ignored her and bickered even louder.

She stood and yelled out:

"Gentlemen!"

They ignored her and bickered louder yet.

She shouted out:

"Gentlemen!"

They ignored her and bickered their loudest.

She jumped atop the table.

Moved to its center.

And screamed out:

"SHUT UP, GENTLEMEN!"

The men went silent and looked up at her, stunned.

She continued in a forceful voice. "No one said you have to be besties. Or a band of brothers. I asked for each of you because I need your specific help. And each of you said you would be there to help me whenever the time came. Well, that time has come. And time is short. So if any of you believe you can't work with any of the men in this room, walk out right now so I can start looking for your replacement."

All the men retook their seats and sat quietly.

Molka jumped down from the table, walked to her office, opened the door, went inside, and closed the door behind her.

CHAPTER 13

Molka slumped at her desk, stared at the opposite wall, and shook her head in disgust.

But not disgust at the disgusting display her team had presented moments before.

Her disgust was reserved solely for herself.

A moment later, Dov entered and closed the door behind him. "Whew. That's one high-octane, testosterone-fueled Alpha fest in there."

She offered up hopeful eyes. "Please tell me self-awareness has kicked in, apologies have been issued, laughter exchanged, and they're all getting along."

He shrugged. "I can't tell you any of that. I can tell you they're eating their lunch in total silence while glaring hatefully at each other."

She shook her head disgusted again. "I should have seen this coming and preemptively diffused all those little personal beefs and biases."

"How could you have known about them?"

"It's the team leader's job to anticipate all potential problems with their troops. No excuses."

Dov said, "I think you're way too hard on yourself. And even if you had been able to anticipate this, you still never know how a merc-type team like that will get along until you actually put them all together in the same room. Believe me. Once, Jaron and I were put in charge of a group of highly talented and expensive mercs in—well, I can't tell you where, but there was a disagreement among them over a very minor detail, and since they hadn't bonded into a team, none wanted to back down and the little disagreement turned into a major fight with fists and weapons and two of them ended up wounded and the op scrubbed."

She sighed. "If you're trying to cheer me up, stop. Where's Jaron?"

"He's still in there trying to lighten the mood with some jokes. He's an amateur comedian."

"What kind of jokes?"

"His, 'Hey, what's the deal with Israeli girls?' routine."

She smirked. "Glad I'm missing that." She picked up a printed list of names from the desktop and held it out to Dov.

He took it. "What's this?"

"That's the order I want them sent in here for our individual meetings." She rose, grabbed one of the chairs from against the wall, and placed it before her desk. "When one is in here, wait outside the door, and when you see that one leave, call the next one in."

"Understood. Ready for the first one now?"

"After that debacle I just witnessed, I'm not sure I want any of them. But send the first one in anyway."

Molka smiled at Warren's entrance. "Thanks again for coming, handsome."

Warren smiled back. "I've missed you calling me handsome." He took the seat across from her. "And speaking of that, Nadia said to tell you, 'Just because I'm 7 months pregnant, *ketzelah*, don't think I won't hunt you down if you flirt with my husband.'"

Molka laughed. "I know she will, and I love that about her. And congratulations on your marriage and upcoming child."

"Thank you." He frowned. "When Azzur called and said he wanted to talk to me about you, at first, I thought…well…the last time I saw you was in the hospital in Australia and…."

"Yes," she said. "I know I didn't look good then, but I'm much better now. So what have you two been up to since Australia, I mean, besides getting married and conceiving?"

"That's about it," he said. "After the Nurse Bandini incident, they took us off active status and put us on paid leave."

She nodded. "A well-deserved vacation. That's nice."

"For about two weeks it was nice. Now I'm itching to get back into the action. That's why I was thrilled to get your call."

She reached behind her to the credenza, and from a stack of briefing tablets, picked up the one with the Warren name label on it, and handed it to him. "This is the full briefing on the target and your responsibilities on the op."

He winced. "Molka, I'll be honored to act as your XO, but why is Kang on the team? It took me every ounce of restraint I had not to come across the table and choke him out."

"Glad you didn't. He's on our side now."

Warren frowned again. "Pentad is on their own side."

"Well, whichever side he's on, he was the best available to me for this op. He might even be the best available for this op, regardless."

"Maybe so. I know he's a super-star talent in our business. I'm holding his GBR background against him, though. And with good reasons, both professional and personal."

"I can understand that. But on the other hand, it checked out that he didn't kill your British friend, Ian, right?"

Warren grudged a nod. "Yes, his story checked out."

"And after he took you hostage on his last mission for the GBR, his last act of that mission was taking out a five-man GBR death squad minutes before they reached Nadia and you because, he said, you two didn't deserve to be shot down like animals chained to the floor."

Warren grudged another nod. "Yes, and we literally were chained to the floor waiting to be shot down like animals."

TASK X

Molka leaned forward in her chair, serious. "I know everything in your training and experience tells you to never trust a GBR man, including a former one. But I trust this one. And if you trust me, I'm asking you to trust him, if only for this op."

He leaned forward in his chair, serious. "I just don't know if I can bring myself to do that, Molka."

CHAPTER 14

Colonel Krasnov took the seat across from Molka with a sly smile. "I suppose I cannot call you 'lieutenant who drives truck' any longer since I am now your subordinate."

She offered him a return sly smile. "I actually thought it was cute the way you said it. I knew there was some affection behind it."

The colonel rubbed thick fingers on thick chin stubble. "So, team leader, we have the good misfortune of serving together again."

Molka nodded. "Just as you foretold last time we spoke, sir. And thank you again so much for coming."

"It is I who must thank you for getting me out of that Belgian cage. If only for this brief time."

"Thank Azzur. I have no idea which strings he pulled to do that."

"When it comes to pulling strings, Azzur has few peers and many surprises."

"Just like my surprise when I found out you were his asset in Canada. I heard about your acquittal on some of the charges. Congratulations."

He shrugged. "Acquitted on two, 28 more trials to go. Very little news has filtered into my world these past years. Speaking of our time in Canada, what of Principal Darcy?"

"Last I heard, she was still deeply embroiled in the Canadian legal system."

"And what became of the brilliant engineer Aden Luck?"

As it had since he got onto the helicopter that horrid night and left her, the sound of Aden's name sent a painful flutter through her heart.

She played it stoically. "All I know is he's working for my country." She reached behind her, picked up the briefing tablet with the colonel's name label on it, and handed it to him. "This is a full briefing on the target and your responsibilities for the op."

He sat up straight and attentive. "I will endeavor to give you a plan providing you the very best of chances for total success."

She offered a respectful nod. "I expected no less from you, sir. And…um…what about working with Jager? Is that going to be a problem?"

A slight sly smile creased the colonel's lips again. "Team leader, yet another angry, humiliated German is the least of my problems."

CHAPTER 15

Captain Savanna entered the office, presenting his trademark slightly crooked rogue smile, and sat. "Lady Molka, you have grown even more ravishing since we last spoke on Katelyn."

"And captain, I'm more than a little surprised you actually came, considering what a man of extreme means you are now after obtaining 100 million dollars in gold bullion stolen from a drug cartel and then the US government that crazy night in the Virgin Islands, which I've heard rumors was turned into nearly 400 million through timely investing." She grinned. "Speaking of which, how and where have you been enjoying that incredible windfall since your disappearance right afterward?"

"Lady Molka, if I were to comment on that, it might be taken as an admission by some very powerful and very embarrassed legal authorities that I knew of what you are referring to."

Molka offered a playful face. "Ah, I see."

He continued. "However, it is my personal opinion that if one were to obtain 100 million dollars in gold bullion stolen from a drug cartel and then the US government one crazy night in the Virgin Islands, which rumors say could have been turned into nearly 400 million through timely investing, it still wouldn't be enough to keep a nice young man—sent by a not so nice man named Azzur—from finding them on one of their mega yachts anchored off tiny Seychelles in the Indian Ocean to deliver a message from you."

She kept up her playful face. "Well, I would have understood if that message were not replied to, considering the exciting, carefree life such a man would be living. I wonder why it was?"

"Lady Molka, I'm sure you recall Señor Delgado from your infamous visit to his island."

Her face became serious again. "Yes. Not someone or something easily forgettable."

"I can well imagine. In any case, many years before that—when I was just starting out and very poor and Señor Delgado was already established and very rich—he told me that when a man does become very successful, he will weep in longing for the days of the struggle. At the time, I didn't understand what he meant. But now I know. And your call for assistance brought me back into a wonderful struggle I very much look forward to."

She gave a respectful nod. "Thank you again for coming."

"And thank you for not betraying Captain LJ Savanna's secret identity to the world."

She feigned confusion. "Secret identity? Hmm…I don't remember that. I do remember you telling me about some guy named Richard Miller from Savanna, Illinois who had his heart broken in college and went on to create an alter ego character to live wild and free."

"But when I think of you, I always see a man wearing an open-collared, long-sleeved black silk shirt, a wide black leather belt, and black pants tucked into knee-length black leather Wellington-style boots. With his ponytailed hair covered by a black bandana and a pair of nickel-plated .45s strapped cross draw on his chest, all while standing on the deck of the speeding beauty *Vengeance* with his feet spread shoulder width apart, hands on his hips, and face ablaze."

His eyes focused on an imaginary sight over her shoulder, and he spoke wistfully. "Ah, Lady Molka, those were the very best of days. The golden age, if you will. Never again to be seen in my lifetime." His eyes came back to hers. "Tell me, do you ever see Lady Laili?"

"I worked with her again a couple of months ago."

"That wild, young lioness is well-worthy of her own series."

Molka's eyebrows rose. "You never know." She reached behind her, picked up the briefing tablet the Savanna name label on it, and handed it to him. "This is the full briefing on the target and your responsibilities for the op."

He viewed the tablet with glee. "And so, the new adventure begins."

Molka said, "I know I told the team to take the rest of today off, but I'm putting you right to work. Jaron has scouted out several boats for sale on the island. They're all large, commercial fishing boats that won't seem out of place where we're going. I want you to go with him now and inspect them for suitability for our needs and then make a final decision after tomorrow's recon, so we can get the vessel into your hands as soon as possible."

"You mean, get her into my hands as soon as possible for modifications and to train the team to crew it?"

Her eyebrows rose. "No. But yes, now that you mention it."

"Consider it done, my lady. And no longer concern yourself with this part of the operation. I'll have it well in hand for you."

"I was hoping you'd say that. And…I'm also hoping you'll promise me that silly little argument you and Luc had won't lead to something more serious."

He stood and tucked the tablet under his left arm and again presented his slightly crooked rogue smile. "Lady Molka, if you know Captain LJ Savana the way you say you do, you know he will never make a promise he cannot keep."

CHAPTER 16

Kang smiled, swaggered into Molka's office and into the chair.

She smiled back, "Thank you again for coming."

He crossed his right leg over his left and sat back. "My pleasure. And I was going to thank you for eliminating my old *friend* Chul in Taiwan. However, my contacts in the GBR recently informed me that after taking out their best field operative and their best asset in Australia before that, your name is now on their death list right next to mine. They even have a special name for you which roughly translates into the bitch of death."

She waved a dismissive hand. "I'll remind myself to be terrified later. And believe it or not, I've been called that name before." She assumed a serious demeanor. "The Pentad file on you Azzur obtained says you passed advanced drone pilot training. Is that true?"

"No, I didn't pass advanced drone pilot training. I *mastered* advanced drone pilot training."

She smirked. "Cute. But Nathan is also a master drone pilot, and I thought bringing two camera drones with us would be advantageous."

"I agree. You can't have too many eyes in the sky on an op."

"You told me you still have contacts in the GBR. What about Chinese intelligence? I assume you used to work with them."

He nodded. "I did work with them and still do have some contacts."

"Great. That's the main reason I really wanted you on the team."

He presented a playboy smile. "Oh, I thought you wanted me for my irresistibly smooth charm wrapped in my incredibly sexy, all-man package."

She smirked again. "Azzur's report on you also mentions your reprimands for excessive fraternization with many attractive female employees at all five Pentad HQs."

His playboy smile continued. "Those reprimands don't acknowledge it takes two to fraternize and that I wasn't always the initiator."

"Nevertheless, getting back to your Chinese intelligence connections, whatever they can give you on the Base X and it's guest living on the north side would be extremely helpful."

His smile faded to seriousness. "I'll do my best. Although, my contacts with them are somewhat limited now."

"Understood." She reached behind her, picked up the briefing tablet with the Kang name label on it, and handed it to him. "This is the full briefing on the target and your responsibilities for the op."

"Molka, I really want to compliment you on the team you've put together. Obviously, you and I are outstanding." He winked. "Warren's reputation in the covert-ops community speaks for itself. The colonel is a legend. And the others all give off the aura of competence and daring. I believe we're well-staffed to pull this off."

"I think we are too. I'm concerned about team unity, though. And you and Warren are right at the top of the concerns list."

"Warren and I will end up having no problems. As the old saying goes, we're two sides of the same coin. More so now that I've come over to the other side. We both have a deep respect for each other which will rise to the surface and wash away any petty personal rivalries."

Molka's eyebrows rose, anxious. "I hope so. Because if the two biggest Alphas on a team of Alphas can't get along, the other

TASK X

Alphas will take sides, and then we'll be a team broken beyond repair and usefulness."

CHAPTER 17

Jager sat across from Molka and feigned disappointment. "Molka, I am so disappointed that you have not taken me up on my invitation to the finest restaurant in Munich for a lavish dinner with its dashing and debonair gentleman owner."

"Sorry, I've been a little busy. But didn't you tell me you would lose your restaurant after I took General Shamieh away from you?"

"I did tell you that, and I did lose it." He sighed, frustrated. "It was a humiliating blow."

She cast him a wary glance. "Nothing personal against me, I hope."

"Not at all. I got bested and left myself open to such a failure." He smiled. "But remember I also told you that my new plan was to make some more money and open the next finest restaurant in Munich. Which I did."

She nodded knowingly. "You tracked down Rivin for Zoran the Great."

He gave a satisfactory nod.

"Good for you," she said. "That disgusting bastard needed tracking down."

"Yes, his demise was long overdue."

"And how did Azzur track *you* down?"

"He actually ran me down, so to speak. I was on my usual morning run in Englischer Garten when a beautiful woman came alongside me and asked if she might accompany me. Naturally, I did not protest."

Molka grinned. "Naturally."

"At the end of the run, I asked her out for coffee, and she asked me if I still owed my life to you. And here I am."

"But how was the coffee date?"

"Nonexistent. After she was thoroughly satisfied, she delivered her message. She could not run away from me fast enough."

Molka shrugged. "That's us women for you." She reached behind her, picked up the briefing tablet with the Jager name label on it, and handed it to him. "This is the full briefing on the target and your responsibilities for the op."

"Understood."

"There's also a facial recognition app to upload to your encrypted phone you'll need to bring on the op to scan and verify the target."

"Very well," he said.

Molka continued. "And as our scout, I suggest you be the first in line to get copies for intense study when Nathan makes the updated digital maps after the recon tomorrow."

"I already planned to do exactly so."

"I also suggest we don't tell the rest of the team that when we first met, we were on opposites sides of a tribal conflict, and you had an HK G36 assault rifle pointed in my face."

He held up his right forefinger. "That is not accurate. The first time we met was a few days before when I almost ran you over with my vehicle in that little village."

"You're right," she said. "It was. Sorry. Seems like a million lifetimes ago."

"I know the feeling."

She sat back and folded her arms across her chest. "One other thing, I would appreciate it if you put your personal feelings about Colonel Krasnov aside for the duration of the op."

"Molka, I came here because you spared my life up on that Turkish mountain when you had an untold number of reasons not to."

Molka smirked. "Starting with your insane partner trying to murder my team and me."

"Fuchs was a good man right up until he wasn't."

She shrugged. "Aren't they all?"

"Good point. However, getting back to Krasnov. Since you did spare my life, if you ask me to serve with him, I will do so. But I think it's only fair you know my personal opinion is that criminals like Krasnov are not only a disgrace to themselves and their own armies but a disgrace to all honorable soldiers of all armies everywhere and for all time. So, if we happen to get into a chaotic firefight on that island, and he happens to cross my field of fire in all the confusion, I'm not sure I can disengage my trigger in time."

CHAPTER 18

A gleeful-faced Nathan ran to Molka's deskside when he entered. "Hug!"

She rose, and they hugged.

"Molka! How are you, girlfriend?"

"Good." She looked down at his right hand. "How's your hand?"

He held up his surgery-scarred right hand, flexed his fingers, and rotated his wrist. "A lot better than the dead bastard son of a bitch who broke it hoped it would be at this point."

Their embrace ended, and she pointed for him to sit, and she did the same.

His smile at her returned. "It's sooo great to see you again. You will always be very special to me because of what we did in Brazil. But as horrible and painful as it was, it pushed me into a whole new and exciting chapter in my life."

Her eyebrows rose, intrigued. "So you actually like being Project Nathan?"

He closed his eyes and hugged himself. "I love it, love it, love it!"

She grinned. "But how do you like working for Azzur?"

His eyes opened and theatrically rolled. "Azzur is Azzur is Azzur, and I'll leave it at that." He leaned forward, excited. "But OMG, how about Raziela being fired from the Counsel!"

Molka's jaw tightened. "She was fired and then did some firing herself."

His eyes lit up. "Ok, that is super-cryptic. Dish the details!"

"Maybe I will when all this is over." Her face resumed professional business mode again. "Did your photographic and video equipment make it through customs ok? That super high-tech stuff is not exactly what tourists would bring in with them."

His face became professional business mode. "They had no issues with it at customs."

"And none with your drone either?"

"Drones. And no issues with customs for them either. I brought six, two of three different types to give us flexibility."

"Good thinking," she said. "Share one appropriate for the op with Kang. He's been trained too."

"No problem."

She reached behind her, picked up the briefing tablet with the Nathan name label on it, and handed it to him. "This is the full briefing on the target and your responsibilities for the op."

He smiled at the tablet. "I never thought I would say this, but I'm looking forward to diving back into cartography again."

"Glad you feel that way," she said. "Because I don't have to tell you because you already know that inaccurate maps have doomed countless operations and even lost some wars."

He viewed her with respect-laden eyes. "I'll give you all my best, Molka."

"Thank you. And thank you again for coming. Now, concerning your issue with Shizi: whatever Laili told you about him was probably true. But he's promised me he's sober and quit drinking over two months ago. I'm taking him at his word and ask that you do too."

Nathan frowned. "It's just that he reminds me so much of my dad. Not just his alcoholism, he actually looks like my dad in the face. Which is weird because my dad is of Slovakian descent. He brings back tough childhood memories."

"Well, try to set the daddy issues aside, give Shizi a chance, and be supportive. Because if he doesn't get that diversion

TASK X

right…I'll never be able to dish you the details of the Raziela story."

CHAPTER 19

"Luc, thank you again for coming, and I want to apologize that my sudden goodbye in Monaco came from my former project manager's lips over the phone and not mine in person."

Luc sat relaxed across from Molka. "Goodbyes denote the past. Hellos denote a hopeful future." He smiled. "Hello, Molka."

Her jaw tightened. "Ok. We need to talk about that. So let's do that now. The time we were together, it was what it was. And it was 31 of the most blissful, carefree, and passionate days—and nights—that I've ever experienced and may ever experience again."

"I feel the same way."

"But it was what it was. And it can never be again. So I hope we can move forward both knowing that."

His face flashed disappointment. "I fear I have just been deposited into the so-called *friend zone*."

"No. You're enshrined in among the most respected men I've ever known zone."

He frowned. "That sounds even more platonic."

"Is that going to be a problem?"

"Molka, I have come to help you in any way I can to avenge your sister without conditions."

She gave him a small, appreciative smile. "Thank you, Luc. So, how did Azzur reel you in?"

"Two Monaco police officers pulled me over just after I left my villa and delivered your message. His choice of messengers, armed men with arrest powers, was not lost on me for its inference."

Her eyebrows rose knowingly. "Azzur is a master of passive-aggressive messages." She reached behind her, picked up the briefing tablet with the Luc name label on it, and handed it to him. "This is the full briefing on the target and your responsibilities for the op."

He gave an ultra-assured nod. "Whatever is required of me will be done."

"You're the key to the op. We can't blast our way into the compound without waking up the Chinese garrison. And yes, it's small, and we can probably neutralize it, but they might alert the Chinese Navy's fast patrol ships swarming in that area, and then none of us will make it home."

He gave another ultra-assured nod. "I will not be the reason, if the op fails."

"I believe you. And can you set aside your little personality clash with Captain Savanna?"

He frowned again. "That will be more difficult. This man grates on me. He grates on me as a ridiculously confident, unapologetically independent man with a hint of fraudulence."

Molka grinned. "Take out the word fraudulence, and that reminds me of someone else I know."

CHAPTER 20

"I'm going to ask you one more time," Molka said to a seated Shizi. "Were you telling the truth when you said you haven't had a drink in months?"

"I swear I haven't, Molka. Not since you last saw me. Look." He held his hands out, palms down. "See, steady as a rock."

She flashed a skeptical face. "But can you stay steady another week? Because your irresponsible, erratic behavior getting me killed is one thing. Getting those other seven good men killed is unacceptable to me. Understood?"

"Aye, ma'am. I'm still your loyal marine."

She maintained her skepticism. "And what about working with Nathan?"

His smile faded into a scowl, and he lowered his palms to his thigh tops and balled his fists. "I hate judgmental people. Because I've been judged all my life. Most of it lately has been justified, I'll admit. But I still hate it." He relaxed his scowl and his hands. "That being said, I think he's probably a good kid and taking out what his dad did to him on me. I can let that slide."

"Fair enough." She reached behind her, picked up the briefing tablet with the Shizi name label on it, and handed it to him. "This is the full briefing on the target and your responsibilities for the op."

He took the tablet and humbled himself in demeanor and voice. "Molka, thank you for giving me this chance. Sobriety is rough. It's even rougher because I've damaged my reputation to the point where contract jobs are few and far between, and the off time with nothing to do is an addict's worst enemy. So, thank you for believing in me."

"I'm going to be honest with you, Shizi, my belief in you runs only minute to minute. And, honestly, I'm probably being foolish bringing you in on something this important to me. But I know you've been struggling, and I can never forget your incredible, selfless bravery from the chopper over Taipei Harbor that night. So I'm taking this chance. But if you make me live to regret it…."

He nodded, almost like a bow. "You should kill me. And I'll 100 percent deserve it."

FRIDAY
JULY 29TH

CHAPTER 21

Private Airport
Eleven Kilometers North of Puerto Princesa
4:55 AM

Jaron drove the resort's shuttle bus carrying Molka and her team—who had not spoken a word to each other during the hour trip—through the airport's pre-opened entrance gate.

Airport operations normally didn't start until 9 AM when the staff showed up. But a cash payment deal brokered by the contractors Molka hired to fly the recon mission provided early, unsupervised access for them to the airport facilities with no questions asked.

And the contractor crew also suggested to Molka what she thought to be some excellent subterfuge to use during their flight.

Fourteen months earlier, an Australian news organization hired an aircraft that departed from the same airport to fly out to the Spratly Islands for a story about the mysterious Chinese artificial island military bases. And that flight, as it approached the islands, was openly threatened over the radio by the Chinese military to immediately leave the area, even after they identified themselves as the media.

The contractors reasoned the Chinese also photographed the snooping aircraft and noted the tail identification number for their report. So they chose the same exact model aircraft with the same paint scheme and then switched the tail number to match it. This would presumably lull the Chinese military into thinking their recon flight was just another media organization searching for a story.

Jaron drove from the gate straight onto the lit-up apron and then toward the single, lit-up runway hosting a waiting aircraft—a sleek, white with black stripes, twin-turboprop, 12-passenger, Beechcraft Super King Air 350—parked at the far end in takeoff position.

He parked parallel to the plane's left side at a 10-meter distance from the open cabin door and deployed airstairs from which two Asian males, the contractors, outfitted in khaki shirts and dark pants, descended.

Jaron opened the bus's exit doors, and Molka—again dressed in her duty uniform and carrying a black gear bag holding eight pairs of binoculars—led the team—who clad themselves in various climate-appropriate t-shirts, shorts, and sneakers—from the bus into the warm, humid predawn.

All team members came empty-handed except Nathan, who carried two silver metal hardcases containing his camera and video equipment.

One of the contractors addressed the team from the airstair's foot in good English. "Men, I'm your co-pilot. I'm going to seat you to evenly distribute the weight. Follow me."

He climbed into the cabin trailed by the still unspeaking team.

Molka greeted the remaining contractor, who would be the pilot. "Good morning."

He addressed her in good English. "Yes, it is a good morning. We'll have unlimited visibility all way to and over the destination."

"Excellent. Flight time?"

"Thirty-nine minutes. If you want to sit upfront with us, there's a jump seat on the flight deck."

"Sounds good," she said.

TASK X

"Just one concern you should know about. The Chinese Navy has stepped up its already pretty aggressive destroyer patrol presence around those island bases. Once we show up on the base's radar as what they feel is too close, we will get one set of warnings to leave. And if we don't leave fast after they give that set of warnings, they'll contact one of those destroyers to have them start tracking us, and that means locking an AA missile on us just for precaution. But the thing about precautionary missile locks is—"

Molka interrupted. "Accidental launches can and have happened. Yes, I have been there myself a few times."

He offered a knowing nod. "Fair enough. Ready to fly?"

Fifteen minutes later, the aircraft was airborne, wheels up, and heading west with the rising sun at its tail, turning the South China Sea a beautiful golden orange before them.

Molka sat in the jump seat behind the co-pilot, wearing a spare headset, and her gear bag lay at her feet.

Through the open flight deck door, she observed the cabin, which featured six high-backed seats on each side of the aisle with their own round window.

In order from the first seat on the left sat Warren, Jager, Savanna, and Nathan. And from the first seat on the right sat Luc, Shizi, the colonel, and Kang.

She hoped to see some cross-aisle chat to start building some semblance of team unity, but Savanna and Shizi napped, and the others stared out their windows in silent contemplation.

About twenty minutes into the flight, the co-pilot pointed out his side of the windscreen and spoke into his headset. "Chinese Navy destroyer."

The sleek gray warship leaving a long, white, V-shaped bow wake trail disconcerted Molka. Not due to the missile lock threat but due to the unknown reaction a destroyer would have to their ship passing through on op night. Did they stop and search?

A few minutes later, the pilot pointed to several black shapes on the water within sight of the destroyer, which he said were fishing vessels, and neither one seemed concerned with the other. Which made her feel much better and confirmed Azzur's suggestion of using a commercial-type fishing vessel was the right choice.

Another 15 minutes later, the pilot spoke into his headset again. "Destination visible at 5-nautical miles to starboard. Standby for the first orbit at 3,000 feet."

Molka viewed the white and green-colored island's form, vacated her seat, moved into the cabin aisle, and addressed the team. "We're here. Right-hand side."

The left-side seated team members moved across the aisle to share the six right-side windows with the others.

And without being told, they stayed clear of the first window for Nathan's use, who already had a pair of sophisticated digital cameras with long attached lenses uncased and ready for aiming.

Molka moved back to her seat, unzipped the gear bag, removed and passed out binoculars to the other seven men, and kept one set for herself.

The pilot began a gentle, banked turn and Base X came into clear view under a bright morning sky.

Binoculars went to eyes, and Nathan's cameras went to work.

Molka scanned the island's north end. The target's beige-colored, two-story residence inside the high-walled compound matched the satellite images. That being a two-story Chinese copy of a Latin American villa. Maybe to make the Guatemalan-born Ramirez feel more at home.

The main communications antenna tower, the two wind turbines, and the power station—all painted a dull white—located on the island's center matched the satellite photos too.

She moved her view to the island's south end, and the two large radome towers, attached comms building, and smaller building for the garrison—painted a duller white shade—also matched the satellite photos.

But to the right of that, something which did not appear on the satellite photos in the form of a huge addition added to the island's land mass: a two-kilometer long by one-kilometer wide

TASK X

U-shape which enclosed an artificial harbor. Two cargo cranes painted bright red, and a long, concrete pier lined the harbor's right side, and behind that stood a long, wide, flat, sandy space.

And on the new peninsula formed by the harbor's left side sat six larger buildings—all painted a bright, recent paint job white shade—also did not appear on the satellite photos.

Nathan spoke up first. "I guess you all see what I'm seeing."

The colonel said, "Is this island confirmed as our destination?"

Molka spoke into the headset. "Destination confirmed?"

The pilot answered: "Confirmed."

Molka addressed the team. "Confirmed. Kang, you're our Chinese expert. Thoughts?"

Kang said, "If I had to guess, I would say they constructed that harbor to bring in heavy equipment and supplies and add a large airstrip to this base. Which they've done on several others."

The colonel said, "This makes sense. I see a large stockpile of construction materials about 150 meters from the new harbor."

Warren said, "And that construction project would require substantially more personnel arriving here to do so."

The colonel said, "By the looks of the new buildings, some of which I believe to be barracks, I would say these substantial extra personnel are already there."

Molka addressed Kang. "Would these be civilian workers?"

"Doubtful. Too much of a security risk to these prized installations. More likely, they would send part of a military construction battalion."

She frowned. "Who would also probably be fully trained and armed soldiers."

"Yes," Kang said. "I'll hear back from my Chinese contacts this afternoon. They should have something on this new development."

"Ok. Get that information to me as soon as you do."

Jager said, "Look at all those plots of neatly lined trees spread out over the whole island. Why the landscaping?"

Kang said, "Those are citrus groves to supplement their food rations. They're a long way from nowhere out here, and supply deliveries might be few and far between."

Warren emitted a sarcastic scoff at Kang. "You commies can never supply enough food for yourselves, can you?"

Kang ignored the remark.

Molka did, too, and addressed the colonel. "Colonel, what is your best estimate of how many soldiers those new barracks could house?"

"Sixty to one hundred is my best estimate."

A smattering of self-grumbling and low curses arose from the team then a radio voice in Chinese-accented English blared over the headsets:

"Foreign military aircraft southwest of reef."

"This is Chinese Navy."

"You are threatening the security of our station."

"To avoid miscalculations, please leave the area immediately."

Molka moved back into the flight deck and stood behind the pilot.

The co-pilot answered the radio call:

"Chinese Navy, we are a civilian aircraft carrying passengers proceeding to Palawan Island."

The Chinese Navy repeated their threat.

The pilot spoke to Molka. "If you have what you need, I suggest we depart this area before a Chinese destroyer does what we discussed."

"Understood." She moved back into the cabin and next to Nathan, who still shot photos. "We've been warned to leave by the Base X garrison. How much longer do you need?"

Nathan lowered his camera. "I'm good. I was just getting some backup images."

She spoke into the headset. "Ok. Let's go home."

Pilot: "Roger. Heading home."

Molka addressed Nathan again. "How long will it take you to produce updated images and digital maps?"

"Give me about four hours when we get back."

"Great. Get a thumb drive copy to Dov as soon as you're finished so he can disseminate everything to the team."

"Will do. Uh…Molka?"

"Yes?"

"I'm more than a little freaked out about an additional sixty to one hundred armed soldiers waiting for us down there. Aren't you?"

She whispered. "Yes. But let's not show it to the others."

The 39-minute flight time out to Base X became 29-minutes to make it back to the airport. The pilot mentioned a good tailwind. Or maybe he decided to go with a maximum cruise speed in fear of anti-aircraft missile locks and accidental launches.

Faithful Jaron waited in the shuttle bus on the apron during the recon and pulled alongside the aircraft when it taxied to a stop.

While the team deplaned and reboarded the bus, Molka concluded the payment transfer to the contractors, then boarded the bus and addressed them. "Gentlemen, in approximately six hours, the recon images and updated digital maps of Base X will be transmitted to your tablets. Please study them and prepare relevant thoughts, suggestions for the op, and any additional equipment requests. We will meet after dinner in the briefing room at 8 PM to discuss and set up the parameters for the final tactical plan."

On the hour ride back to the resort, Molka again hoped to see some cross-aisle chat to build team unity. But again, Savanna and Shizi napped, and the others stared out their windows in silent contemplation.

FREDRICK L. STAFFORD

CHAPTER 22

**Club Utopia
Conference Room
8 PM**

Molka exited her office wearing a fresh duty uniform, moved to the podium, and faced the seated team, who all changed into alternate casual clothes and placed their briefing tablets on the tabletop. "Good evening, gentlemen. Did you have a good dinner?"

They spoke a unified: "Yes."

The first collective thing they had done since arriving.

Molka continued. "This briefing will be conducted as follows. First, our intelligence specialist Kang will provide the information he obtained today from his sources in Chinese intelligence about the new construction and increased personnel we viewed this morning on Base X."

"Next, Captain Savanna will brief us with his thoughts on the amphibious operation."

"After that, the colonel will brief us on the ground operation."

"Then we will take input from each of you regarding the final tactical plan. To reference the recon photos and new digital maps Nathan prepared and to share any visuals you may have, Dov has synched your tablets with the big wall monitor there. Just open the mirroring app now appearing on your tablet desktop to connect it."

"Gentlemen, be advised: This is the first time for me planning and commanding a special operation of this size. And some of my procedures and terminology will not strictly adhere to the standard ones you're accustomed to. But they're comfortable for me and I ask that you indulge me on them. That being said, the op is tentatively scheduled to be executed one week from tonight. That gives us a two-day cushion before we lose several of you to other commitments."

She addressed Kang. "Kang, please give your briefing."

He stood. "My sources confirmed the target currently lives in the residence in the compound and has two security men living with him at all times. They are hired from a firm in Hong Kong and serve in three-month rotations. They also confirmed two women, those being a full-time cook, and a full-time housekeeper, live in the residence."

"My sources could not give me specific information on the new additions to Base X. However, similar construction on other islands involved a military construction unit of approximately 50 to 100 to finish a new harbor. So, the colonel's estimate was accurate. Then, perhaps, another 100 are brought in to help construct the airstrip."

Molka's eyebrows rose. "Bringing the total garrison to approximately 220. I guess we can consider ourselves very lucky we'll pull the op before those reinforcements arrive and only face about 120 tops."

She hoped her downplaying tactic would calm concerns about the nasty surprise from the morning recon.

"Please go on, Kang."

He continued. "I'll conclude with one bit of positive news for us. These very remote, and small island bases are garrisoned entirely by navy personnel. And they trust their perimeter security to their navy surface ship patrols. Therefore, they feel no need to post sentries at night, and they all sleep blissfully knowing their fellow sailors have their backs."

TASK X

Molka said, "So it's up to us not to wake anyone on that side of the island until Shizi's diversion hits them when we're headed home." She addressed Savanna. "Captain Savanna, please give your briefing."

He stood holding his tablet. "After the recon, this is the vessel I've chosen for the op."

He swiped his tablet, and on the big monitor, a photo appeared showing a commercial fishing boat with a white bridge and superstructure and a dark blue hull.

Savanna continued. "She's a 30-year-old, 85-foot prawn trawler named the *Banda Pearl*."

Molka said, "She looks well-used."

Savanna said, "That's exactly how we want her to look. A world-weary, old working girl trying to make a living on the South China Sea, like thousands just like her. She'll blend right in."

Molka nodded. "Understood."

He went on. "She has a just re-built Caterpillar 3508 twin-turbocharged diesel motor. And I'm having them install bow thrusters for better control and maneuverability. And after all the below deck refrigerated storage equipment is stripped out, she'll make good speed for us."

Molka said, "How long will it take to do all that?"

"It's being done as we speak. The seller was happy to take care of it since I told him he could keep the equipment to resell."

"Ok," Molka said. "Please go on."

"Tomorrow at noon, she'll be ready for me to take delivery from a marina about 20 miles south of here. And Lady Molka, I'm requesting the entire team, except for you, come with me."

Molka flashed a quizzical face. "Why is that?"

"On the cruise back here, I will give each man basic pilot training. So, if we have badly wounded and-or casualties, any survivor can get us home. Of course, you are exempt because you already have your captain's certification."

She nodded. "Excellent suggestion, captain. I approve your request. And also train Dov and Jaron so they can act as your crew on the night of the op."

Savanna grinned. "Thank you. I was about to ask you for just such an accommodation. I'll make them first-rate hands." He swiped his tablet, and the updated overhead image of Base X appeared on the monitor. "Before I start, I must say the quality of these recon images and updated maps is incredible." He addressed Nathan. "Fine work, sir."

Nathan offered a humble nod.

Molka liked the acknowledgment too.

Another small step in team unity.

Savanna continued. "Now, as you can see, the entire island is surrounded by a seawall of undetermined height behind a very thin beach-like coastal strip. And obviously, consideration of getting over the wall will have to be made regardless of the chosen landing spot. But I believe a promising place for that is here…." He zoomed the image over a small beach. "It's about 30-yards wide and fronts an unoccupied section of the island's westside between the target's residential compound and the power station."

Warren spoke up. "So, you'll pull our ship close to that tiny beach, and we'll jump out and splash ashore?"

"No," Savanna said. "Remember, that island is built atop a natural coral reef. And without knowing how far or how deep that reef may extend out from the island running afoul is too great a risk for the *Banda Pearl*. And if we lose her, it's a long swim home."

Warren said, "Point taken. How will the assault team land then?"

Savanna answered. "We'll bring some electric motor-powered inflatables for the landings and extractions. Using the ship's crane, they can easily be lowered and raised from the deck. I've already purchased those craft from a dealer at the marina, and they'll be loaded aboard *Banda Pearl* when we pick her up."

Molka said, "Captain Savanna, your initiative is appreciated. We'll also all need to be trained on how to pilot those landing boats and rehearse boarding and launching them from the ship."

"Of course, Lady Molka. And that's all I have for now."

She addressed the colonel. "Colonel Krasnov, your thoughts on the ground operation, please, sir."

He stood holding his tablet and gestured at the image still on screen. "First, I agree with Captain Savanna's suggestion for a landing beach. It is the most suitable to our needs."

He swiped his tablet to bring the overhead shot of the new barracks buildings. "I will start my thoughts with the glaring new difficulty we have discovered in the reinforced garrison."

"My original plan was that another man and I would go in just ahead of the main force and set up an observation and blocking position across from the garrison's comms building—which we must assume is staffed around the clock operating the radar systems—and the attached barracks building in this citrus grove about 50 meters away. However, with the prospect of many more personnel in the new barracks facilities, several other observation-blocking teams should be used." He addressed Molka. "Team leader, how did you intend to allocate our personnel?"

She answered. "I thought we would divide the assault force into two teams: Alpha and Bravo. Alpha team consisting of yourself, Nathan, and Shizi will land first so the observation-blocking position can be established and Shizi can work on the diversion. Then about 15 minutes later, Bravo team consisting of Jager, Luc, Warren, Kang, and myself would land and carry out the breaching of the compound, securing the residence, and eliminating the target."

The colonel said, "Would it be possible to move one man from Bravo to Alpha to assist us?"

Molka said, "We require our scout Jager to lead us to the compound without being detected. And also, after the compound is breached, he will locate the target and confirm the target's identity with a facial scan. Luc is the only one who can make a surreptitious breach of the compound and deactivate any alarms. Warren, as my XO, has to be with the kill team in case something happens to me. And Kang is needed to interpret to the Chinese domestic servants inside the residence to keep them from getting hurt." So, no. Bravo can't spare a man. Sorry, sir."

"Understandable," the colonel said. "And I must commend you for already doing a large part of planning of this operation."

Molka gave a humble nod and then faced Savanna. "Captain Savanna, can you spare Dov and Jaron to join Alpha?"

Savanna said, "I can spare one of them. The other should stay aboard to assist in the recovery of the landing boats and their occupants."

"Right," she said. "We don't want that to get messed up because we might be in a hurry to get out of there."

Savanna nodded. "That was my thinking as well, Lady Molka."

She addressed the colonel again. "Colonel, you can have Jaron for Alpha."

He nodded. "Thank you, team leader."

"You're welcome, sir. Anyone else have comments?"

Jager raised his hand.

"Yes, Jager."

Jager stood with his tablet and swiped until an overhead image of the compound came onto the screen. "I believe when we approach the compound, we should take a covered position in this citrus grove approximately 40-meters from it and send the breach and alarm specialist uh...the uh, Frenchman...uh—"

Luc spoke up, a bit offended. "Luc Durand, *monsieur*."

Jager continued. "Right. Anyway, I believe we should take a covered position and send him alone to breach and deactivate any alarms just in case he trips an alarm or is discovered, so the rest of Bravo team won't be compromised too."

Luc spoke up again, a bit more offended. "I think, *monsieur*, it will be wise for each to worry over his own responsibilities and not project their inadequacies on another."

Jager cast an offended look on Luc. "Are you implying that I can't do my job? Because if so—"

Molka interrupted. "We'll discuss specific tactics as a TEAM when the ground operation plan is finished. Anyone else?"

Warren raised his hand.

"Yes, Warren."

He stood. "I would just like to register my concern as to the validity of the information in the report given by the GBR man."

Molka said, "Concern noted. Any other comments?"

No one spoke up.

She continued. "Alright. Submit any additional weapon and equipment requests to Dov so he can call them in tonight. The shuttle bus to take you to the marina to pick up the ship tomorrow will leave outside the resort's lobby at 11 AM. By the time you return, the weapons and equipment should be delivered, also by boat, and we'll reconvene to inspect them together. That will be all."

The colonel spoke up. "With your permission, team leader. Since our cartographer, Nathan, has already been assigned to my team, I would like him to assist me with his expertise in preparing the tactical plan for the ground operation, and that we begin to do so immediately in my quarters to be submitted to you in the morning before we leave for our sea duty."

Molka smiled, humble. "Request approved. Thank you for your outstanding initiative, sir."

The colonel stood, picked up his tablet, and departed.

Nathan stood, picked up his tablet, and trailed the colonel.

Molka addressed the remaining team members. "That's all I have for tonight, gentlemen. I'll be in my office at 6 AM if you need to see me. I'm going to bed now. But, uh…feel free to stay and discuss among yourselves."

Her latest attempt to encourage some team unity also fell flat.

Each man left the conference room in silence without a glance or word to another.

**SATURDAY
JULY 30TH**

CHAPTER 23

6:08 AM

A duty uniformed Molka sat at her desk staring at her laptop, admiring the colonel's tactical plan for the ground operation he submitted to her on a thumb drive minutes before.

Her assessment: classic Red Wolf.

Brilliantly simple and simply brilliant.

It could work.

It had to work!

She pulled up the recon photos of the target's compound and residence. Since the satellite images of the same area provided to her by the Counsel were taken, a large, masonry, working decorative fountain had been constructed in the compound about 30 meters from the residence's front porch.

Perhaps its beauty and soothing, gurgling water pleasured the head resident, but it could also provide an excellent cover position to the assault team after they entered.

Another enhancer for a good plan coming together.

But if the team didn't come together first, the best plan she had conceived would be useless. And during the previous night's briefing, the unity prospect seemed no closer, with the couple of promising moments overshadowed by Jager and Luc's throwing shade on one another and Warren's open statement of mistrust for Kang.

If she ever thought team leaders had it easy in the past, she never would again.

Dov opened the door and entered carrying a covered room service tray. "Good morning."

"Good morning." She viewed the tray. "What's that?"

"Your breakfast, hot from the kitchen."

"I haven't ordered breakfast yet."

"I know. I checked with the kitchen and found out you gave them a standard alternating breakfast order of egg white omelet with goat cheese and an orange juice and oatmeal with blueberries and banana and plain yogurt." He placed the tray on her desktop and removed the lid. "Today's an omelet day."

The wonderous aroma watered her mouth. "Well…thank you."

"I'll bring your breakfast every morning, so you won't have to worry about it. You have enough to do in the next six days. Is this time a good time?"

"Yes. Thank you again."

She moved her laptop aside, slid the tray before her, removed the lid from the orange juice glass, took a sip, picked up her silverware rolled in a cloth napkin, dug the fork into her scrumptious-smelling omelet, and took in a large bite. As she chewed, she glanced up to see him watching her.

She swallowed. "Sorry, I'm usually ravenous like this in the morning. Don't mean to be rude."

He smiled. "No offense. Healthy appetite, healthy mind. And I've already powered down my breakfast. I have a report for you; I can come back if you like?"

"No. Go with your report."

"I heard from the *Baron of Berlin*, Bennie Berlin, an hour ago. He was able to add the additional weapons and equipment requests made by the team to our order. He said he'll be here by 4 PM. It's about an 8-hour cruise from his home port of Manila Bay."

"Ok. We'll have him use the larger of the marina's two docks to unload it on."

"I already informed him of that."

She nodded and kept up her omelet devouring.

He viewed a hand-sized, printed-out photo of a smiling Janetta on the desktop's right corner. "That's your little sister."

She swallowed and gazed at it. "Yes. I printed it out from my phone. I keep a photo of her on my office desk in my clinic, and sitting at the desk without it made me feel odd."

Dov said, "The gift shop here has an old-school laminating machine. I guess they used it for people who wanted to print out their vacation pics and laminate them to display on the wall. If you like, I can laminate your sister's pic for you, so it displays better on your desk or maybe on your nightstand at night."

His kind gesture stirred her heart. "I'd actually like that a lot. Thanks."

"No problem. I have that list of the additional equipment and weapons requested by the team if you'd like to look it over?"

"I'll look it over on our way to the training ground."

"Training ground?" he said.

"Is one of the electric carts charged?"

"Yes, they all are."

"Ok. Pick me up outside the lobby entrance in 10 minutes."

She dove back into her omelet.

Ten minutes later, Molka rode in the cart's passenger seat as Dov drove the winding asphalt path toward the resort's far side and read from a list on his tablet. "The colonel requested an additional SIG LMG-68 light machine gun."

Dov said, "For Jaron to use on Alpha team."

"Right." She read on. "And the colonel also requested another 1000 rounds of 7.62-millimeter ammo with tracers. That makes 1,500 rounds total for those LMGs." Her eyebrows rose. "If we get in a fight where we need all that, we're probably all dead."

She read on. "Jager wants a different model of night vision goggles? I ordered the best, newest ones Berlin had."

"He said it's an older model he's used for years and feels more comfortable with."

She read on. "Kang wants a small, powerful megaphone."

Dov said, "To use inside the compound to call out to the servants and security inside the residence."

"Good idea." She read on. "Two FIM-92 Stinger rocket launchers. What the…. No name attached to the request. Who wanted those?"

"I did. Air defense for the *Banda Pearl*."

She flashed him a disbelieving glance. "Serious?"

"Yes. It's better to have something and not need it than to need it and not have it."

"I agree, but those Stingers are crazy-expensive. And everything we don't use Berlin buys back at only 20 percent of what we paid. I don't want Kaelee to think we're abusing her incredible generosity."

Dov said, "I know, but Captain Savanna appointed me his first mate and told me one of my primary duties was defending our ship. So…."

She smirked. "You mean the ship you haven't even seen? The captain talks theatrically like that and gets people all excited. But you have to discern what's real and what's fluff."

He frowned. "Then you might not like the special items he requested."

She read on. "And for Captain LJ Savanna…" She looked over all the items and laughed. "Well, I can't wait to see that."

They arrived at the main beach, and Molka said, "Stop here."

Dov halted the cart.

She pointed toward the beach. "By tomorrow night, I need you and Jaron to measure off and mark off a stretch of beach the same size as our landing beach on Base X. Then we're going to conduct a practice exercise that night and every night until the op."

"We'll have it ready for the exercise, Molka. You're really concerned about the landing, aren't you?"

"Yes. Every op I've been part of has been helicopter insertion and extraction. Those I'm great at and comfortable with. But loading, landing, re-loading, rendezvousing, and unloading

TASK X

again all at sea just seems fraught with countless things that can go wrong and any one of them could be fatal."

CHAPTER 24

5:05 PM

Firm commitment times became optional for the evening.

It started when Bennie Berlin delayed his arrival from 4 PM to 8 PM.

Then Savanna's message said the *Banda Pearl* would arrive at the resort marina's smaller dock within 30 minutes. But when Molka arrived there 15 minutes later to watch the ship cross the bay, the 85-foot prawn trawler already sat docked and tied off.

Molka walked the ship's length. She presented a much older version of the vessel Savanna showed in the photo. The white paint on the superstructure and upper hull carried ample rust streaking, and the dark blue paint on the lower hull oxidized to a medium blue hue.

Dov and Jaron appeared on the aft deck, stepped through an open gate in the side railing, and jumped down about a meter to the dock.

Molka addressed them. "Berlin is delayed until eight. Where's the rest of the team?"

Jaron said, "They went straight to their villas to order dinner."

TASK X

She said, "None of them wanted to eat together in the restaurant after being together all day?"

Dov and Jaron exchanged a nervous glance, and Dov said, "No."

She frowned. "Ok. What happened out there?"

A grinning Savanna appeared on the aft deck. "Lady Molka, please come aboard."

She addressed her assistants again. "Go to dinner. I'll meet you on the big dock at eight when Berlin arrives."

They departed, and she climbed up through the open railing gate, and onto a non-slip steel deck.

Savanna grinned anew. "What do you think of her?"

She shrugged. "I was about to ask you the same."

"She'll do the job for us just fine. Please inspect the landing boats for your approval." He gestured toward the stern where the two boats sat side-by-side, covered by blue tarps.

Molka followed Savanna across the aft deck dotted with numerous freshly vacated bolt holes indicating recent equipment removal leaving only a blue, electric-powered crane retracted to the left.

They reached the boats, and he removed the cover from the one on the right side to reveal a larger-size, dark gray-colored, inflatable boat with four bench-style seats and an attached black outboard motor.

Molka examined the craft. "Bigger than I thought."

"Eighteen-footers," he said. "I went with the larger size so, in case of a malfunction, one boat can carry both assault teams."

She nodded approval. "A good precaution."

"Those 150 horsepower-equivalent electric motors will move them very fast and silent."

"And we'll use the crane to lower and recover them?"

"We will. I'll rig up a strap and chain system to do the job. And also, a ladder for the teams to climb in and out of them."

She nodded again. "Good. We'll need to run practice exercises in lowering, loading, launching, and landing those boats numerous times, starting tomorrow night."

"Yes, I've already informed the rest of the men such an exercise would be necessary."

"And how did the pilot training go?"

"We'll need one more session for me to feel comfortable. And of course, I need to finish instructing Dov and Jaron in their duties."

"Ok," she said. "Schedule them for in the morning and let Dov know the details and he'll inform the rest of the team. And um…speaking of the team again, how did everyone get along today?"

He placed the tarp back over the boat, moved to the stern railing, placed his hands atop it, and gazed out at the bay. "I will say this about that. During my piracy days on the Caribbean, it was my experience that a disharmonized crew was no crew at all. It really was a group of disgruntled individual agendas that could get everyone caught." He turned a concerned face to Molka. "And with our endeavor, that could get everyone killed."

CHAPTER 25

8:11 PM

If Captain Savanna's vessel choice for its mission delivering two assault teams was all about covert ordinariness, Benny Berlin's vessel choice for its mission delivering black-market weapons and equipment was all about overt extraordinariness.

Molka waited holding her laptop under strong fluorescent lighting in the sticky evening on the resort's larger marina dock—flanked by Dov and Jaron—watching a vibrantly illuminated, newer model, gold-colored, 100-foot yacht cruise slow across the bay toward them.

About a dozen young, bikini-clad girls danced with drinks on the forward deck to loud, thumping club music.

Over four hours late.

But the man could make an entrance.

Had to give him that.

The yacht's pilot skillfully brought the golden beauty through the marina's entrance channel and then eased her starboard side alongside the dock, where two Asian male deckhands hopped out to tie her off, place bumpers, and deploy boarding stairs from her afterdeck.

All the while, the 13 bikini party girls representing multiple races—not one younger than about 19 but not one older than 21—continued unabated party gyrations to their blaring music.

A moment later, the late-50s, diminutive but dandy, Benny Berlin exited the rear cabin and raised his right hand.

The music silenced.

The girls stopped, slumped, and frowned.

Berlin's head carried a tanned, cherubic face under silver hair slicked straight back and he styled a dark blue, gold-button blazer over an open collar white dress shirt, white dress pants, and white dress shoes.

He addressed the girls in American English with a thick New York City accent. "Ok, babies. Go play on the beach while daddy takes care of business."

The *babies* obeyed *daddy* and giggled and wiggled and jiggled off the forward deck, down the yacht's boarding stairs, down the dock, off the dock, and onto the beach.

A sight that didn't go unnoticed by Dov and Jaron's leers.

Berlin descended the stairs, moved to Molka, and extended his hand. "Greetings, Molka. I've heard a lot about you from Azzur. It's a pleasure."

She shook his hand. "Thank you."

He gestured toward his babies frolicking in the sand, still being gawked at by Molka's assistants. "It's not all fun and games with the girls of *The Golden Gun*."

Molka said, "The girls of the golden gun? Sounds like an old spy movie. Or a…. Well, never mind."

Berlin said, "*The Golden Gun* is the name of my yacht. And its girls, or babies as I prefer to call them, help discourage, by distraction, any nosey authorities who may want to board her." He smiled, flashing overly white, expensive teeth. "Who would want to go below and look around when all the most interesting things were up here?"

Molka nodded. "Makes sense. I guess."

"Sorry again about being late, Molka. My men will have your order offloaded in just a few minutes. Then we can do an inventory together and finalize our deal."

She nodded, satisfied. "Fair enough."

TASK X

And right on cue, eight younger Asian males emerged from the rear cabin dressed in gold-colored coveralls, all carrying and double carrying a variety of dark green military-style crates and cases.

Molka, Dov, Jaron, and Berlin—who showed himself to be a chain smoker to rival Azzur—stood back and watched the unloading and stacking onto the dock.

And as it progressed, a crucial omission on her behalf became apparent to Molka. An omission of how much hard work it would be for her and her two physically compromised assistants—thanks to her—to carry all the heavy hardware from the dock down the beach about 200 meters to Dov and Jaron's beach villa.

She could ask the team to help, but they all sequestered in their villas after dinner, and she didn't want to disturb the relaxation of her skilled professionals by doing manual labor.

About 15 minutes later, Molka's order waited in a long, neat row, with each crate and case opened to reveal the contents.

Berlin's men re-boarded the yacht, and he flipped his latest cigarette into the water and addressed Molka. "Shall we?"

She nodded and pulled up her order list on her laptop.

They moved to the crates and cases on the far left, and Berlin recited as they moved down the line:

"Six MP5 submachineguns mounting a tactical sight and mounted on tactical slings. Each with one attached 30-round magazine and four spare 30-round magazines inside tactical magazine pouches mounted on tactical chest rigs."

"Nine Glock 19 semi-automatic pistols inside tactical thigh holsters. Each with one attached 15-round magazine and two spare 15-round magazines inside tactical magazine pouches."

"One Beretta 96A1 semi-automatic pistol inside a tactical thigh holster. With one attached 10-round magazine and two spare 10-round magazines inside tactical magazine pouches."

"Three SIG LMG-68 light machine guns with 100-round ammo pouches.

"Two FIM-92 Stinger rocket launchers."

"Fifteen, one and a quarter pound C-4 block charges with 19 electronic timer-detonators."

"Two Milkor MGL 40-millimeter grenade launchers on tactical slings."

"Fifteen hundred rounds of 7.62-millimeter ammo."

"Twelve hundred rounds of nine-millimeter ammo."

"One hundred rounds of .40 S&W hollow point ammo."

"One case of 40-millimeter smoke grenades."

"One case of 40-millimeter CS grenades."

"Ten sets of US Army new issue night vision goggles."

"One set of NATO older issue night vision goggles."

"Eleven black, tactical-style Kevlar helmets with mounts for night vision goggles and communication headsets."

"Eleven, high-power, two-way tactical radios with encrypting and twelve sets of wireless, tactical headsets."

"Ten black BDUs in individual sizes."

"Ten black tactical t-shirts in individual sizes."

"Ten sets of black tactical boots in individual sizes."

"Ten sets of black tactical socks."

"Nine tactical watches."

"Two 10-round, 40-millimeter grenade bandoliers."

"One case of heavy-duty flex-cuffs."

"One case of heavy-duty rubber gloves."

"And finally, one box of special-order items for a Captain LJ Savanna."

"Everything check out for you?"

Molka reviewed her list again. "Yes."

He continued. "And as we agreed, I'll buy everything that survives your use back for 20 percent of the purchase price."

"Right." She smirked. "What a deal."

He flashed the overly white teeth again. "Hey, this is a dirty business and a dirty game."

"Uh-huh. I have your money in my office."

"I always like to seal a deal with a drink. Shall we go to the bar?"

"The resort is closed," she said. "So the bars are closed too."

His smile frowned. "That's very disappointing. Closing a deal without a drink just isn't business."

She gestured at his yacht. "You don't have several well-stocked bars aboard that beast?"

"No, I run a dry ship. Mixing my men with alcohol and my babies could lead to rough seas out there."

Her eyebrows rose. "That makes sense too." She addressed Dov and Jaron, who still stood staring at the daunting job awaiting them. "Go ahead and dive in. I'll be back to help you shortly. We can probably have it done by midnight if we go hard."

Berlin assumed a concerned face. "I may be of service with that. Please allow my men to assist your men in carrying your order to your storage place."

Molka smirked again. "And how much more will that cost?"

"Nothing, of course. Call it customer appreciation."

She glanced at the long line of heavy cases and crates again. "Alright. Thank you."

Berlin called out: "More work to do out here, crew."

His men exited from the rear cabin again and faced him.

"Carry out service on the customer's order." Berlin then addressed Dov and Jaron. "They'll do all the work. Just show them where to go and where to put it."

Dov smiled, relieved. "Thank you, Mr. Berlin."

Jaron smiled, relieved. "Thank you, Mr. Berlin."

"My pleasure, men." Berlin turned his attention back to Molka with a fresh fluorescent smile. "Now, before you pay me, do you think you can see your way into opening the bar especially for me to have that deal-closing drink?"

CHAPTER 26

11: 47 PM

Nathan poked his head into Molka's open office door to find her seated at her desk. "What are you still doing awake?"

She glanced up from her laptop. "What are *you* still doing awake?"

He dropped into the chair across from her, wearing a lavender designer t-shirt, white shorts, white sandals, and white-framed glasses. "I was woken up along with the rest of the team by Bennie Berlin's beach party featuring his men, his women, and Dov and Jaron. All laughing, yelling, singing, and generally raising hell."

Molka winced. "Sorry about that. I took Berlin to the resort bar for a deal-closing drink he wanted, and then he asked if his men could also have a few drinks from the bar before they left. I said yes, to thank them for helping carry all our stuff into storage. Dov and Jaron were hosting them. Guess it got out of hand." She stood. "I'll go break up the festivities."

"Berlin already did, and…" He made a wavy motion with his left hand. "They all sailed away."

She sat back down and flashed a sly smile. "Did you join in the party with the boys?"

He flashed a sly smile. "I'll admit, I was very tempted. But I'll party when the job is done."

"Any of the rest of the team join in the party?"

"Not a man."

Molka sighed. "I kind of wish they all would have."

"You mean to build some team unity?"

She gave a thoughtful nod. "Yes."

"You wished that because, as the old cliché says, team unity is the foundation for any successful team."

"Yes. All clichés are based on a truism."

He said, "That's what I came to talk to you about, team unity."

"What about it?"

"Today on the boat was much worse than the first meeting. We all got into it again with our *rival*. And when Captain Savanna pulled rank and told us it was his ship and he didn't tolerate disharmony on the crew and for all of us to shut up, that Luc guy started organizing a mutiny to take the ship away from him and toss him overboard."

She flashed a quizzical face. "What? No."

"Well, I might be exaggerating a little. But it was an ugly scene. Oh, by the way, Luc had a lot of nice things to say about you." He grinned, sly, again. "Did you two once have a little boom-boom time or something?"

Molka smirked. "Or something."

Nathan's eyes alit. "Oooo…dish the details, girlfriend."

"Not now." She rubbed her temples. "Today's over. So we only have five days before the op. This team better bond fast. Or…."

"Or," he said, "it could be a deadly disaster when we get out there, and things get rough, and no one trusts anyone."

"Exactly." Her face tightened with frustration. "I just don't understand why they can't come together for this op. They all have much more in common than they do differently. I guess all men are dogs at heart and need to mark their territory."

Nathan smirked. "And all women are catty and love to backstab each other. All clichés are based on a truism, and there's a cliché for every occasion. But what you said before about wishing the team joined that party tonight gives me an idea that might help the situation."

She cupped her ears. "I'm all desperate ears."

"You're right about all us guys having more in common than we do different. And now we all know that too. But none of us want to be the first to drop our guard and drop our grudge." He leaned forward, excited. "So, I think what we need to break that impasse is a good old-fashioned social mixer, like our parents used to go to. At least mine did."

"Remind me what a social mixer is."

"It's when people of like minds and interests get together in a party-like setting, mix, bond, and build new friendships. Usually fueled by lots of alcohol and some good food. We could do the same thing with our guys."

She shrugged. "Alright. I'm willing to try anything at this point. How would we go about putting something like that together?"

"Leave it all to me." He grinned. "I've wondered if I could do a side hustle as an event planner, and this will prove it. We're in the Philippines, home to some of the world's greatest seafood. Which means they have great seafood restaurants. I'll pick the venue and ensure we get our own private section to mix socially."

"Why not here?" she said. "We have a big restaurant with a world-class staff right here. And plenty of alcohol in the two bars."

He shook his head, negative. "No, we can't do it here. That won't work."

"Why not?"

"Because this is where we work every day. It's not special anymore. We need to take a little road trip to Puerto Princesa and build up some anticipation and excitement."

"Ok. Make it happen for tomorrow evening. You're excused from boat pilot training in the morning. I'll give you the op cash card. Use whatever you need."

"Will do. Good night." He hopped up and moved to the door.

She called after him. "Nathan, you really think this will work?"

He paused, turned, and grinned again. "By the end of the night, it will be bro hugs all around."

TASK X

SUNDAY
JULY 31ST

CHAPTER 27

3:05 PM

How those HQ staffers in the Unit did it every day, she would never know. Ten straight hours stuck at a desk equaled torture for Molka. Especially after only five hours of sleep.

But finishing the final briefing for the op required it.

She closed her laptop, leaned back in the chair, and stretched. Behind her on the credenza sat the breakfast tray Dov brought her at 6 AM before he left with Jaron and the rest of the team for their ship pilot training session.

And on the desk's right-hand corner, propped against the resort phone, was her photo of Janetta enclosed in enhancing lamination. Dov made it for her before she woke and brought it with breakfast. It already gave her comfort, and it would sit on her nightstand to do the same at night, and she devised one other use for it in the coming days.

Nathan took the rental SUV into Puerto Princesa hours before to make the arrangements for the night's social mixer-team bonding session, an event she hadn't yet announced to the others until she heard back from him, which she expected anytime.

Molka rose and picked up the food tray to walk it back to the kitchen herself rather than calling the staff to come to retrieve it. Room service always made her feel a little odd anyway like she was being lazy. Besides, her legs needed stimulation after the 10 static hours.

And even though her stomach howled for skipping lunch, she would refrain from ordering any food to save room for the night's feast.

The message notification sounded from her phone on the desktop: Nathan.

She placed the tray back on the credenza, grabbed her phone, and read:

Maganda Seafront Restaurant in Puerto Princesa.
Reservation 8:30.
Dress is dressy-casual.
On my way back.

Dressy-casual. Hmm. Ok. She needed to go to her villa and put together something dressy-casual and do her part in the social mixer, whatever Nathan said it should be, to make the night's event a success.

And if the night's event wasn't a success…

Her phone message notification sounded again.

Message from Dov:

Please come to the marina lagoon to inspect.

The marina lagoon?

Fifteen minutes later, Molka arrived at the marina's nearside, driving one of the coral-pink electric carts. Across the lagoon, Dov and Jaron stood on what appeared to be an exact replica of their landing beach on Base X, including digging out the soil behind it to expose a 2-meter-high seawall section mimicking the one the assault teams would have to climb up and over.

She drove around the asphalt path to their side and arrived behind them. There they parked another cart with shovels in the back seat and a wheelbarrow waiting beside it.

TASK X

Molka exited and moved toward the lagoon's edge where the two sweaty, t-shirt, jeans, and work boots-wearing men, waited for her. She dropped beside them on a compacted sand strip 30 meters long by 2 meters wide.

Jaron wiped his face on his shirt hem and said, "I hope this is what you wanted for the landing exercise."

Her eyebrows rose, impressed. "It's more than I hoped for."

Dov said, "We decided to put it here instead of the regular beach because the seawall sections that form this lagoon can simulate the seawall the assault teams will have to climb over on Base X. It's a small detail, but most ops succeed or fail on the smallest of details."

Molka smiled. "Ha. That sounds like Azzur talking. But this will give us a very realistic simulation. Great job. Where did you get all the sand from, the beach?"

Jaron said, "Yes, but don't worry. We'll put everything back as it was, and the resort owner will never know."

She viewed the *Banda Pearl* across the lagoon, moored at the larger dock. "When did they get back?"

Dov said, "Couple of hours ago."

She addressed her assistants with a stern face. "I appreciate you two taking the initiative to build this today, but you should've gone on the pilot and crew training cruise. There might not be time for another one."

"We did go on it," Jaron said. "We took care of this when we got back."

She flashed them a curious face. "You put this together in only two hours after spending all morning on the ship after a long evening of hard drinking with Berlin's guys? And I must say, you don't even look slightly hungover."

"Dov said, "Well, this isn't the first time we've drank hard all night and worked hard all day."

Jaron said, "No excuses is part of our profession."

She grinned, impressed. "You two are just about to force yourselves into my good graces."

Dov smiled, humble, "I'd really like that, Molka."

Jaron smiled, humble, "That goes double for me, Molka."

"Alright. You've earned some relaxation time, so take the rest of the day and night off."

Dov said, "You don't want us on the landing exercise tonight?"

"No landing exercise tonight. Instead, inform the team we're traveling to Puerto Princesa for dinner. Attendance is mandatory. Dress is dressy-casual. They will report to the shuttle bus outside the hotel lobby at 7:15 sharp."

CHAPTER 28

**Maganda Seafront Restaurant
Puerto Princesa
8:22 PM**

The website photos Nathan showed Molka highlighted Maganda Seafront Restaurant as a large, attractively quaint, tin-roofed, wood-paneled structure built on pilings above a tree-heavy mangrove just off The Port of Princesa.

But as shuttle bus driver Nathan—usual driver Jaron stayed with Dov to guard the resort and watch over the weapons and equipment cache in their villa—drove down the restaurant's single-lane, tree-lined entrance road, no restaurant could be seen.

During the hour drive, the team, once again, kept to themselves in their seats staring out the window or at their phones while Savanna and Shizi dozed.

The social mixer would not get a head start for success.

The road ended in a clearing hosting an expansive, half-full, florescent light-lit, asphalt-surfaced parking lot. Nathan parked on the lot's far side, away from all other vehicles, and opened the side exit doors.

Molka—in a light blue, sleeveless, above the knee, sundress over cute tan-colored wedge sandals with her hair worn down, black-framed glasses on, and a black purse slung across her body—stepped out from the AC coolness into summer night humidity and stood aside to wait for her disharmonized team.

At least they came handsome.

All dressed in the best they brought with them.

Luc set the standard—or maybe she was just biased—in a tight, dark blue, open collar, pressed dress shirt—with the sleeves rolled to the elbows exposing muscular forearms—white, pressed, slim-fit pants cinched with a thin brown leather belt and brown leather dress shoes.

Kang: sharp, black, slim-fit dress shirt over sharp, stone-colored dress pants and sharp, high-polished, black leather dress shoes.

Jager: pale-yellow banded collar shirt over pressed khaki-colored dress pants and tan leather dress shoes.

Nathan: Tel Aviv hipster-style, purple, slim-fit long-sleeved dress shirt tucked into slim-fit, black dress pants, and sleek, designer titanium-framed eyeglasses matching large titanium-hoop earrings hanging from each earlobe.

Warren: a painted-on burgundy polo highlighting his muscular pecs and accentuating his huge biceps over skinny, straight-leg, gray slacks, and gray suede slip-on shoes with no socks.

Savanna: a slim-cut, white linen suit over an open-collar, white silk shirt with a bright red star-shaped flower in his lapel, white dress shoes, and, of course, his wonderfully quaffed hair featured a perfect bang flip.

The colonel: an untucked, red, short-sleeve, button-up shirt over brown pants and brown boots.

Shizi: a bright green and orange-patterned Hawaiian-type shirt over blue jeans and brown sandals.

All featured fresh shaves and Jager's beard a fresh trimming and a few spritzed colognes on.

Nathan moved aside Molka, and she said, "Where's the restaurant located, camouflaged in the trees?"

He pointed to the left toward a wooden, covered pedestrian bridge traversing over the mangrove water and through thick trees. "The entrance is across the bridge. Give me one second while I check on our table." He removed his phone from his back pocket, placed a call, spoke briefly, and ended the call. "Our table is waiting."

Molka addressed the loosely lined-up team. "Gentleman, as I said before we left, tonight is a thank you dinner from me to all of you for coming to my aide. And I would like to keep it strictly a social occasion. No mention of the op, please. Nathan made all the arrangements for tonight and will take the lead. We're all yours, Nathan."

He gestured toward the bridge, "This way, please, men."

He led the way to the bridge. They crossed to the welcoming yellow light of an open front entrance door held open by a smiling, white-uniformed, middle-aged woman who greeted them in Filipino-accented English: "Welcome to Maganda. We are so happy you chose to dine with us this evening."

She led them through a Polynesian-themed-décor main dining room filled with seafood lovers seated at wooden tables in high-backed wooden chairs and an aroma of deep-sea delicacies frying and baking and basting and boiling, which launched hunger pang waves through Molka's empty stomach.

They passed a crowded bar to their right, notably seating—to Luc and Savanna's smiling gazes—two younger, very attractive Hispanic women modeling skimpy, girls-night-out dresses.

The hostess led on through glass double doors and onto a large, open-air, covered porch—offering a gorgeous view of a small, tranquil bay giving the restaurant its "seafront" moniker—and crossed the space toward a waiting, long, wooden table with nine wooden chairs.

The patio also contained three other occupied tables, one of which hosted a loudish, alcohol-fueled, all-male celebration.

The hostess smiled and said their server would be there shortly and departed.

Nathan spoke up and gestured at the table. "Everyone, please find your place card and be seated."

He referred to individual white cards at each setting with their names printed in black.

The team moved toward their assigned places, but a collective pause occurred as they viewed the name on the card sitting next to theirs as their bickering target from day one.

Warren glanced at Nathan, frowned at Molka, and said, "I think we've been set up for a psyop, boys."

Molka smiled and took her seat at the table's head. "Just go with my psyop and sit down, *boys*."

The team paused.

The team complied.

Nathan sat to her right with his nemesis Shizi beside him.

The Russo-German belligerents: the colonel and Jager rounded out that side of the table.

To Molka's left sat Luc with his contra counterpart in crime Savanna.

And next to them sat top tier operative opponents Warren and Kang.

Earlier, Nathan informed Molka the integrated rivals seating arrangement would be key to his social mixer plan, working to kickstart the bonding process leading to some workable team unity.

But by the disgruntled faces displayed by the arrangement, another bickering outbreak kicking in seemed much more likely than bonding kicking off.

A moment later, a younger female server arrived, passed out menus, and asked for their drink orders.

Molka: bottled water.

Luc: A glass of Sauvignon Blanc.

Savanna: A premium bourbon and water.

Warren: An American draft beer.

Kang: A premium German lager.

Jager: Gin and tonic.

The colonel: Three shots of a Swedish brand vodka.

Nathan: Strawberry Margarita.

Shizi: Iced Tea.

When the server left, Nathan viewed Shizi with an impressed face. "Shizi, I have to admit, I didn't think you would abstain. And…I'm very sorry for what I said about you the other day. You were right. I was way out of line." He offered his hand for shaking.

Nathan humbled himself to close a gap.

A selfless move.

But would it work?

TASK X

Shizi stared at Nathan's hand, then shook it, offering a slight smile. "Don't worry about it, kid. You weren't that far out of line."

A hopeful trill trickled through Molka.

While they waited in more uncomfortable silence, the loudish, alcohol-fueled celebration table a few paces to their left grew louder, and the hostess lady arrived at it and politely asked the men to lower their voices and politely departed.

They ignored her request.

Closer examination revealed it seated 15, younger, larger, very athletic males. They dressed in various athletic gear combinations of famous athletic logos t-shirts, shorts, and warm up suits. And their loud talk came in what sounded like Russian accents.

The server returned with an assistant server and two trays holding their drink orders and, after placing them, asked if they were ready to order.

Nathan addressed the team. "Men, the owner here highly recommends the fresh caught, grilled, butter-garlic lobster tails served with traditional side dishes. I think we should all go with his recommendation if that's ok with everyone?"

No one protested.

But the uncomfortable silence at their table settled in again.

Molka and Nathan exchanged disappointed glances.

The promising start went nowhere.

Maybe some people just can't be socially mixed?

The loudish table became a raucous table, and the hostess lady arrived at it again, and again, politely asked them to lower their voices, and politely departed again.

And again, they ignored her request.

A few moments later, the team's server and assistant server arrived with place settings and silverware and their lobster tail entrees along with several traditional Filipino vegetable and rice side dishes and asked if they wanted a refill on their drink orders. All did.

And right after the servers departed, the team cast courteous eyes toward Molka.

Molka smiled at them. "My, what gentlemen you all are, waiting for the lady to start." She unwrapped her fork from her cloth napkin and held it up. "Well, the lady is starving and starting. Please join me."

The team did so, and all consumed the excellent meal with a heartiness—as strong, healthy men do—but with a quietness—as strong, friendly men do not do.

All the while, the raucous table became more and more raucous.

Moments later, Kang spoke. "Those guys are ruining a great meal for me."

Nathan said, "The hostess has asked them to quiet down twice already."

Warren said, "Obviously, they didn't understand her or are pretending not to."

Shizi said, "You can't take rowdy drunks to nice places and expect them not to act like rowdy drunks."

Savanna grinned at Shizi and said, "Very true, sir. I've captained several crews who aggressively proved that adage."

The offending parties' raucousness elevated even more.

Jager tossed his napkin on the table and displayed an irritated face. "This is preposterous. An excellent establishment being ruined by drunken, inconsiderate rabble." He faced the colonel. "Krasnov, those are your people. Why don't you do something honorable for a change and ask them to behave like semi-civilized men."

The colonel addressed him. "They are not my people. They are speaking Kazakh, not Russian."

Jager continued. "Well, if they're from Kazakhstan, they'll all speak Russian too. Just like they do in every other country you people had under your iron boot for 75 years."

The colonel glared at him momentarily, downed another shot, laid his napkin on the table, stood, and approached the raucous ones.

When he arrived, they all went quiet and watched him.

He spoke to them in Russian.

The biggest of the group—dark-haired, block-jawed, wearing a green t-shirt over black shorts—spoke back to him in Russian.

The colonel then turned away and returned to his seat.

The raucous table resumed being raucous.

TASK X

Molka and everyone else looked to the colonel.

He answered their silent query. "They are a rugby team from Kazakhstan playing matches in the Philippines. The man in the green shirt is their team captain. He informed me they are celebrating a victory and will continue to do so in any way they wish."

The team emitted some grumbles and went back to their meals.

Molka excused herself to the ladies' room.

Nathan went with her.

They paused to talk when they reached the small hallway containing the restroom doors.

Nathan frowned. "This is brutal. It's like they're ignoring each other just for spite against me for the seating arrangement."

Molka's eyebrows rose. "I wish that was the reason."

"Why do you say that?"

"Because it would mean they were working together."

"True." He sighed. "I guess I'll have to implement my social mixer doomsday plan."

"What's that?"

"After we finish eating, I'll take everyone to the bar and pour shots down their throats until they become friends or kill each other."

Molka shrugged. "Well, at least your doomsday plan guarantees it will be over one way or another. I'll give it that."

She entered the ladies' room, took care of business, and headed back for their table. When she stepped through the glass doors onto the patio, it put her in direct sightline of the raucous table, and one of the raucous rugby players fixed lecherous eyes on her toned, tanned legs showcased by the shorter dress and tapped his raucous mate beside who also fixed lecherous eyes on her legs and made a comment loud enough for her to hear. Which set off a lecherous ripple effect through all 15 raucous rugby men who fired a grinning, laughing, inappropriate comments barrage directed at her.

And even though Molka didn't understand Kazakh, they weren't saying anything she hadn't heard before from rude, drunk men all over the world, and didn't choose to dignify them with a reaction and simply returned to her seat.

After she sat, she found her entire team all casting irate glares at the foul-mouthed rugby team.

Taking offense for her.

What sweeties.

"It's ok, guys," she said. "Just ignore them, and let's finish our dinners."

But instead, Kang turned in his seat and called over to them: "Watch your mouths around the lady, *gentlemen*."

Luc turned in his seat and called over: "Yes, watch your mouths, around the lady. Or someone may come close them for you."

Savanna turned in his seat and called over: "And count me among those to do the closing."

Jager called out toward them: "And I."

Nathan called out toward them: "And I."

Shizi called out toward them: "And I too."

Warren turned in his seat and called over: "I see you looking at me, big boy in the green shirt. You want to say something to me? Or maybe you want to do something?"

The rugby team's raucousness morphed to fury, which speaks a universal language, and their fifteen sets of furious eyes locked on Molka's team.

Who responded with eight furious locked-on sets of their own.

Molka knew tensions escalating out of control when she saw them.

And she saw them.

But before she could speak to de-escalate, the hulking rugby team captain in the green t-shirt stood and approached the table.

Molka's team all stood to face him.

The rest of the rugby team—all well-muscled athletes in their early 20s—stood as one and came to join their captain.

Molka stood and addressed her team, "Everyone take it easy. I'm not offended by their immature ugliness. Let's be the more mature ones and not start something even more ugly."

The rugby captain addressed the colonel in Russian.

The colonel translated to the team. "He says we have insulted his men, and they wish to do something about that. However, he says, if our team leader will give him a deep, wet, tongue kiss, right here, right now, in front of everyone, he and his men will not kick our scruffy old men asses."

An infuriated growling emanated from the team, punctuated by Shizi. "Scruffy old men? I'll show you a scruffy old man, punk."

Then Luc addressed the colonel. "Colonel, please inform this…*captain*, I will wait for him out in the parking lot if he wants to do something about this…."

Luc faced the rugby captain, picked up his wine glass from the table, and threw the contents into the man's face.

The man howled and lunged at Luc.

Luc didn't flinch.

Warren and Kang intercepted and held the rugby captain.

Several rugby players grabbed Warren, Kang, and Luc.

The rest of Molka's team rushed to defend.

All the men hurled yelling threats and insults.

Hands grabbed and fists clenched.

A mortified Molka prepared to yell for everyone not to fight.

The colonel yelled first:

"NYET!"

"NO!"

"Not in here!"

"Not in here!"

The even more nervous-faced hostess lady hustled to the table. "Is there a problem?"

The combatants disengaged but remained squared off.

Molka said, "No problem. We're leaving right now. Sorry for the disturbance."

"Thank you again for dining with us." The hostess lady departed with nervousness bordering terror.

Jager said, "You see that? These Neanderthals have now indecently offended and upset two fine ladies tonight."

Luc said, "Let us invite them all out into the parking lot and then teach them some manners."

Savanna said, "Yes, colonel. Tell those scalawags to meet us outside."

Kang said, "And if they don't wish to do so, we can drag them outside."

The rest of Molka's team agreed in kind.

Molka said, "Gentlemen, let's just leave."

The colonel spoke to the rugby captain in Russian.

The rugby captain answered, spoke to his men, and they all turned, strode across the patio, and out the glass doors.

The colonel translated to the team:

"They have accepted our challenge and will await us outside."

Molka's team started to stride toward the glass doors.

An even more mortified Molka prepared to yell for everyone to stop.

Nathan yelled first:

"Wait! Wait! Wait!"

"Don't go! Don't go! Don't go!"

The team paused and turned to him.

Molka sighed, relieved.

Thank goodness for Nathan, the voice of reason!

Nathan continued. "I need to pay our bill first. We won't be welcomed back in. So, wait, and don't go without me."

Molka held up stop sign hands. "No, no, no, no. We're not starting a fight."

The colonel addressed her. "Team leader, the fight has already started. Now it is just a matter of who will win it."

CHAPTER 29

Molka came to believe the best leaders were those who mastered the use of the reins over their teams.

Leave the reins too loose, and the team will run wild and get away from you.

Pull the reins too tight, and the team will buck you off and kick you.

The best leaders learned how to ride with a neutral grip while maintaining control and loosen or tighten the reins based on the situation.

She decided to keep the neutral grip and go along for the ride as Nathan paid their bill and the colonel led the team toward the door. Because he was right, the fight had already started.

But with 15 big, strong, athletic, much younger rugby players against their nine—tough as they may be—the odds didn't favor them winning or walking away unscathed.

The best she could do was hope for limited injuries so the op would not be hindered.

Still, she felt obligated to make one last attempt to stop it.

When they exited the restaurant's front door onto the pedestrian bridge, she spoke up from her position at the rear. "Alright. Everyone please hold up for a second. I have a couple of things to say first."

They all stopped and faced her.

She continued. "One, this is a foolish waste of time and resources. And two, 15, big, strong athletic, much younger rugby players against our nine—tough as we may be—probably means some of us are going to get hurt, and that may hinder the op."

Warren said, "It's actually 15 against eight. You're sitting this out, Molka."

Kang said, "Yes, Molka, you can't be a part of this fight, and it's nothing against you as a woman. We all know you're the very toughest among us. But you're our team leader. If you get incapacitated, the op is off. And that can't happen."

The entire team chimed in with agreement.

Then the colonel spoke up. "And also, on the subject of jeopardizing the operation, I suggest we do not risk engaging these men in mortal combat. Pending homicide charges could hinder our freedom of movement. Instead, let us agree to freestyle fighting until every member of one side is down and unable or unwilling to continue the fight. Agreed?"

The team agreed.

The colonel led on across the bridge.

Molka followed.

Soon she would have to drop the reins.

In the warm, humid night, the 15 rugby men waited in a single abreast line on the parking lot's far, unoccupied side.

The team moved toward them in a single abreast line, and when they reached within about 10 meters of their opponents, the colonel stopped and said, "Wait here while I confirm the rules of engagement with them."

Nathan called after him: "Be careful, colonel."

The colonel stopped without fear before the green t-shirted rugby team captain and spoke to him in Russian.

The rugby captain answered him in Russian.

A moment later, the colonel returned to the team. "They have agreed to the rules of engagement: freestyle fighting until every member of one side is down and unable or unwilling to continue the fight. And they are ready to commence."

Warren addressed Molka. "Molka, as your XO, I'm strongly requesting you move back another 10 meters and wait there until this is over."

TASK X

She nodded her consent and moved back.

The team moved toward their opponents.

Their opponents shouted some cocky insults and taunts.

Warren paused the team and formed a huddle.

A moment later, the huddle broke and, to her surprise and delight, split into four two-man squads—the makeup of which exactly mimicked their seating assignments.

Nathan's suggestion to try and salvage his social mixer?

Then, without warning, the two lines rammed together in a testosterone-fueled, street fight-like blurred clash of flailing fists, arms, legs, and feet.

Hyper-ventilated exhaustion, exacerbated by the warm-humid conditions, limited the opening salvo to about 25-seconds and left Nathan and two rugby players on the asphalt.

Both sides disengaged and reformed.

Nathan popped up.

One of the downed rugby men did the same.

The other was out for the duration.

That made it fourteen against eight.

The rugby captain shouted orders and sent double-team attacks into everyone but the smallest two on Molka's team: Nathan and Shizi.

In the free-for-all fighting which followed, Molka witnessed, in no particular order:

Kang peeling a man from Warren's back with a vicious roundhouse kick, and Warren returning the favor with a devastating side kick when another attacker put a chokehold on Kang.

Jager and the colonel working together to sling an attacker to the asphalt and put their shoes and boots into his groin and head while they used their hands to fight off the others.

Savanna and Luc, standing back-to-back, fending off and inflicting damage to their attackers with skilled pugilism.

And Nathan and Shizi responding to the insult of being sent single attackers by easily dropping them with fierce Taekwondo-style kicks and elbow strikes, exchanging laughs, a high-five, and running to reinforce their teammates.

The untimed round ended with six bodies dropped.

All rugby players.

They were either unconscious or too stunned to continue or faking to be one or the other because they'd had enough.

And the still standing rugby players' faces betrayed they'd about had enough too and a realization they had not picked a fight with typical early to late middle-aged tourists.

And if they'd known most of the men pummeling them had killed other men with their bare hands, they may have turned and started running and not stopped until they reached the safe confines of the Ascension Cathedral.

Instead, they retreated about 10 meters and huddled.

Warren called the team together to huddle again too.

The next round would be eight versus eight.

Even odds only on paper.

Molka didn't know much about rugby. Other than it was a very tough sport played by very tough people. But what they did next, she later learned, was a rugby tactic called forming a scrum.

The eight still-standing rugby players formed an arms locked, heads down, wedge-type formation and slow-walked toward Molka's team like a human tank.

Her team surrounded them and unleashed kicks and punches.

But the tough rugby players seemed to be accustomed to being struck hard while in such a formation and used it to absorb and deflect with no damage.

And they regained their wind as her team expended theirs.

The momentum definitely began to turn against her team.

And they knew it too.

Then Savanna yelled: "Stand fast, my lads!"

They ceased their fading assault and watched Savanna sprint across the parking lot to an area surrounded by a tall, white wooden fence. He reached it and pulled open a section forming a gate, entered it, and reemerged, pushing a large, green, steel rolling dumpster back toward the brawl site.

Luc beamed and yelled: "Splendid captain!" And sprinted to join Savanna in propelling the dumpster forward.

The other six men did the same.

The resulting eight-man push built up speed.

A green steel tank racing at the tough as steel human tank.

Something would have to give.

The dumpster aligned on the waiting scrum formation.

TASK X

The speed increased even more.

Twenty meters until a collision.

Then 10…

Then 5…

To their credit, the rugby players held their ground.

3

2

1

THUNK!

ARRRGGHHHHH!

The impact elicited a collective groan from the rugby players and shattered their formation into scattered individuals rolling on the asphalt.

Molka's team moved the dumpster aside and moved to finish it with brutal efficiency.

As a rugby player tried to stand, he got chopped down by punches and-or kicks in vicious volleys.

Once down again, none got back up.

Finally, the green-t-shirted rugby captain took punishment from every team member until he rolled onto his back, winced, raised surrender hands, and spoke Russian in a humbled, pleading tone to the colonel.

The colonel held up his hand toward his teammates:

"Cease fire!"

"Cease fire!"

Then he translated the fallen rugby captain's last words: "They wish to forfeit the rest of this match. They admit they are defeated, and we are the victors."

Molka's team broke into cheers, smiles, high-fives, back pats, handshakes, and yes, as Nathan predicted, bro hugs all around.

The most beautiful sight she'd seen since they arrived.

Her team then moved to help the vanquished who could stand to stand, and some handshakes among adversaries were exchanged.

Molka jogged to the scene with a grin and said, "Alright, you *scruffy old men*, you've proved your point, and now you'll have to take your victory lap on the way back to the bus. In case someone called local law enforcement about this little melee."

The team jogged alongside her toward the bus waiting at the parking lot's opposite end, a half kilometer away.

As they moved, she eavesdropped into several conversations....

Warren to Kang: "I liked your super-fast, efficient, very violent moves. That wasn't Taekwondo, though."

Kang to Warren: "It was Hapkido. A hybrid Korean self-defense martial art."

Warren: "I'd like to learn more about it, maybe incorporate it into my arsenal."

Kang: "I could show you a few things. How about after breakfast on the beach tomorrow?"

Warren: "I'll be there."

Molka's thought: *Kang was right. Deep respect for each other would rise to the surface and wash away petty personal rivalries.*

Jager to the colonel: "Colonel Krasnov, you fought like a warrior tonight."

The colonel to Jager: "I fought like a fat old man. But I thank you for standing with me."

Jager: "Of course, sir. One soldier to another."

Molka's thought: *A soldier's respect is the deepest kind of respect. They have that for each other now.*

Luc to Savanna: "Captain Savanna, I admire your flair."

Savanna to Luc: "And I, yours. Both on this night and in your career, *Monsieur* Durand."

Luc: "My personal friends call me Luc. I would be honored if you did so as well, Captain Savanna."

Savanna: "My personal friends call me, LJ. And I would also be honored if you did so as well."

Luc: "I was thinking of the perfect way to round out this evening."

Savanna: "You are, of course, referring to those two beautiful *senoritas* at the bar."

Luc: "Of course. Shall we go introduce ourselves?"

Molka's thought: *Ha. I knew those two would get along great.*

Savanna to Molka: "Lady Molka, Luc, and I will find our own way back to the resort. We've decided to—"

TASK X

Molka to Savanna and Luc: "I heard you. Briefing tomorrow, 2 PM. Be there."

A beaming Luc and Savanna broke off and headed back toward the restaurant at a faster pace, side-by-side.

Thirty minutes later, on the dark two-lane highway north of Puerto Princesa halfway back to the resort, inside the darkened shuttle bus, Molka's team talked and laughed about their victory and many other subjects' men of like minds and like life experiences talk and laugh about.

She sat silently among them for a while to assess their conditions.

A small knot sprouted from the colonel's forehead.

Dried blood crusted Jager's mustache from a nosebleed.

Warren sported a few facial contusions.

Kang's knuckles swelled from his fast, effective, violent hand strikes.

Shizi, who had limped aboard the bus, sat with his right ankle propped on the seat across from him.

But considering the violent carnage, they'd unleashed and absorbed; they'd dodged any op-hindering injuries.

Satisfied and relieved, Molka moved into the first passenger seat opposite driver Nathan who would develop a black left eye the next day.

He glanced at her with a frown. "I'm really sorry about tonight, Molka."

Her eyebrows rose. "Sorry for what?"

"Traditional social mixers usually don't end in a massive parking lot brawl."

She grinned. "I would say it was more of a one-sided beatdown than a brawl."

He grinned. "Yes, the guys really battered them. Especially their captain. He took the worst of it. I'll bet that's the last time he'll ever rudely ask a strange woman to give him a deep, wet, tongue kiss right here, right now, in front of everyone."

Molka turned her head to view her newly and tightly bonding team again. "Nathan, for what that rugby team captain and his men did for me tonight, I'd give them all deep, wet, tongue kisses right here, right now, in front of anyone."

**MONDAY
AUGUST 1ST**

CHAPTER 30

Club Utopia
7:51 AM

The previous night, after returning to the resort from the evening's eventful events with the wondrous ending, Molka went straight to bed and got solid sleep.

And as she sat at her desk in a freshly laundered duty uniform, she reflected on the most beautiful and perfect morning since she arrived in Palawan.

Maybe the most beautiful and perfect morning she remembered in the past year.

Earlier, dawn broke over her 5:30 AM morning run around the resort's perimeter, a little cooler and less humid than usual with a pleasant sea breeze. It reminded her of the wonderful cool spring morning walks on the beach in Haifa with her parents and her little Janetta.

The beautiful perfection continued after she finished the run, showered, and dressed when on the way to her office, she spotted Nathan and Shizi in the swimming pool playfully racing as would a father and son—which also bode good news for Shizi's gimpy ankle—and Warren and Kang down on the main beach sparring

TASK X

and building and reinforcing their newfound mutual respect and trust.

And even more beautiful perfection greeted her when she passed and greeted Jager and the colonel on their way to breakfast together, engaged in a deep soldier's conversation about the Crimean War.

And to cap off the beautiful perfection, when she entered the hotel lobby on the way to her office, she used the check-in desk's computer to see Luc and Savanna last used their villa keycards at 5:48 AM. Meaning they made it back from their joint conquest.

The only thing not beautiful and perfect that morning was Dov hadn't brought her breakfast order from the kitchen to her office as he did every other morning since they arrived.

Dov was courteous and sweet for saving her the walk to the restaurant so she could work and eat at her desk.

He was a good, thoughtful assistant.

And Jaron was ultra-loyal and ready for any assignment.

But maybe her praise came too soon for them because it was 7:51, and they were supposed to report to her at 7:30 AM.

She had instructions for them on how to set up the afternoon briefing and prepare the weapons and equipment for the team inspection she postponed from the day before and also the procedures for the night's landing exercise.

A heavy day and night of work to get done with only four training days left before op night and her assistants were the key to getting that work in.

She picked up her phone from the desktop and sent them both messages to report.

They always replied right back.

No replies came back.

She called Dov's phone.

No answer.

She called Jaron's phone.

No answer.

She picked up the resort phone on her desk and dialed Dov and Jaron's villa phone.

No answer.

This is odd.
Where are those two?

They live to please me and get my approval.

Situational awareness poured down from her head, and dread welled up from her stomach, and they collided in her chest.

Oh no.

Oh No.

OH NO!

She sprung to her feet, grabbed her Beretta from her purse on the credenza, snatched the master keycard from her desk's top drawer, burst from her office, ran across the briefing room, down the hallway, out the lobby's rear entrance, down the hill, behind the resort's stores, onto the tree-lined, asphalt path, around the marina lagoon, onto the villa's private beach, and down to Dov and Jaron's villa at the far end, racking her weapon on the way.

She crouched for cover beside the villa's front porch steps and called out at the front door:

"Dov!"

"Jaron!"

"Are you in there?"

"Answer me!"

No one answered.

She repeated the same lines.

No one answered.

Only the wave-lapping sounds from the beach 30 meters away broke the morning silence.

The blinds on the front window were closed tight. Weapon at the ready, she moved to the villa's left side. The window there had the blinds raised, but since the structure sat on pilings, the window was way too high for her to look into.

She moved to the villa's backside to find another small wooden porch hosting a BBQ grill in front of a closed back door and another blind's blocked window.

Moving to the villa's other side, another window too high to view into.

She moved back to the front porch steps and called again:

"Dov!"

"Jaron!"

"Are you in there?"

"Answer me!"

No one answered.

TASK X

Instincts told her they were inside, and something was very wrong. What to do next?

Go get back up from the team to make entry a bit later?

Or make entry then in case a bit later would be too late?

Make entry immediately.

Molka soft-stepped up the four steps onto the porch, moved to the door and tried the front door handle.

Door locked.

Good or bad sign?

Prepare for the worst.

She removed the master keycard from her right front pocket.

And slid it over the lock.

The lock clicked unlocked.

Next decision.

Go in hard or easy?

Go in hard!

Beretta ready in her right hand.

One calming breath.

And…

She pushed open the door with her left hand.

Dove headfirst onto the floor.

Rolled into a sitting firing position.

And scanned the room to acquire targets.

She found two:

Dov and Jaron

Both lay stomach down on their beds in the room's rear.

Both clad in only underwear.

Their wrists were flex-cuffed behind them.

Their ankles were flex-cuffed together.

And those flex-cuffs were flex-cuffed to their bed posts.

Black duct tape covered their mouths.

An airhole cut in the tape allowed breathing.

But not wide-mouth screaming.

And their bloodshot eyes leaked shame.

A shame over what filled the rest of their villa.

That being, nothing but empty space where all their weapons and equipment no longer occupied.

CHAPTER 31

"It was Benny Berlin's guys," Dov said when Molka pulled the tape from his mouth.

She moved to the next bed, pulled the tape from Jaron's mouth, and he said, "This is very devastating for both of us."

"Not to mention me." She retrieved her weapon from where she had left it on the nightstand, tucked it behind her waistband, and cast livid eyes upon them. "Berlin's guys, really?"

Dov said, "Yes, really."

Molka shook her head, confused. "I'm confused. Why would it be Berlin's guys? But whoever it was, why did you two just let them come in here and take our stuff? You carry personal weapons. Why didn't you stop them?"

Dov said, "They took them too."

She moved to the villa's center and scanned the room. "They took everything?"

"Everything," Jaron said.

She glared at her prostrate assistants. "Before I grab a knife from your kitchenette and cut you loose, tell me what really happened. Because if I have a knife in my hand at that time, I may use it in a very bad way."

Dov started. "It really was Berlin's guys. Two of them showed up here last night."

Jaron said, "Two of them that we hung with the night before. And they brought two of those pretty girls from Berlin's yacht with them."

Dov continued. "They said Berlin had other business on this island and gave them the night off and that they were heading back to Manila in the morning, and since they didn't know anyone else on the island to hang out with, they came here and wanted to drink with us again."

Molka smirked. "And let me guess, these two Berlin guys had made a special effort to be friends with you during the big beach bash?"

Jaron said, "Yes."

Dov said, "They're great guys. At least they were."

Molka reached behind her head and pulled on the base of her ponytail. "Idiot!"

Dov: "I'm really sorry, Molka."

Jaron: "That goes double for me, Molka."

"No. I'm the idiot. Azzur warned me Berlin was not to be trusted, and Berlin himself as much as admitted to me the same when he said his business was a dirty business and a dirty game. Now I know what he meant by that."

She started to pace before the beds. "That's why he offered me his men to help us carry our stuff here. So they would know exactly where to find it when he sent them to steal it back."

She continued her pacing. "And that's also why, when they were finished, he asked if it was ok if his men had a drink with you guys for a job well done. And he assigned two of them to befriend you and build trust with you. And then last night, he sent two of his *babies* you were both gawking at with them to be the diversion when they executed *Operation Take Back*."

She stopped pacing and glared at them again. "How did that op go down."

Dov said, "After they showed up, we got some more beer from the bar and were in here drinking with them and laughing and having a good time. Then the girls asked to use our bathroom, and they took their purses in there with them, and when they came out, they had Glocks in their hands and put us at gunpoint."

Jaron said, "We thought they were joking until they handed the weapons to the guys, and we saw on their faces it wasn't a joke."

Dov: "Then the girls took flex-cuffs and duct tape from their purses, tied us up like this, and gagged us."

Jaron: "But at least they let us take off our shoes and clothes to be comfortable and put the breathing holes in the gags, since we would be alone for hours, if not all night."

Molka said, "How did they know the rest of the team would be away last night in Puerto Princesa?"

"They didn't," Jaron said. "They thought you were all asleep and brought in a second wave of armed men to cover every villa. It was well-planned."

She sighed, frustrated. "And how did they haul everything out of here? They bring a big truck too?"

"No," Dov said. "Berlin showed up with his yacht again, and they loaded it up and were gone in less than 20-minutes."

She sighed again, even more frustrated. "And now he's back in Manila laughing at Azzur's stupid friend."

She moved into the kitchenette, opened drawers until she found a serrated-edge steak knife, moved back to the beds, and cut their binds.

They both got onto their feet, a little stiff and unsteady.

Dov's eyes filled with shame again. "Molka, I can offer no excuse or apology that is remotely mitigating our dereliction of duty."

Jaron's eyes filled with shame again. "That goes double for me, Molka."

Dov said, "We'll pack up and be gone within the hour."

She glared at them. "As well you should be. Unfortunately, we're too close to the op to make any personnel changes. You'll atone for yourselves with hard work to see this through."

Dov said, "Yes, Molka. Thank you, Molka."

Jaron said, "Yes, Molka, Thank you Molka."

Dov said, "What are your orders?"

In thought, she picked up the knife from where she had left it on Jaron's bed. "Pull yourselves together and then inform the team what happened and tell them we're having an emergency meeting in the briefing room in one-hour. If you need me before then…" She tossed the knife across the room and clanking into the sink. "I'll be in my office humbling myself to Azzur."

CHAPTER 32

"It's a dirty business and a dirty game," Azzur said from a video call on Molka's phone atop her desk. "Those were his exact words?"

She glared down at him. "Yes. Those were his exact words."

"And that is exactly what he used to say in the old days before he pulled one of his famous double crosses." A slight smile curled Azzur's lips. "We even adopted it in our Berlin station as a beloved, catch-all, slang expression."

Her glare became a smirk. "Well, I'm so glad I could—Wait. Is that a smile? It is!" Her smirk became a glare again. "Well, I'm so glad I could take you on a good old day's memory trip, but you might have mentioned that little tipoff of Berlin's to me before I did business with him."

Azzur lit a cigarette. "I believed my warning to you regarding Mr. Berlin to be adequate."

"Thanks for nothing then.

He continued. "If Mr. Berlin stole back what he sold you, you gave him an overwhelming reason to do so."

Molka's jaw tightened. "What do you mean by that remark?"

"View the situation this way: If you bought a stolen car from a car thief and then parked that car with the keys left inside it in clear view of the car thief and turned your back, what would you expect to happen? Surely, Molka, you have not been away from the military long enough to forget that an armory must be guarded 24-7."

She sat back and folded her arms across her chest. "My armory was being guarded 24-7. By your guys. Who got duped by Berlin's guys."

"I see." He puffed a cigarette and blew smoke. "That is unfortunate."

Molka smirked. "Yes. Isn't it?"

"Dov and Jaron informed me they were making very positive steps in earning your trust and respect."

"One step forward, one thousand steps back. And thanks for letting me know they're reporting to you on my personal op."

Azzur ignored the inference. "If you contacted me to ask that I intercede with Mr. Berlin on your behalf to return your weapons and equipment, I do not think he will be receptive because, as I told—"

She interrupted. "I'm not asking you to intercede. I need you to give me his location in Manila, tell me what type of security he has, and provide me with some tools when I get there. Then I'll go intercede him personally."

Molka entered the briefing room with the team seated at the conference table and Dov and Jaron standing against the wall to the left of the podium, which she moved behind with a serious face. "Good morning, gentlemen."

They replied with a collective good morning.

She continued. "Obviously, a major security breach has occurred. This breach was entirely my fault, and I apologize to you for my lack of professionalism."

Nathan spoke up. "What can we do to help, Molka?"

A collective agreement followed his remark.

She offered a humbled, appreciative face. "Thank you, gentlemen. I'm leaving within half an hour to recover our weapons and equipment. Warren, you'll be taking charge of the team in my absence. I want you to conduct the first briefing on the ground operation's tactical plan this afternoon. I'll send it to your briefing tablet shortly."

Warren nodded. "Understood, Molka."

She addressed a bleary but attentive-faced Savanna. "Captain Savanna, I want you to conduct a night training exercise of launching and operating the landing boats from the bay onto the simulated beach in the marina lagoon Dov and Jaron constructed."

He nodded. "Of course, Lady Molka."

She addressed Kang. "Kang, you'll be coming with me. Go grab your ID and passport and meet me at the SUV outside the hotel lobby."

"See you out there, Molka." He rose and departed.

The colonel spoke up. "Team leader, may I ask how you intend to recover our weapons and equipment?"

"By playing a dirty game against a dirty business."

CHAPTER 33

**Ninoy Aquino International Airport
Manila, Philippines
1:11 PM**

After a one-hour and twenty-minute direct flight from Puerto Princesa International Airport to Ninoy Aquino International Airport, Molka—still wearing her duty uniform and carrying her purse—and Kang—still wearing his sharp, white polo shirt over olive green shorts and sandals from the morning briefing—sat at a table in a café in busy Terminal 2.

Molka picked at a chicken Caesar salad and watched her phone for an incoming message, and Kang devoured a Wagyu burger and watched people.

The notification chime sounded on her phone. She checked the incoming message and said, "He's here."

The "he" she referred to approached in the form of a late 30s, short, dark-haired, white male wearing a light blue, short-sleeved shirt over navy blue slacks and carrying a black portfolio case.

The man arrived at their table, sat in the seat next to Kang facing Molka, and spoke in Hebrew-accented English. "Afternoon Molka, I'm Edelman from the Israeli Embassy."

"Afternoon," she said. "You're an old friend of Azzur's, he tells me."

He grinned. "Yes, among other things." He turned to Kang. "I'm going to speak Hebrew to Molka. Not that I don't trust a former GBR man now working with Pentad."

Kang waved a dismissive hand. "No problem. I'm used to the shunning now. I'll finish this tasty burger while you talk."

Edelman faced Molka again, unzipped the portfolio case, removed a printed document, passed it to her, and spoke in Hebrew. "That's the safehouse address, the entry codes for the safehouse, Berlin's itinerary for today, the contractors' contact number, and an action plan to achieve your goal." He reached into his front pocket, removed a black key fob, and handed it to her. "That's a white cargo van with rear-opening cargo doors and no windows in the cargo area waiting in the lot outside this terminal, space 157. When you're done with it, just let my office know where you left it, and we'll pick it up. And all the equipment for you and your partner here is waiting in the safehouse's upstairs master bedroom on the bureau."

Molka answered him in Hebrew. "This is all outstanding. I appreciate it."

"Thank Azzur. He called in a couple of favors to help you here. He really wants you to succeed in your operation. Whatever that may be, and even though, he said, it will very much upset the world authority."

She shrugged. "Well, the world authority will get over it. Or not."

Barangay Merville Neighborhood
Just Outside Manila

The white cargo van took 15 minutes to make the 6-kilometer drive from Ninoy Aquino International Airport to a modest, beige-colored, red tile-roofed two-story home in a quiet, well-off the main road, residential area.

TASK X

A head-high, beige-colored wall topped with brown steel spikes surrounded the home. And a brown steel gate blocked the driveway entrance from the street.

Driver Molka nosed the van to the gate, removed her phone from her purse, opened an app, entered a password, and swiped while passenger Kang observed the quiet street in both directions.

A moment later, the gate auto-opened, and Molka pulled into the driveway, under a carport, and shut off the vehicle.

The duo exited and moved left to the white front door, where Molka—still holding her phone with the app open—swiped it again to unlock the door.

They entered an AC-cooled, white-walled, beige-carpeted living room featuring unpretentious brown furniture. A kitchen and a half bath opened off the space.

They moved to a staircase featuring a closed steel door under it, climbed to a second-story hallway, and walked through an open door into a master bedroom with a queen-sized bed, white dresser, nightstand, and bureau.

And atop the bureau sat two large, blue plastic storage bins with lids. Black-inked, white labels on the lids indicated one for Molka and the other for Kang.

They moved to and opened their respective bins and inspected the contents.

After a moment, Molka peered into Kang's bin and said, "An HK P30L nine-millimeter, very nice. That's the same weapon you had in Australia. Your preferred sidearm, I take it?"

"Absolutely."

"Is that based on performance for you or because it's one of the coolest looking handguns ever?"

He presented a playboy smile. "Let's just say I always make cool work for me."

She smirked. "I should've guessed that. Everything else there?"

"Yes. Perfect. Your man Azzur is good. Very Good."

"He is. But you're only as good as your next success."

"True," he said. "Excellent safehouse your people have here. Nice, secluded neighborhood, blends right in. And I can tell by the way our voices almost echo in here that the walls are heavily soundproofed to cover various loud activities." He pointed at the floor. "What's behind that steel door under the stairs."

"That's the room where uncooperative problems get taken care of. At least that's what we're going to say it is."

"Understood," he said. "Professional question."

"Go with professional question."

"Why did you want me with you on this job, Shizi speaks better Filipino than me, and Berlin and his guys speak English, anyway?"

"Shizi is a specialist," she said. "Not an operative. This is a job for operatives."

"Then why not bring Warren? Of the three operatives on our team—you, Warren, and me—I rate him just behind you and just ahead of me."

"I have a different opinion of that ranking order. But don't be too politely humble to admit that you could trick, trap, and hold Warren as a hostage for several days. I can promise you; there is no other man or woman alive that can say that."

Kang grinned. "Except for maybe Nadia."

Molka grinned. "Good point." She time-checked her phone. "We're right on schedule. Let's suit up."

CHAPTER 34

Manila Grande Golf and Country Club
2:31 PM

A thrice-occupied, white golf cart rolled down the cart path and stopped adjacent to the 1st hole tee box.

The cart was driven by a large, muscular, early 30s Asian man in a black short-sleeved shirt, black slacks, and black shoes.

A similarly built, aged, and identically clad man sat in the cart's rear seat.

The cart's passenger—Benny Berlin—sporting a gold-colored golf shirt over white golf pants and white golf shoes, exited the cart and walked with a cigarette in his mouth across the stunningly gorgeous course's perfect emerald green grass toward the tee box.

Waiting for him there—slinging a custom-made, gold leather golf bag over his right shoulder containing custom clubs and the initials BB in black script on the side—was Kang.

He wore the white coveralls and green ball cap uniform of the club's caddies and greeted the approaching Berlin. "Good afternoon, Mr. Berlin. I'm Kang."

Berlin arrived with a perplexed face. "Where's Danilo?"

"He went down with a little headache this afternoon."

Berlin offered a semi-skeptical face. "I've never seen you here before."

"I usually work mornings, sir."

"Danilo's been caddying for me for four years. I feel naked teeing off without him. Are you sure you can take care of me?"

Kang smiled and handed him the driver. "You're about to find out, sir."

Berlin teed off, handed the club back to Kang, and walked down the fairway toward his ball.

Kang trailed behind.

And about 40 meters to the right, Berlin's security men in the cart paralleled them.

Berlin made par on the hole, and when they moved to the 2nd hole tee box, another golf cart appeared behind Berlin's men and stopped about 10 meters to its rear.

The new arrival mounted a large red with white letters sign across the front which spelled: RANGER. The cart driver, behind large sunglasses, appeared to be a slender-built Filipino male and wore the blue ball cap over blue polo shirt and khaki pants uniform of the club staff.

Berlin teed off again.

Kang took the driver from him. "Nice shot, sir."

As they moved down the fairway, Berlin lit a fresh cigarette and glanced at the cart path to see his men being followed by the cart identified as the course Ranger's and its occupant looking over at him. "Why is the ranger watching me? I don't break any rules here."

Kang said, "Maybe he's a fan, sir. Your game carries quite a reputation in the clubhouse."

Berlin flashed a surprised face. "It does?"

"Yes, sir. That's why I was so happy to step in for Danilo when he went down, to get this up-close view of your stellar performance."

Berlin grinned. "Now you're just trying to boost your gratuity. You can't bullshit me, son. Trust me. I'm a much better bullshitter than a golfer."

Kang smiled. "Yes, sir."

Berlin made another par, and they headed to the par 3, 3rd hole tee box, which was surrounded by trees on three sides.

TASK X

Kang pulled the 9 iron club from the bag with his left hand, set the golf bag down, and carried the club to Berlin with his right hand tucked in his coverall's hip pocket.

Berlin frowned at the club. "Danilo always hands me the 8 iron on this hole."

Kang's right hand came out of his pocket, holding his HK nine-millimeter, semi-auto pistol. "I prefer the nine."

Berlin's face-shocked on the weapon, and then he turned to yell for his men.

But they were already out of their cart and on the way, walking quickly with their hands in their back pockets. And with the ranger behind them pointing a Beretta at their backs.

Berlin's shocked face turned back to Kang. "What is this?"

Kang placed the club back inside the bag, slung the bag over his left shoulder, and gestured his weapon toward a tree line about 80 meters to the right. "Move. Now."

Berlin complied.

Kang walked behind him.

Berlin said, "I had a feeling you really didn't work here." He glanced over his shoulder to see his captured men and their captor trailing them by about 10 meters. "What, are you guys going to rob me?"

Kang answered. "Not exactly."

They moved into the tree line, which formed the boundary between the golf course and a one-lane street traversing an upscale residential neighborhood.

A white cargo van sat parked on the street's shoulder.

Kang ordered: "Stop here. Hands atop head. Don't move."

Berlin complied.

The ranger arrived with the two security men.

Kang ordered them: "Go stand next to your boss."

They complied.

Kang addressed the duo. "We don't want to kill you, but we will. So, don't try to be heroes now. Take your hands from your pockets, put them atop your heads, and get on your knees."

They complied.

The ranger moved before Berlin.

The ranger's hat and polo shirt carried the club's logos. He removed his sunglasses and hat, tossed them aside, reached his right hand to his face's left side, and pulled off a molded mask revealing Molka.

Berlin smiled, relieved. "Molka, thank goodness. For a minute there, I thought we were all dead."

Molka said, "They're going to live through this. You, on the other hand…well, you're the last person in Manila I would want to be right now."

Berlin offered her a cagy face. "Don't take it personally. I've tried to double-cross practically everyone I've ever made a deal with."

Kang said, "Not a very sound business practice."

Berlin looked to Kang. "What kind of business do you think I'm in? I sell highly illegal merchandise to the worst types of people—no offense Molka—to do highly illegal things with. It's not like they can go to the police and file a complaint that the bad man in the big gold boat stole back the 25,000 AK-47s they were going to use to overthrow a legitimately elected government."

He faced Molka again and flashed the overly white teeth smile. "It's what I do. It's exciting for me. It's just part of the dirty game I play in the dirty business I'm in. And you win this round. Nice job. Now, we can make a new deal, right?"

"Wrong." Molka removed two sets of flex cuffs from her back pocket and bound the bodyguard's wrists behind their backs, ordered them to lay on their stomachs, removed two more sets of flex cuffs, bound their ankles together, and said to them, "Berlin's other guys were nice enough to leave safety airholes in my guy's gags. So I'm not even going to gag you. You can yell your heads off for help when we leave. But this is a quiet area. Maybe you'll get found in a few hours."

She tucked her Beretta into her waistband behind her back and then pulled two Glocks from her front waistband and tossed them into the golf bag. "Your weapons are in the bag, guys. I'm not going to *steal* them from you."

She next picked up her hat and glasses and headed toward the van.

Kang ordered Berlin: "Follow her."

Molka reached the van's rear, opened the right-side cargo door exposing a rear cargo area holding only a black gear bag,

TASK X

drew her Beretta, and pointed it at Berlin. "Get inside and lay face down."

Berlin tried to muster a brave face. "Ok, I'll play along. The victors get to celebrate. I respect that. Then we'll make our new deal."

He complied.

Kang climbed in beside him, and while Molka watched with her weapon ready, Kang secured Berlin with handcuffs, ankle shackles, and a black hood and sat on the cargo deck beside him.

Berlin's muffled voice sounded from under the hood. "We're going to make a new deal, aren't we, Molka?"

Molka closed the van's rear door, jumped into the driver seat, and drove the van back toward the soundproofed seclusion of the safehouse.

CHAPTER 35

Kang removed the hood from Berlin's head, who found himself chained to a steel chair inside the small room behind the steel door under the safehouse's stairs.

The space resembled an oversize shower with white tile walls and floor and a large, grated floor drain.

Berlin blinked at Molka, and Kang, standing across from him, changed back into their own clothes.

After taking a moment for his eyes to adjust to the harsh light from the single ceiling fixture over his head, he said, "So, I guess this is the part where I apologize and refund all your money?"

Molka said, "No, this is the part where you call your guys and tell them to take our order back to your yacht, reload it, and get lost. And then call your yacht captain and tell him to meet you on board this evening. And then you're going to cruise with us all the way back to Club Utopia."

Kang spoke up. "*And* this is also the part where you agree to add a 50 percent penalty of the purchase price for the inconvenience to that full refund."

Molka grinned. "Nice touch."

Berlin's face paled. "What if I can't do that?"

Kang said, "Then you'll leave this room in plastic bags."

TASK X

Berlin shook his head, scared. "I'm sorry, I can't do what you ask."

Kang smirked. "We knew the *Baron of Berlin*, or the Baron of Bullshit, or whatever, would call our bluff with a bluff. So, now we're calling yours right back."

Molka opened the door, and two Asian males clad in yellow rain suits stepped into the room. Both wore goggles atop their heads; one carried an orange chainsaw and the other a large fillet knife.

She said, "And in case you think those are actors posing as professionals...."

The man with the knife removed a phone from his side pocket, held it before Berlin's face, and scanned through several gory photos of the two men smiling and holding up severed heads.

Berlin grimaced and turned his face away. "I meant I can't do what you asked because I already resold your order this morning. The best I can do is replace it and give you a full refund and that inconvenience penalty. Replacing your full order will take me a couple weeks, though, because all I have in stock of your items are the MP5s and tactical gear."

Molka's jaw tightened. "I don't have a couple of weeks to get my full order replaced. I have tonight."

Kang glared at Berlin. "I say we let the butcher boys here slice off a couple of his fingers to make sure he's not lying."

The man with the chainsaw spoke up. "He's not lying."

The man with the knife said, "He knows he's in mortal peril. They never lie at this point. They're too terrified."

Kang glanced at Molka. "I guess these two would know."

Molka addressed Berlin. "Here's your last chance. Call the people you resold our order to and tell them you made a fatal mistake—which you have—and that the order was already bought and paid for—which it was—and you need to give them a full refund and come pick it up. Today."

Berlin's face hinted at coming panic. "And I would love to do that for you, Molka. And that order is sitting in a warehouse here in the city and will be for the next few weeks."

She put her hands to her hips, annoyed. "Then what's the but?"

Berlin continued. "But the people I resold it to are a local triad. Which is—"

She interrupted. "We know what triads are."

"Ok, and there is no way they will sell it back to me."

Kang said, "Not true. Triads will sell you anything for the right price."

Berlin continued. "Yes, but they've already sold it to some Indonesian pirates who have sold it to a terrorist organization in the Middle East. And even if I offer a full refund or pay twice or three times or more to buy it back, the answer will still be a non-negotiable no. Because those types of deals with those types of people can't be undone if you want to keep your heads, so to speak."

Kang nodded at the man holding the chainsaw. "And now you've lost yours anyway. Fool." He addressed Molka. "Let's go so these men can do their work. While they do, we'll pick out a good spot to dump the body parts' bags."

Berlin viewed Molka with watery, begging eyes. "Molka, please…please. Can you help me? I'm Azzur's friend."

"Being Azzur's friend is not a persuasive reason for me to help you." She sighed, frustrated. "Where's this triad warehouse with our stuff located?"

CHAPTER 36

Manila North Harbor Area
4:17 PM

The densely packed warehouse district Molka drove the cargo van through sat adjacent to a huge container ship facility on the Port of Manila's North Harbor section.

And most of the flat-roofed, concrete block buildings she passed on the lightly trafficked two-lane street carried a grayish hue, stood two or three stories high, and ranged from well-used to borderline dilapidation.

Kang sat in the rear cargo area guarding a re-restrained—minus the hood—Berlin lying on his stomach again

They approached the address Berlin gave for the triad gang warehouse holding the stolen order, and Molka made a left turn into an empty parking lot of an out-of-business auto shop across the street, turned around, backed it in, and said, "Is that the right building, Berlin?"

Kang helped Berlin sit up to look out the front windshield. "Yes, that's the one."

Kang laid Berlin back on his stomach, moved into the passenger seat, and both he and Molka put binoculars from their safehouse equipment to their eyes and viewed the large, dark gray, three-story warehouse set back about 50 meters from the road.

The building's front featured a cargo truck-sized, white metal overhead loading door, which was closed and a smaller open entrance door to the right.

The structure was flanked by two other three-story buildings and separated from them by narrow alleys, and a tall chain-link fence that continued to a street-side and was sealed by double, inward swinging, steel gates secured with a thick steel, ram-proof barricade bar.

The 50-meter paved space between the front gate and the building served as a parking area hosting about a dozen smaller cars to the right side, probably belonging to some of the men Molka and Kang gave their attention to.

Molka said, "I count four AK-armed men sitting in chairs in that parking area just in front of the big loading door."

Kang said, "I count the same."

She said, "And Berlin, you said there are four more guards in the back?"

Berlin answered: "Yes, and two on each side."

Kang said, "Making 12 total. Always the same security arrangement, Berlin?"

Berlin said, "Yes, every time I've been there. Which is many times."

Molka said, "How many inside?"

"The only ones I ever saw inside came from the outside after I got there."

Molka said, "What else is stored in there?"

Berlin answered: "Various stolen boxed merchandise, mostly electronic and appliances. And a few stolen luxury cars. And a sailboat, oddly enough."

Molka said, "And you said our order is stacked on two shrink-wrapped pallets just inside that loading door?"

Berlin answered. "It was this morning. I doubt they've moved it. As you can probably see, they barely move at all. But they will fight you to the death if it comes to that. They've all sworn an oath to do so. They're real killers with a high body count."

TASK X

Molka lowered her binoculars and addressed Kang. "I'm so glad you suggested we bring that drone from the safehouse's gear closet. We should get it over that building and confirm the security numbers and layout. Now we'll test out your drone pilot skills to see if you're really a master."

He presented a playboy smile. "Just find me some cover, and I'll show you just one of the many things I've mastered."

As Molka drove the van behind the building to a vacant lot, Kang reached into his gear bag and removed a black, hand-sized camera drone with its four propeller boom arms folded against its body, a black remote flight control, and a black tablet.

She parked and exited with Kang. He handed her the tablet, and she powered it up while he deployed the drone's propellers, placed it on the pavement, and used the controller to start the motors and take off.

Molka held the tablet showing the drone's camera view at an angle Kang could see it to fly without the afternoon sun's glare obscuring the screen.

He flew it across the street and then on a wide, high loop over and around the building to the left of the triad warehouse and approached it from the rear, and she tapped the video record button on the screen.

The camera showed four more AK-armed men sitting in chairs at the building's rear. Kang then maneuvered to confirm two more AK-armed men sitting in chairs at each side of the building.

Kang said, "Security is just as Berlin said it was. Maybe those contractors are right. He's too terrified to lie at this point. I'm going to remember that mind trick."

Molka said, "Fly back over the roof."

He climbed and hovered the drone high over the flat roof covered in a tar paper-like sealer.

She pointed to a steel square near some roof-mounted air conditioning units. "What's that look like to you?"

He said, "A roof access hatch."

"That's what I thought too. Ok. Bring her home."

Kang flew the drone back across the street, landed on the same spot it took off from, and shut it down. "What are your thoughts?"

Molka gazed into the distance and exhaled hard. "We just need to figure out a way to get past that barricade bar sealed gate, get in that warehouse, get our stuff out, and leave without starting a firefight and-or massacre with the guards, which will bring a massive law enforcement response. And get it done tonight. Other than that, it should be easy."

Kang's face assumed a sly confidence. "I've got an idea of how we can do all that. But we would need fast access to some heavier weapons and some tactical equipment."

She gestured toward the van. "We've got just the man to supply us that."

He continued. "And it's very high risk. So, pulling it off would take a team with exceptional skills, the ability to execute precision timing, and a lot of guts."

Molka grinned at him. "And we've got just the men for that too."

CHAPTER 37

**Manila North Harbor Area
Rooftop on Building to the Right of the Triad Warehouse
11:51 PM**

Luc stood on the flat roof's edge wearing a very tight black Lycra tee shirt, black Lycra yoga-style pants—which accentuated his lean, ripped, muscular physique—black sneaker-like shoes, a wireless comms headset, and a small, black backpack.

He confirmed what the drone footage showed as the distance to the warehouse roof over the narrow alley separating them at about 5 meters or a little over 16 feet.

He backed away from the edge about 30-meters, assumed a sprinter's standing start position, inhaled, exploded into a sprint toward the roof's edge, launched himself a half meter from it, carried the distance, stuck a silent landing on the warehouse roof about one meter from the edge, broke into another sprint toward the roof access hatch cover, knelt beside it, reached over his shoulder into the backpack, removed a pry bar, wrenched open the hatch's locking system, opened the hatch, replaced the pry bar into the backpack, and spoke into his headset: "Molka, Luc."

Molka's voiced answered: "Go, Luc."

"I'm in."

Molka: "Acknowledged. Stand-by."

"Roger that."

11:55 PM

Shizi staggered down the dark sidewalk outside the warehouse wearing a pink t-shirt, baggy orange shorts, and flip-flop sandals. His thick hair mussed, and his left hand held a paper bag containing an open liquor bottle.

When he approached the closed and locked tight warehouse front gates, he was illuminated by a light on a pole beside it and drew attentive stares from the four AK-armed guards seated outside the warehouse's big, overhead loading door.

He stopped before the gate and started swaying and singing a drunken tune in Taiwanese.

The guards yelled and cursed at him in Filipino.

As he kept up the singing, he reached behind his back, pulled off a small piece of black duct tape stuck to his t-shirt, which held a length of det-cord with an attached electronic timer-detonator, and stuck it to the gate's thick steel barricade bar without the still yelling guards noticing.

He staggered and sang his way down the sidewalk until he was out of the guards' view, reached into his shorts front pocket, removed a two-way radio, and spoke into it: "Molka, Shizi."

Molka's voice answered: "Go, Shizi."

"Gate primed."

Molka: "Acknowledged. Stand-by."

"Roger that."

11:59 PM

Molka sat in the cargo van's driver seat again parked in the lot across the street from the warehouse. She re-outfitted into a black BDU over black tactical boots, wore a wireless comms headset over her high pony-tailed hair, and watched the warehouse through binoculars.

In the van's rear cargo area—also outfitted in black BDUs over black tactical boots and wearing wireless comms headsets—sat Warren, Kang, Nathan, the colonel, Jager, and Savanna. Each man carried an MP5 submachine gun with a 30-round mag slung in a tactical sling across their chests.

Molka lowered her binoculars and turned in the seat to face the men. "Ready, gentlemen?"

They all answered in the affirmative.

She spoke into her headset. "Luc, Molka."

Luc answered: "Go, Molka."

"Green light. Repeat. Green light."

Luc: "Roger that."

12:00 AM

Luc opened the roof access hatch and climbed down an attached steel ladder to the warehouse's dimly lit third floor. The space held some boxed merchandise but also over a dozen cots, a kitchen, a bathroom, and a shower, and smelled like men lived there when they were not on guard duty.

He crossed to a steel staircase and trotted down to the second floor stuffed with more boxed merchandise, mostly electronics.

He picked up three boxes containing brand new, high-end laptops and headed down the stairs to the ground level, which was about 80 percent filled with even more boxed merchandise, four luxury cars, a 30-foot sailboat on a trailer, and upfront, just inside the large overhead door, sat two, shrink-wrapped pallets holding their weapons and equipment.

He jogged to the left front corner and into a little enclosed office with a desk, some chairs, and an open door leading outside to the warehouse's front.

He moved to the door, tucked the boxes tight under his left arm, took a calming breath, and burst into the parking area.

About 20 meters to his right, the four seated guards froze in stunned silence for a moment at the intruder thief who got past all their men.

All almost fell from the chairs, scrambling to their feet.

Luc feigned a shocked face, dropped the laptops, and ran back inside the warehouse.

The four guards ran inside after him.

12: 04 AM

When the fourth of the four guards chasing Luc disappeared into the warehouse, Molka lowered her binoculars and spoke into her headset. "Shizi, Molka."

Shizi's voice in her headset: "Go, Molka."

"Green light. Repeat. Green light."

Shizi: "Roger that."

Molka tossed the binoculars in the passenger seat, started the van, put it in gear, and sped toward the warehouse's front gates.

12:05 AM

Half a block from the warehouse, a large, white cargo truck with an attached hydraulic-powered lift gate waited parked against the curb.

TASK X

Inside, Shizi sat in the passenger seat next to the door, and next to him sat Berlin men in the middle and driver seats.

As soon as Molka gave him the "Green Light" code, Shizi reached his right hand out the open side window holding a small, black remote control-like device, pointed it down the street toward the warehouse gates, and pushed a button on the device's face.

Instantaneously, the det-cord he placed on the gate's barricade bar detonated with a loud pop, sliced it in half, and dropped it on the pavement.

He addressed the truck's driver. "Let's move."

12:06 AM

Molka's van reached the breached gates and—since it belonged to the embassy—she slowed to ease them wide open with the soft front bumper and then raced across the parking area toward the warehouse.

When she reached within two meters of the building's front, she cut hard right, stopped, and ordered:

"Alpha, Bravo, go!"

Warren opened the van's right-side rear cargo door, and all six men jumped out and immediately split into two three-man squads.

Warren, at the run, led Kang and Nathan toward the alley on the warehouse's left side.

The colonel, at the run, led Jager and Savanna toward the alley on the warehouse's right side.

Both squads entered their alley destinations and kept moving.

Molka exited the van holding a Glock 17 and watched Shizi and the white cargo truck enter through the open gates, fly across the parking area, make a 180-degree turn, and back in and stop a meter from the warehouse's big loading door.

Shizi jumped out, holding a Glock, and ran to Molka.

Warren's voice came over the headsets: "Alpha. Left flank secured."

The colonel's voice came over the headsets: "Bravo. Right flank secured."

A moment later, Warren's voice again: "Alpha and Bravo linked up, rear of the warehouse. All guards secured."

Molka spoke into her headset. "Acknowledged, Alpha and Bravo. Stand-by."

Warren: "Roger that."

The colonel: Roger that."

Molka ran to the right—trailed by Shizi—through the open door into the warehouse office, stopped, and spoke into her headset. "Luc, Molka."

Luc answered: "Go, Molka."

"Perimeter secured. Where are you at?"

Luc: "Third floor. They are still looking for me on the second."

"Ok. Let them know you're up there, exit onto the roof, close the door behind you, and get back down here."

Luc: "Roger that."

Molka: "Alpha, secure remaining guards on the third floor."

Warren: "Roger that."

Molka: "Bravo, bring the detainees inside."

The colonel: "Roger that."

Molka exited the office—with Shizi covering her—moved to the two shrink-wrapped pallets, climbed atop the first one, and began opening and inspecting the boxes and crates.

Shizi looked up at her. "Well?"

She grinned. "We're back in business."

12:17 AM

The 12 triad guards—flex-cuffed at the wrists and ankles—lay face down on the warehouse floor in the same spot where the two shrink-wrapped pallets sat moments before.

Berlin's two men loaded them on the cargo truck, backed in just outside the opened loading door, and waited in the warehouse under Shizi's watchful eyes along with the rest of the team.

A giddy Nathan started high-fiving his comrades. "Yes! Yes! Yes! That's the way professionals do it! That's the way we do it! No scruffy old men here!"

Molka addressed him. "We haven't done it yet. We still have to get our highly illegal weapons loaded onto the yacht and get through the eight-hour cruise home without getting caught."

"You're right," Nathan said. "I'm humbled but still very proud of us."

Molka said, "Ride with Shizi and his two new friends in the truck, just in case they get a foolish idea to steal our stuff again for their foolish boss."

Kang addressed Molka. "Speaking of that fool, should I call the butcher boys at the safehouse now and tell them to bring Berlin to the marina?"

"Yes. And tell them the faster, the better."

He grinned. "Sure you don't want them to first cut off a finger or two for causing this mess?"

She raised her eyebrows, sarcastic. "Don't tempt me."

Warren faced Molka. "How far is Berlin's yacht from here?"

"Only about seven kilometers." Molka addressed the team. "Alright. Even though we should keep these borrowed weapons, we'll give them back to get rid of them since we just used them in the commission of a crime of sorts. Toss them in the back of the truck, and let's mount up."

The team began to comply.

Molka's phone vibrated in her right front pocket.

She removed her phone and checked it.

Message from Dov.

But before she read it...

Warren yelled: "We've got company! Hold your weapons, men!"

Three cars had entered the front gate. One each parked parallel on each side of the gate, and the third parked halfway in the gate to block it.

Ten men, similar in look and dress to the detained guards armed with AK-47s, leaped from the vehicles and used them as cover.

Warren moved to a covered position just inside the door to the left and yelled: "Alpha, on me!"

Kang and Nathan ran to line up behind him.

The colonel moved to a covered position just inside the door to the right and yelled: "Bravo on me!"

Jager and Savanna ran to line up behind him.

Shizi, Luc, and the two Berlin men moved inside the building and away from the door.

Molka took a covered position behind the truck's right rear and assessed the threat. "Well, the good news is, they're probably more triads and not the police."

Warren said, "One of the guards must have gotten off a message before we got him."

Molka said, "Let's try the easy way first: negotiation. Shizi, tell them we have them outnumbered and outgunned, but we just want to leave. If they withdraw so we can, we won't open fire."

Shizi cupped his hands around his mouth and yelled toward the triads in Filipino.

Before he finished, several yelled back at him.

Molka said, "That doesn't sound like we have a truce."

Shizi said, "From my understanding, they're just cussing us out with very profane terms."

"So they're not scared of us," she said. "But they're not attacking us either. What's that say to you, colonel?"

The colonel said, "They are waiting for reinforcements."

She nodded, concerned. "That's what I was afraid of. We need to break out before that happens."

Warren addressed the colonel. "Basic fire and movement tactic, colonel?"

"Yes," the colonel said. "Bravo will take the lead."

"Hold on," Molka said. "Before you expose yourselves to fire, a nice diversion to make them look the other way would be highly desirable."

The colonel said, "What do you suggest, team leader?"

She turned and addressed Shizi. "Do you have any det-cord left over?"

"Yes," he said. "And a backup timer-detonator."

"Perfect." She looked at Luc. "Can you go back over the roof onto the roof of the building next door and then get down and into the street behind them?"

Luc offered a confident nod. "Easily."

"Ok. Shizi, instruct him on how to use the det-cord and detonator. Once Luc's in position, this is the plan...."

CHAPTER 38

12:27 AM

Luc stood on the edge of the triad warehouse building's flat roof and reconfirmed the distance to the other warehouse roof over the narrow alley separating them at about 5 meters or a little over 16 feet.

He backed away from the edge about 30-meters, assumed a sprinter's standing start position, inhaled, exploded into a sprint toward the roof's edge, launched himself a half meter from it, carried the distance, stuck a silent landing on the warehouse roof about one meter from the edge, broke into another sprint across the roof to a steel roof access ladder attached to the building's side, made a rapid descent the three-stories to a gravel alley, and spoke into his headset: "Molka, Luc."

Molka's voiced answered: "Go, Luc."

"I am over and down."

Molka: "Acknowledged. Proceed."

"Roger that."

TASK X

12:29 AM

Molka, still in her crouched-covered position behind the truck, turned and addressed Shizi. "Ok. Give them the final warning."

Again, Shizi cupped his hands around his mouth and yelled toward the triads in Filipino.

Again, before he finished, several yelled back at him.

Molka said, "Still no truce?"

Shizi said, "Far from it."

She addressed Alpha and Bravo teams. "Prepare to assault."

12:35 AM

Luc moved fast and silent on his rubber-soled shoes down the sidewalk toward the triad warehouse front gate. The 10, armed, triad members behind their cars just inside the gate never glanced his way.

When he reached within 5 meters of them, he dropped down into a crawling position and glided on elbows and knees right under their chatting voices and cigarette smoke clouds to the gate's right side support post and stuck a short det-cord length with an attached timer-detonator to it using a pre-attached duct tape strip.

He then reversed his crawl for 5 meters, stood, moved fast and silently back down the sidewalk another 50 meters, and spoke into his headset: "Molka, Luc."

Molka answered: "Go, Luc."

"Diversion set."

Molka: "Acknowledged. Standby."

"Roger that."

12:36 AM

Shizi sat in the running truck's driver seat, slumped as low his he could while still being able to see over the wheel. The Berlin men huddled on the floorboard to his right.

To the truck's left, Molka sat in the started van's driver seat.

And crouched behind her in the van's cargo area, Alpha and Bravo teams facing the rear cargo doors with weapons at the ready.

Molka talked into her headset. "Ok, Shizi, headlights off, move nice and slow."

Shizi: "Roger that."

Molka: "Luc, prepare to detonate on my command."

Luc: "Roger that."

Shizi continued easing toward the gate.

The gate-blocking triads had not yet taken notice.

When he moved far enough away, Molka eased behind him.

The truck-van tandem continued to creep toward the gate.

When it reached 40 meters distance, the triads stirred.

Molka yelled into the headset: "Go, Shizi!"

Shizi floored the accelerator and aimed for the blocking car.

The gate blockers rose to fire.

Molka yelled into the headset again: "Luc, detonate!"

BANNNNG!

The detonating det-cord flung the gate post into the air and caused all the triads to flinch and look behind them.

Molka stopped the van, and Alpha and Bravo leaped out the rear cargo doors and ran toward the triads, with Alpha going left and Bravo right.

Shizi battered into the gate-blocking car.

CRUMMMMMMMP!

And pushed it through the gate and into the street, then turned right and continued.

TASK X

Six triads recovered and moved to open lethal fire.

The teams cut all six down first.

The surviving triads cowered in place.

Molka raced up behind the teams and yelled into the headset: "Extract!"

The teams leaped back into the rear cargo area, and Molka raced through the gate and turned right.

Half a block down the street, Luc waited on the sidewalk.

Molka stopped beside him.

He opened the passenger door.

Molka said, "You drive. I need to liaison with the contractors."

She hopped into the passenger seat and pulled out her phone, and Luc came around the van's front, hopped in the driver seat, and continued down the street after the truck.

Molka messaged the contractors holding Berlin and explained they would be delayed a few minutes from arriving at the marina and to hold there.

Luc maintained about a four-car lengths distance behind the truck. A moment later, a smaller red car flew past them on the left and got behind the truck.

The van's headlights silhouetted four men inside the red car, three holding long guns with barrels up.

Molka said, "More triads, I'll wager."

Warren said, "We should have taken the survivor's phones."

Jager said, "Or just not left any survivors."

Molka said, "They know about the truck that ripped them off, but they don't seem to know about this van being with them." She talked into her headset. "Shizi, Molka."

Shizi answered: "Go, Molka."

"Red car behind you appears to be more triads."

Shizi: "I see them."

"They'll follow you until you stop and then take you."

Shizi: "And I assume you'll prevent this?"

"Roger that." She addressed the van's occupants. "Well, we've tried to be as nice as possible with these killers, which they don't deserve. But no more warnings, no more messing around. Luc, get alongside them." She rolled her window down. "Warren, hand me your weapon."

Luc said, "Before you fire, allow me to please first try something more subtle my mentor taught me. We do not want to draw any more attention to ourselves."

Molka said, "What do have in mind?"

Luc said, "Everyone, please brace yourself."

Everyone complied.

Luc stomped the accelerator.

Brought the van to within 5 meters of the red car's bumper.

Eased to the left and matched the red car's speed.

Put the van's right fender centimeters from the red car's left rear fender.

And flicked the wheel a quarter turn to the right to make fender-to-fender contact, causing the red car to slide sideways, and he then accelerated, forcing the red car into a 180-degree spin, and continued to catch up to the truck.

PIT maneuver executed.

Behind them, the red car's spin became a tire screeching, black rubber cloud generating slide across the other lane, ending in a hard, curb jumping, drivetrain-ruining stop against a chain-link fence.

Molka had turned in her seat to witness the non-fatal crash out and then faced Luc. "Your mentor taught you how to do a perfect PIT maneuver?"

Luc nodded. "Yes, he did."

"Who did you want to PIT?"

"No one. He taught me how to perfectly do it so I would best know how to avoid it when the police chased me."

She grinned. "Ha. This is quite a *diversely* skilled team I have here."

And it was.

And it was a great one too.

Yes, having to take time to recover from the shady actions of the shady Bennie Berlin lost them a full day and night's training for the op. But the day and night were not a total loss.

Atop the team unity foundation, they laid during the parking lot brawl, they built some solid teamwork and timing pillars.

And some individual talents showed themselves:

The sober Shizi playing the drunk Shizi to perfection to setup their success.

TASK X

Warren and the colonel's natural leadership instincts to immediately pivot their teams to attack-mode when the gate threat arrived.

And Luc's seemingly boundless skillset proved huge twice.

From an unsettling, uncertain start to all arrows pointing up with still a few more days to prepare, her hopes for the team to reach peak readiness by op night seemed within reach.

You hear that, Alberto Ramirez?

Her phone vibrated in her right front pocket again.

She removed her phone and checked it.

Another message from Dov.

TUESDAY
AUGUST 2ND

CHAPTER 39

**Larger Marina Dock
Club Utopia
9: 22 AM**

Just after docking, Molka moved through *The Golden Gun's* second and third decks waking the team, who took advantage of the vessel's six cabins and two sofa beds to get some light sleep.

She stayed awake and on guard with her borrowed pistol on the bridge with the yacht's captain and two deckhands to discourage any more deception.

The team's recovered weapons and equipment sat stacked on the aft deck, ready for fast unloading by Dov, Jaron, the team, and one other recruit.

She unlocked and opened a third-deck walk-in storage locker door. Berlin sat on the floor—with his hands cuffed in front—among rope coils, various cleaning products, and folded deck chairs.

He looked up at her with a cowed fright he quickly pulled a smile mask over. "Ah, Molka. Can we finish our business now?"

"Not soon enough for me." She removed his phone from her back pocket, handed it to him, and removed her phone from her black BDU's right front pocket.

Berlin's hands shook a bit as he swiped, then he looked up at Molka again. "Will that amount be satisfactory?"

Her phone's message notification chimed. She viewed the message and re-pocketed her phone. "Alright, Berlin. You can have your yacht back now and get out of my sight." She removed a handcuff key from her left front pocket and tossed it toward him.

He caught the key and exhaled, relieved. "Thank you, Molka."

"Right after you help the others unload my order."

"My pleasure. And I must admit," he flashed his overly white teeth again, "I was 50-50 at best I would live through this."

He started to stand.

Molka's face hardened, and she pushed him back down. "Yes. Live through this. Your dirty little trick in your dirty game in your dirty business cost time that makes it less likely my friends and I will all live through what we have to do. But if I do live through it, and you ever do see me coming, run the other way as fast as you can as if your life depended on it. Because it will."

Molka brought Berlin up onto the aft deck, where the team and Dov and Jaron worked hard in the humid morning air to offload the boxes and crates and stack them on the dock.

Berlin joined the effort without prompting.

Before Molka could as well, a concerned-faced, t-shirt, shorts, and sandals wearing Dov spotted her and held up a stop sign hand.

She paused next to the side railing.

Dov handed the box he carried to Jaron, moved through the open gate in the railing, and joined her.

She said, "Ok. Your messages last night and again this morning all hinted you wanted to tell me something, but you didn't want to tell me over the phone. Right?"

Dov said, "I was trying not to even hint that much." He lowered his voice to just above a whisper. "Azzur sent us a message for you he didn't want to send over your encrypted phone."

Her face flashed confusion. "Why not, what's the message?"

He glanced over his shoulder at the others and lowered his voice to a full whisper. "Can we talk in your office? It's to be delivered to your ears only."

CHAPTER 40

10:26 AM

The colonel entered Molka's office with his BDU shirt shed, leaving the black t-shirt underneath to expose sweat stains around the collar and both armpits. "Reporting as ordered, team leader."

From her desk seat, she gestured at the chair across from her. "Please be seated, sir."

He sat. "Your assistant Dov has just informed us our personal gear is to be immediately issued right from where it sits on the dock, and the heavy weapons and the rest of the equipment are to be immediately loaded onto the *Banda Pearl*. Obviously, a major turn of circumstances has occurred."

She offered a solemn face. "I received a message from Azzur. He said the war crimes tribunal wants Colonel Nikolai Vasilyevich Krasnov—the Red Wolf—back in custody by tomorrow night."

He rubbed thick fingers on thick chin stubble. "The furlough he arranged for me does not expire for another five and a half days."

"Higher authorities, of the *world authority*, found out about that furlough he arranged and were quite outraged by it and rescinded it. They know you're here, and they've sent an official to come pick you up and take you back to Brussels. They'll arrive in Puerto Princesa tomorrow afternoon with a warrant, and they have secured Philippine law enforcement to back them up for the apprehension here sometime tomorrow evening."

He nodded. "I cannot say I am surprised by this."

"For what it's worth, sir—even though Azzur tried to deflect it by play-acting, he didn't want to give your position away by contacting me directly—I know he was the one who gave you up." She smirked. "So you can thank him for that someday."

"I actually would like to thank him someday for getting me out of that Belgian cage. Once and forever."

Molka shrugged. "Maybe they put some heavy pressure on him with my government, and he had to—once and forever?"

A cunning smile creased his lips. "Old wolves do not fall into a trap twice."

Molka offered a slow, empathizing nod. "I understand. You're never going to let them put you back in the cage. Because they're just making an example out of you. And for every charge you're acquitted on, they'll keep finding new ones until one finally sticks and locks your cage door forever."

"My accusers have made that intention quite clear."

"You could have disappeared as soon as Azzur got you out. But you still came here to help me first. And now that's put you in grave danger. So no matter how badly I need your help, you must leave as soon as possible."

"Yes, team leader, I will be gone by tomorrow morning. And I will never be seen or heard from again."

CHAPTER 41

12: 00 PM

Molka, changed into a clean duty uniform, exited her office carrying her laptop, trailed by Dov—who carried a smaller cardboard box—and Jaron.

They moved to the front of the briefing room, where the team sat at the conference table, all sweat-soaked and drinking cold bottled waters after completing Molka's new orders regarding the disbursement and stowing of their weapons and equipment.

They hadn't been told the reason for those orders nor the purpose of the unscheduled midday meeting.

Molka moved behind the podium to the table's left, placed her laptop on it, and faced the team. Dov and Jaron took their regular places, putting their backs to the left side wall.

After a somber pause, Molka addressed the team. "When I served with the Unit, my commanding major used to say, 'Hopes and dreams rarely survive contact with reality.' I must now admit that three days from now, my hopes and dreams were that we would be ready enough to have at least a 50 percent chance of successfully completing our operation. I picked that percentage not because I have doubts about the men's talents and abilities in this room. Far from it."

"It was because I've always tended to be pessimistic about my hopes and dreams to save myself from bitter disappointment when they don't come true and be pleasantly surprised when they do. And I fully expected to be pleasantly surprised this time."

"However, the reality my commanding major spoke of has now contacted those hopes and dreams, and their survival is in great danger."

The team's attention on her became rapt.

She looked to the colonel. "Colonel Krasnov is being forced to leave us before tomorrow evening. And as you all know, the ground operation cannot spare a single person. Most especially the man who planned it. But to his peril, credit, and my everlasting gratitude, he's agreed to stay with us until tomorrow morning."

"So if we are to go ahead with the op, we must go tonight. And if we go tonight, there's a strong likelihood, because we're not yet fully prepared, some, or all of us, won't come back."

The team exchanged stern expressions but remained silent.

She continued. "And since this op is not official, it's strictly personal for me, I should not, in good conscience, ask any of you to take on the additional risk of going tonight."

"However, I know I will never again get this opportunity of having exactly the right team in exactly the right place at exactly the right time."

She breathed deep and exhaled. "That's why I am asking you to take that risk of going tonight. And I know, knowing the type of men you all are, you will all agree to go. But I think it only fair we actually vote to do so. And for that vote to be legitimate, it MUST be unanimous."

Dov moved to the podium, placed the box he held atop it, and he and Jaron removed from inside the box slips of white paper with the words YES and NO printed on them and black markers and began to pass them out to the team.

Molka said, "I thought voting by secret ballot would be best so every man can vote his conscience without this group's strong, all-Alphas, peer pressure affecting the outcome. Please take your ballot and leave the table for privacy, circle your choice, fold your ballot, and put it in the box on the podium. The colonel, Dov, Jaron, and I have already voted yes."

Jager spoke up: "Before we hold this secret ballot vote, may I say something?"

Molka nodded. "Of course."

He continued. "Molka, what kind of men do you think we are?"

Shizi spoke up: "And, Molka, I'm sad to say, this is the first time you've ever disappointed me."

Nathan spoke up: "I was just about to say the same thing, Molka."

Luc spoke up: "Molka, it is precisely because this operation is personal to you that the additional risk is irrelevant to us."

Savanna spoke up: "He's right, Lady Molka. Perhaps, if this were an official operation for some government entity or a mercenary contract for a stranger, some of us would have reservations about doing it now."

Kang spoke up: "Molka, we've already discussed this among ourselves. The target murdered your little sister. To all of us, that's the same as if he murdered our own little sister."

Warren spoke up: "All you needed to say, Molka, was the colonel is leaving in the morning, we're executing the op tonight, and this is the final briefing. So, please do so, right men?"

Every man verbalized agreement.

A warm lump broke free from Molka's heart and settled in her throat, causing her eyes to water. She fought back the tears, swallowed hard, and offered a smile. "Thank you, gentlemen. The colonel is leaving in the morning, we're executing the op tonight, and this is the final briefing."

She opened her laptop. "A lot of what I'm about to go over, you heard from Warren yesterday during his prelim briefing, and you've been studying on your tablets for the last few days. But let's go over it all together for unit cohesion."

She swiped her laptop, brought up an itinerary-type list on the big, wall-mounted monitor, and began:

"Wake up: 11 PM."

"Assembly for final weapons and equipment check on the marina dock beside the *Banda Pearl*: 11:30 PM."

"Departure: 12 AM."

"Travel time to Base X: three hours, twenty-eight minutes."

"Weather is expected to be clear and seas calm."

She swiped her laptop again and brought up the updated digital map of Base X. "Upon arrival at two kilometers off Base X's west coast, the first landing boat will launch with the Alpha team—the colonel, Nathan, Shizi, and Jaron—which upon landing, the colonel, Nathan, and Jaron will establish observation-blocking positions of the comms building and original Chinese garrison barracks, as well as, the new barracks buildings on the island's south side, while Shizi places the diversion explosives on the main comms tower and the power station on the island's west side."

"And since we will maintain radio silence as long as possible, Jaron will also act as message runner between Alpha and Bravo teams should it be necessary."

"After placing the explosive charge, Shizi will return to the landing beach and act as security for the landing boats during the op."

"Fifteen minutes after Alpha launches, Bravo team—Warren, Kang, Luc, Jager, and I—will launch."

"Upon landing, Warren, Luc, Kang, Jager, and I, with Jager leading, will proceed to the residential compound on the island's north side."

"Luc will then covertly breach the compound wall and open the front gate for the rest of the team to enter."

"Then Warren, Kang, and I will secure the target's two security men and his two domestic servants while Jager locates and positively IDs the target and also takes photos and a DNA sample."

"I will then eliminate the target."

"Bravo will then withdraw from the compound."

"Warren, Luc, Kang, and Jager will return to the landing beach and return to the ship, as I link up with Alpha to inform them the objective has been achieved and then return with them to the landing beach and return to the ship."

"Shizi will then detonate the explosives to cut their main power and long-range communications, as well as divert their attention as we make our withdrawal for home."

She swiped her tablet to bring up a chart. "Radio procedures. Even though we have the newest model with strong encryption, as I said, we will maintain radio silence for as long as possible. We don't know what kind of decryption tech the Chinese garrison may have. If and when we go to radio comms, to avoid confusion and cross chatter, Alpha will use channel one. Bravo will use channel two. The *Banda Pearl* will use channel three. And channel four will be what I call the 'command channel' which can communicate with all radios, and I'll be monitoring."

She swiped the laptop to bring up another list. "Now, here are the rules of engagement."

"Starting with the Alpha team. We will conduct the op under the assumption that at some point, the Chinese garrison will be alerted to our presence and move to investigate."

"Under that circumstance, remember, we are not going there to kill Chinese military personnel. They have nothing to do with the vile murderer occupying the north side of their island. And I doubt most of them even know anything about who lives in that compound."

"Therefore, they are not to be fired upon with deadly weapons unless they fire at you with deadly weapons, and then only if you are certain you are in imminent, mortal jeopardy for which deadly force is your only defense."

"That not being the case, you will first deploy smoke grenades to confuse and disorient them. Followed by CS grenades to slow, if not totally stop, their approach because it's unlikely military radar and construction units would be issued gas masks."

"Onto the rules of engagement for the Bravo team."

"The target's two domestic servants are not to be harmed in any way. They're just there to make a living."

"However, the target's two security men are fair game if they resist. When they signed up to protect a terrorist, they knew what they were signing up for. And if they didn't, they should have."

She addressed Kang. "Kang, if you could get any last-minute updates about Base X from your Chinese intelligence contacts, that would be very helpful."

He nodded and pulled his phone from his front pocket. "I'll get right on that."

TASK X

Molka checked the time on her laptop. "Now, let's break into our individual teams to discuss specific tactics and review the maps again for the next couple of hours." She addressed Savanna. "And then, Captain Savanna, can you and your crew organize a landing boat exercise? I know doing so during daylight is not ideal but waiting until dark is too late now."

He nodded, confident. "Yes, Lady Molka. That won't be any problem."

Molka continued. "After the exercise, I suggest everyone eat and go to bed, even though I know most of you got some sleep last night on the way home. Because I have a feeling we will all need all the rest we can get. Ok. That's it."

As the team stood and moved to join their individual units, the colonel waved Warren aside for a private word.

The two men came together. The colonel offered a respectful nod and said, "Bravo team leader."

Warren returned the respectful nod. "Alpha team leader."

The colonel continued. "I wanted to tell you that your leadership and performance have been admirable, and I fully expect that to continue tonight."

"Thank you, colonel. I'll definitely give it my best effort."

"I understand your wife, and you have a personal friendship with our team leader."

"We started with a professional relationship with her that became friendly. My wife really admires her. I'm not sure Molka allows many close friends, though. By her own choice."

"This is my thought, too," the colonel said. "Since your wife and you are friendly with her, I hope when this is all over, you will check on Molka from time to time and make sure she is finally living a happy life."

CHAPTER 42

7:22 PM

Molka sat on the beach sand outside her villa, gazing across the bay at the setting sun's purple, orange, and magnificent yellow pallet painting the horizon.

Dov, Jaron, and the team—except Kang, who talked to his Chinese intelligence contacts and would report to her soon—had bedded down until their 11 PM wake-up.

Earlier, the landing exercise went exceptionally well. They ran through it four times—each time faster and smoother—and it also proved to be a microcosm of the tight, bonded unit they came together to be.

Savanna's fabricated rig to lower and retrieve the boats into and out of the water with the ship's crane was engineering genius, considering how fast he did it. And he trained Dov and Jaron to operate it fast and efficiently and be competent deckhands for the *Banda Pearl*. If the op succeeded, Captain LJ Savanna would be an underrated reason for it.

Warren embraced his role and responsibilities as XO and, as a competent XO would, suggested she step aside to observe and critique and spot any flaws in the exercise her active participation might not expose.

Jager, even though he served as a captain in the German army, behaved more like a top-notch NCO harping on the smallest details and stressing their importance, and then offering encouragement and assurances.

The colonel, Nathan, Shizi, and Jaron—Alpha team—knowing they were the key to the op succeeding, used the time it took the *Banda Pearl* to cruise from the marina to the spot out in the bay for the exercise starting point and then the cruise back to the marina afterward, huddled in hyper-focus together over their digital maps discussing their upcoming duties.

Luc shelved his usual charm, wit, and humor and kept quiet company with himself while paying close attention as if to say, "I will not be the reason, if the op fails."

And Kang presented as a cool, steady, and confident presence the other men gravitated to and tried to impress.

They returned from the exercise carrying high morale. And before they went to their villa's beds, the colonel surprised his teammates with a restaurant group meal he arranged of thick, prime-cut steaks he called "a warrior's last supper."

They were the finest men Molka had worked with since the Unit, to whom they stood as equals, if not superiors. And she would probably never work with such fine men ever again.

If she lived to see sunrise.

In the coming hours, approximately 225 kilometers—120 nautical miles—due west of where she sat, on a speck of an island in the South China Sea, over 10 years of agony and heartbreak and tears and rage would come to a merciful end for her: one way or another.

The villa's door next to Molka's opened, and Kang stepped out sporting a sharp, gray polo, black shorts, and bare feet and trotted down the porch stairs, down the beach, and sat in the sand beside Molka. "No new information on Base X. I'm very sorry."

She shrugged. "It's fine. Just confirming the target was in that compound was all I really needed."

"I only wish I could have found out who is protecting the target and why."

"It doesn't matter now. I'm going to get a couple of hours sleep. You should too." Molka glanced over to see Kang staring at her with sadness. "What's wrong?"

"My heart is going to break for you tonight."

She flashed a perplexed face. "Why?"

"Because you're going to find out what I found out."

"What's that?"

"That the word closure is more than just a cliché for getting over a personal tragedy. It's a cruel, cruel word."

She remained perplexed. "How so?"

He turned his face away from her and toward the coming twilight. "After I completed my first assignment for Pentad, I requested and was given an indefinite leave of absence. That leave was part of my agreement to join the organization. And I used the time to track down and kill a man who killed someone years ago that I loved more than my own life."

He continued. "And when it was done, I waited for the joy of relief to replace the hate. And the hate left me, but the joy of relief never came. It was depressing to the point where I began to miss the hate. Because when I had the hate, at least I had hope. But then I had neither."

She said, "And what do you have now?"

He turned his face back to her. "I have closure. And closure isn't enough. And it will never be enough."

Molka stood, agitated. "It will be enough for me."

**WEDNESDAY
AUGUST 3RD**

CHAPTER 43

Banda Pearl Underway Heading West
South China Sea
1:47 AM

Jaron—clad in the team's freshly issued black BDUs over black tactical boots and wearing a black tactical thigh holster holding a Glock 19—stood on the *Banda Pearl's* foredeck, scanning the dark, clear sky with binoculars for Chinese military patrol aircraft.

Just above him, Savanna and Dov occupied the ship's bridge clad in fresh black BDUs, tac-boots, and wearing sidearms.

Savanna stood at the wheel, manned the controls, and watched the engine gauges. To his left, Dov monitored the GPS and the marine radar, which offered a blue screen with a few tiny orange dots representing small fishing craft—the nearest over 10 nautical miles away—and a solid white heading line pointing to a large orange blob representing Base X.

Dov's eyes moved to the GPS screen. "Sixty-five, point five nautical miles to Base X, captain. We're halfway there."

Savanna glanced over at the GPS and then the radar screen. "Well…I'm so glad I replaced this ship's original dome radar with a long-range, open array unit."

Dov said, "Why is that captain?"

"Because the old radar wouldn't have picked up what's just appeared."

Dov viewed the screen to see a larger orange object 70 nautical miles northwest of Base X.

"What is that, captain?"

"That is a sea-going vessel."

Dov's face flashed confusion. "But it looks huge compared to the others we've watched on the scope."

Savanna kept keen eyes on the object. "It's not a container ship because that's nowhere near the shipping lanes. And it's too big to be even the largest commercial fishing vessels for these waters like ours is. So, my suspicion leaves only one other possibility."

Dov frowned. "A Chinese Navy patrol destroyer."

"Yes, Mister Dov, I'm afraid so."

"What do we do?"

Savanna used his finger to trace an imaginary line from the object across the screen. "On her present course, she will pass by Base X at a range of about 30 nautical miles. If she maintains that, we'll be fine. So, remain steadfast, my steady man."

"Yes, captain."

The men went back to their duties.

After a few moments, Savanna said, "Where is Lady Molka, in the galley with the others?"

"No," Dov said. "She's down in the berthing cabin. She felt a migraine coming on and wanted to rest her mind to get rid of it. Want me to go tell her about this?"

Savanna scanned the dark seas ahead and said, "No. Best let her rest for now. She has an intense night awaiting her. You just keep a sharp watch on our big girlfriend out there and let me know if she changes directions."

CHAPTER 44

1:47 AM

Down on the second deck, Warren, Kang, Luc, Jager, the colonel, Shizi, and Nathan sat at a large Formica-topped table in the galley.

All outfitted in their freshly issued black BDUs, black tactical boots, and black tactical watches. Except Luc, who preferred to wear his tight black Lycra outfit, black sneaker-like shoes, and his own watch.

And in addition, Warren, Jager, Kang, and Shizi wore black tactical chest rigs mounting four spare 30-round MP5 mags in tactical pouches, and the colonel and Nathan slung a bandolier each holding five smoke and five CS grenades.

Lined up neatly to their left, atop a blue tarp on the linoleum floor, were their individual weapons, their helmets with attached night vision goggles and wireless headsets, their radios, two small, black backpacks holding Nathan and Kang's camera drones, and three, large, green metal ammo cases containing extra rounds for the light machineguns.

For the cruise's first hour, the seven men studied—for the numerous time—the digital maps on their tablets interspersed with op-related chat.

Then, after Nathan distributed canned energy drinks and bottled waters from the galley refrigerator for a break, the table erupted with some high-spirited joking, ribbing, and a few non-work-related stories punctuated by generous and loud laughing.

Luc did not participate, though. He instead sat silent, deep inside his own thoughts. And Luc demurred when Shizi asked him to share the details of Savana and his pursuit of the attractive ladies after the parking lot brawl. Surprising, since he freely entertained them with other stories of conquests gained and conquests lost in previous relaxed moments.

Warren time-checked his watch. "Ok, boys. We should be past the halfway point. We're cleared to test fire our weapons."

All but Luc—who still insisted he go unarmed—stood, retrieved their assigned MP5s, Glock 19s, SIG LMG-68 light machineguns, and Milkor MGL 40-millimeter grenade launchers, and headed up the ladder to fire them from the stern into the sea.

The colonel hung back, and when all the others exited, he moved into the seat beside the still somber Luc and said, "Luc, your personal bravery is beyond question. However, I can see you are very nervous."

Luc feigned a smile. "Is it that evident?"

"I believe this is because you are the only one among us who has not faced hostile fire."

Luc said, "The last time I was with Molka, I actually was shot at by some criminals. Luckily, they were bad shots, and I never felt threatened. Later, Molka was forced to kill many of these same men to save innocent lives. I saw their bodies, hacked and bloodied by automatic weapon fire, some with terrorized, dead, open eyes. I put that sight out of my mind that day. However, since we got on this ship, that sight is all I can see."

The colonel said, "I do not want you to think of this anymore. The woman and men you are going in with are all highly experienced warriors who are more than a match for any threats we will encounter on that island. Being among them puts you in the safest position on this team." He placed his arm around Luc's shoulder. "Follow their instructions, do your job, keep your head down, and you will come through this alive and well."

Luc offered a relieved smile. "Thank you, my friend."

CHAPTER 45

1:47 AM

Down on the third deck, in the ship's head in the bow, Molka—outfitted in her black mock turtleneck, black jeans, and black tac-boots with contacts in, her old pilot's watch strapped on her left wrist, and her hair in a high ponytail with bangs swept right to left to keep her aiming eye clear—knelt over the toilet and wanted to vomit.

It wasn't from sickness.
It wasn't from nerves.
It was from frustration.
Because another massive headache assaulted her brain.
She lay on the floor.
It started.
The thousand glowing hot, needle-sized knives plunged into the center of her mind, sadistically twisted in every direction, slashing and shredding and shredding and slashing.
She bowed her head into her hands.
To wait for the pain to subside.
And for the dark urges to start.
The most horrible, dangerous, vicious, depraved, bloody thoughts. Thoughts a normal brain would strongly suppress to

hold on to its own sanity suddenly welling up and becoming tolerable, completely rational, preferable, and justifiable.

The pain faded.

The dark urges focused.

Alberto Ramirez!

You bastard!

Your one slow death will feel like 1000 slow ones.

Because I changed my mind.

About my vicious .40 caliber hollow points.

You're not getting two center mass and one in the head.

You're getting...

One in each shoulder.

One in each kneecap.

One in each foot.

One in each testicle.

And then you will crawl in unbearable blood-drenched agony across the room and beg for the last two rounds in my mag to be put through your eyes.

YOU HEAR ME?

YOU BASTARD!

A few moments later, the dark urges stopped.

Molka got back onto her feet, exited the head, crossed the passageway to a small cabin with a small bunk, and laid atop it with her eyes closed.

In what seemed a second's fraction later, she awoke to Jaron's gentle nudge.

Her eyes opened to him.

He said, "Molka, we're here."

CHAPTER 46

**South China Sea
Two Kilometers West of Base X
3:22 AM**

After Jaron left her and headed back topside, Molka rose, grabbed her black gear bag from the floor, placed it atop the bunk, and unzipped it.

First, she removed a black tactical thigh holster holding a Beretta 96A1 and mounting two spare 10-round mags in tactical pouches. She removed the weapon from the holster, released the mag, removed and inspected the first three .40 caliber hollow point rounds—the kill shots—for the 10th time that night, reinserted them into the mag, reinserted the mag into the weapon, made sure the weapon was safe, re-holstered the weapon, and strapped the holster to her right thigh.

Next, she removed a black, tactical chest rig mounting four spare 30-round MP5 mags in tactical pouches and strapped it on.

Next, she removed an MP5 submachine gun with an attached 30-round mag and mounting a tactical sight on a tactical sling. She released and inspected the mag, reinserted it, ensured the weapon was safe and strapped it across her chest.

Next, she removed a small, black, encrypted two-way radio and clipped it inside her left front pocket.

Next, she removed a black, tactical-style Kevlar helmet mounting night vision goggles and an attached wireless comms headset. She placed the helmet on her head, moved the night vision goggles into the flipped-up rest position, and secured the helmet's chinstrap.

Finally, she removed Janetta's laminated photo, pressed it to her heart, slipped it into her right front pocket, and headed topside.

When Molka entered the second deck galley, the team was all on their feet, gearing up with business-like efficiency and faces. Without stopping, she said, "Assemble on deck in five minutes."

She climbed the ladder onto the aft deck and into a warm, humid early morning accented with a strong sea aroma and the taste of salt on her lips.

The *Banda Pearl* cruised slowly through light seas with only a slight up and down swelling motion.

Beside the ship's crane near the starboard side railing, Dov and Jaron had the tarps off the landing boats and worked on attaching one to the lowering straps.

She moved to the ladder climbing to the bridge, ascended it, and entered it from the open rear door. Only the instrument panel lights and the GPS and radar screens lit the space. She noted that the two olive green cases holding Dov's FIM-92 Stinger air-defense missiles were stacked to the left.

Savanna stood at the ship's wheel, a changed man. As in, he changed from his BDU ensemble into the contents of his "special order" box from Bennie Berlin.

That being: an open-collared, long-sleeved black silk shirt, a wide black leather belt, and black pants tucked into knee-length, black leather, Wellington-style boots. He accessorized with ponytailed hair covered with a black bandana tied at the back, a gold hoop earring shining from his left ear, and sported a sweet looking, black leather, cross draw, double shoulder holster rig carrying a pair of nickel-plated, classic M1911 .45s.

His trademark Captain LJ Savanna—pirate on the hunt—outfit from their time in the Caribbean two years before.

A small, nostalgic smile crossed her lips, but there was no time to reminisce. She moved to his left, and he handed her binoculars. "Dead ahead, Lady Molka."

She raised the binoculars and viewed through the bridge's front windows. About two kilometers dead ahead lay Base-X.

Red LED aircraft warning lights flashed from the two radomes on the island's southern end and from the main comms tower and the wind turbines aside from the power plant on the island's west side. A few other scattered, faint lights that appeared to be streetlight-types dotted the island.

But the target's residential compound and both garrison barracks sat completely blacked out. Sleeping unaware, she hoped.

She lowered the binoculars, timed-check her watch, and addressed Savanna. "Captain Savanna, you got us here safely, ahead of schedule, and undetected. I would like to compliment you, but I expected no less from you, sir."

"Thank you, Lady Molka." He presented his slightly crooked rogue smile. "I would like to compliment myself as well, but I, too, expected no less." His smile switched to seriousness, and he gestured to a larger orange mass on the radar screen. "I must now report what I believe to be a Chinese Navy destroyer located 60 nautical miles west of our position moving at slow speed on a southwest course. However, I do not believe she poses a threat to us at this time."

Molka studied the screen. "Please explain."

"If she maintains her current course and speed, she will pass approximately 25 nautical miles west of Base X in about two hours."

Molka said, "And before then, we'll be withdrawing from here at full speed for home due east."

"Yes, and even if the island garrison, with their comms knocked out, is somehow able to get word to the ship they've been breached, we'll just blend into the dozens of early morning commercial fishing vessels in the area."

"Does the rest of the team know about this?"

"I informed the assault team leaders."

"Ok. Keep a close watch on it and break radio silence if the threat assessment changes."

"Of course, Lady Molka. Shall I commence our run toward the landing beach?"

"Yes."

"Commencing run, aye." He adjusted the throttle. "As planned, I'll slow to trawling speed to mimic fishing activity, move to within one kilometer of the landing beach, and hold her steady for launching the landing boats. I'll let you know when we're in position."

"How long until then?"

"Ten minutes." He turned a hopeful face toward her. "All my best wishes and good luck to you, Lady Molka."

"Thank you. And just in case things don't go the way we hoped tonight…," She hugged him around the neck, "Thank you again for being here when I needed you."

"We'll drink to that when you return." His rogue smile reappeared. "I pilfered two bottles of fine bourbon from the resort bar and stashed them aboard."

Molka smiled, turned, exited the bridge, and climbed down the ladder to the aft deck to find Alpha and Bravo teams facing each other and standing at attention.

Molka moved between them. "Stand at ease, gentleman."

They stood at ease.

Alpha's, the colonel, and Nathan carried their light machine guns slung over their right shoulders and their six-shot, revolver-type grenade launchers slung across their backs. Nathan also wore a slim backpack containing his camera drone. And Shizi carried his MP5 barrel across his chest on the tactical sling, and a black gear bag slung over his right shoulder containing his C-4 blocks and timers.

Bravo's Warren, Jager, and Kang, also carried their MP5s barrel down across their chests on the tactical slings. In addition, Kang wore a slim backpack containing his camera drone and megaphone for the compound breach. And Luc presented as somewhat an odd contrasting figure, unarmed in his tight-fitting outfit, with his helmet serving as the only marker to match him with his compatriots.

Molka addressed her men. "We'll be in position to launch boats in less than 10 minutes. I don't need to ask if you're ready. I know you are. I prepared a team leader speech, but I edited it down to two words: good hunting. And on a personal note...."

She moved to each man, hugged them around the neck, and said: "Thank you again for being here when I needed you."

Molka moved across the deck toward Dov and Jaron.

After she departed, the men of Alpha and Bravo shook hands and wished each other good hunting. And when the colonel came to shake with Kang, he pulled Kang close and spoke into his ear. "I know you have felt like an outsider since you joined us and left your home country. I know this feeling too. However, you are the nucleus that binds this team tightly."

Kang smiled, humble. "Thank you, colonel."

Molka stood before Dov and Jaron beside the landing boats. "Dov, Jaron, I want you both to know I was wrong about—"

Dov interrupted with a warm smile. "Please, save your sentiments for when you say goodbye to us tomorrow, Molka. You've got an op to run now."

Jaron smiled warmly, "What he said goes double for me, Molka."

The ship's slow forward movement nearly stopped, then the motor reversed for a few seconds to bring her to a full stop, and she settled into a gentle rocking.

A moment later, Savanna's voice boomed from above: "Now hear this!"

All eyes on the aft deck lifted to the bridge's rear doorway where Savanna stood with feet spread shoulder width apart, hands on hips, and face ablaze. "Lady Molka and my brother raiders, we have arrived! Best of luck to all and good hunting, and remember to pillage them just for fun, knock them around and upside down, and laugh when you've conquered and won!"

The team gave a hearty cheer.

Then Molka gave serious orders: "Lower the landing boats. Bravo team, standby. Alpha team, prepare to board and launch."

CHAPTER 47

4: 17 AM

Seventeen minutes after the Alpha team departed the *Banda Pearl* for the landing beach, Molka sat in the Bravo team's landing boat's bow seat facing Base-X.

Luc sat on the bench seat behind her.

Jager and Kang sat on the bench seat behind him.

And Warren sat in the stern manning the silent running electric outboard.

After a smooth launch, they began the kilometer run toward the landing beach through foot-high swells. Sea spray warmed Molka's face and salted her lips again. She reached down with her right hand and squeezed the laminated photo in her right front pocket.

Yes. It's really happening, my little Janetta.

At about a quarter kilometer from the beach, two sharp flashes illuminated the island's interior, followed a millisecond later by…

BOOOOOM!
BOOOOOM!

Jager said, "What the hell?"

Warren said, "Was that ours?"

Molka viewed two moon-silhouetted smoke columns rising from the areas of the comms tower and power plant. "That was ours."

Kang said, "Break radio silence to verify?"

Before Molka could answer, at about 30 meters from the beach, Shizi stood beside the other landing boat, frantically waving his arms.

No. Not Shizi.

It was Jaron.

Then small arms fire bursts sounded from the island.

Luc said, "Something has gone awry, obviously."

The boat hit the beach, and the Alpha team jumped out and pulled it up beside the other.

Molka addressed Jaron. "Were those accidental detonations? Where's Shizi?"

A distressed-faced Jaron answered. "He's with the colonel. The colonel ordered him to drop the comms tower and turn out the lights immediately."

Molka said, "What happened?"

"Bad luck. Two guys were on this beach fishing." He pointed at two dropped fishing poles and a bait bucket."

Kang said, "Likely, supplementing their very meager rations during their off time."

Jaron continued. "They spotted us coming in and ran for their barracks. The whole garrison is awake. The colonel, Shizi, and Nathan are keeping them pinned inside. For now."

Molka's jaw tightened. "Surprise is gone. Survival is in question. We may have to scrub."

Warren said, "Not yet. We can still take down the target and get out if Alpha can hold."

"Ok," she said. "Get Bravo to the cover position outside the compound, deploy the drone, and prepare to breach. I'll be there as soon as I get a sitrep from the colonel."

Warren said, "Roger that." He addressed Bravo. "Jager, take the lead, covered position outside the compound."

Jager said, "Roger that. Let's move." He led Warren, Kang, and Luc up and over the seawall and toward the compound at the run.

Molka addressed Jaron. "Take me to the colonel."

TASK X

CHAPTER 48

With their night vision goggles activated, Jaron led Molka up and over the seawall and at the run onto a single-vehicle-wide access road made from crushed and compacted coral.

After about 40 meters, he cut left from the road into a citrus grove with the trees planted in neat rows in grass-topped soil.

They cut a diagonal path through the rows until they reached the grove's opposite edge, where the colonel and Nathan lay prone aiming their light machineguns—with front bipods deployed—at the new barracks buildings about 75 meters away across a flat sandy tract.

Molka dropped down prone to the colonel's right, and Jaron dropped prone to Nathan's left.

The colonel said, "We have been firing short, randomly timed bursts above the door and windows to discourage them from leaving. We are saving the smoke and CS grenades for when they attack us."

Molka said, "Where's Shizi?"

"Deployed with Jaron's machinegun in the grove across from the comms buildings and original barracks conducting the same mission as we."

Nathan aimed and fired a short burst.

TASK X

Molka reached into her left front pocket, switched her radio from the command channel four to Alpha's channel one, and spoke into her headset. "Shizi, Molka."

Shizi answered: "Go, Molka."

"Sitrep."

Shizi: "A couple of guys poked their heads out the comms building door, and I chased them back inside. It's been quiet since. And no movement from the barracks."

"Acknowledged. Standby."

Shizi: "Roger that."

Molka flashed a contemplative face. "Sir, for over one hundred potential weapons against your three, they're reacting very slowly."

The colonel said, "Remember, these are navy specialists, not regular infantry. It may take them some time to organize and coordinate a response. So, we must take advantage of this."

Molka said, "I agree, but we have to assume they have an emergency antenna on one of these buildings with the range to call that Chinese warship. Which means it's probably already steaming at full speed here."

Nathan said, "But even so if that ship is 60 nautical miles away, it still gives us plenty of time."

The colonel aimed and fired a short burst at the barracks wall.

Molka said, "Maybe so, but we also have to assume that ship would have at least one helicopter with ground and sea attack capabilities that they can send out ahead."

The colonel nodded. "Very possible."

Molka pounded her right fist into the grass. "Then we should abort. We have to abort."

The colonel turned his face to Molka. "Team leader, the only reason you would ever consider aborting now is out of concern for your men. But I will speak for every man when I say, do not be concerned with us. We all agreed to complete this operation against all risks. Now, go complete it."

Molka nodded. "Yes, sir." She addressed Nathan. "Get your drone up and monitor both barracks and the comms building. Make sure they're not sneaking out the back doors and windows."

Nathan said, "Roger that." He crawled behind him to a tree where his backpack leaned against, along with the two grenade launchers.

Molka addressed Jaron. "Get back to the boats and position them for a fast extraction."

Jaron, "Roger that."

The colonel said, "First, I will need him to bring us the extra ammo for the machineguns from our boat. We may need all of it before we leave."

Molka's eyebrows rose, concerned. "I really hope not. But do it, Jaron."

Jaron sprang up and ran off.

Molka spoke into her headset again. "Shizi, Molka."

Shizi: "Go, Molka."

"Can you hold for a few more minutes, marine?"

Shizi: "Aye, ma'am. Or I'll die trying."

"Roger that." She switched her radio to Bravo's channel two. "Warren, Molka."

Warren answered: "Go, Molka."

"Bravo in position?"

"Affirmative."

"Sitrep."

Warren: "Drone deployed. Compound lit by emergency lighting and unoccupied. What are your orders?"

"Standard plan: Breach compound, neutralize security, secure staff, locate, capture, verify, and hold target. I'm on the way."

CHAPTER 49

4:33 AM

From the citrus grove's edge about 40 meters from the compound's front gate, Warren, Jager, and Luc huddled behind Kang all watching the camera view screen attached to his drone controller as he flew the tiny aircraft over the compound's courtyard for the fourth time.

Except for the sporadic popping sounds from Alpha's short machinegun bursts on the island's southside, silence roared in the ears due to the heavy pesticide use, insect-free environment.

Warren continued to watch the screen and said, "The target's security still hasn't come out to see what the explosions were and what the firing is."

Luc said, "Is that good or bad?"

Jager said, "It could mean they're scared, or they're barricaded inside, well-armed, and prepared to repel all invaders."

Warren: "Let's not wait for them either way. Breach it. Kang, keep surveillance over the compound until he's inside. If security shows themselves before that, call abort to Luc."

Kang: "Roger that."

Warren: "Ready, Luc?"

Luc: "I am ready."

Warren tapped the Glock in his thigh holster. "Sure you don't want this?"

Luc: "No thank you, my friend."

Warren and Jager held their MP5s at the ready and moved behind trees at the grove's edge to cover Luc's run to the compound.

Warren: "Ok, Luc. We've got your back. See you inside."

Luc burst from the grove at the sprint and onto another compacted crushed coral road leading to the compound's gate.

He covered the 40 meters distance without making a sound in less than five seconds and, about a meter away from the compound's smooth, masonry, prison-high wall, launched himself toward it, stuck to its face several meters up, and used non-existent hand and foot holds to crawl up and over and drop inside.

Jager said, "Look at that. Amazing."

Warren nodded. "Impressive athlete."

A moment later, the metal gate slid open to the left, and Luc stepped into the opening and spoke into his headset. "Bravo, you are clear."

Kang landed the drone inside the compound, tucked it and the controller into his backpack, grabbed his MP5 in the ready position, moved to the tree covering position next to Warren, and nodded.

Warren and Jager then burst from the grove, retraced Luc's route to the compound wall, ran through the gate, and took a covering position inside it.

Warren spoke into his headset: "Kang, you're clear."

Kang burst from the grove and ran toward and through the gate.

The trio then ran crouched across the compound's crushed, compacted coral surface illuminated by a bright emergency light attached to the residence's face and joined Luc hunkered low behind the courtyard fountain, which didn't flow because of the knocked-out power.

As Luc kept his head down, Warren, Jager, and Kang peered over the fountain's edge to view the front of the residence and a metal ramp laid over four steps leading to a large, covered porch and a red-painted wooden front door.

Jager said, "Faint light coming from the window on the second floor and the first-floor window to the left."

Kang said, "Backup generator. Wonder what they've used that ramp to load in there?"

Warren said, "Hopefully, not heavy weapons they're now pointing at us." He addressed Kang. "Ok, let's try the easy way."

Kang rolled onto his side, removed the megaphone from his backpack, switched on the power, rolled back into a crouching position, aimed the megaphone toward the front door, and spoke the memorized script from the plan in perfect Chinese:

> *Occupants of the house.*
> *This is the Chinese military police.*
> *Do not be afraid.*
> *We are here to help you.*
> *This island is under attack by foreign terrorists.*
> *For your safety, come out now with your hands raised.*
> *If you come out with a weapon, you will be shot.*
> *If we come in, you may be shot.*
> *This is the Chinese military police.*
> *Do not be afraid.*
> *We are here to help you.*
> *Come out now with your hands raised.*
> *If you come out with a weapon, you will be shot.*
> *If we come in, you may be shot.*
> *This is the Chinese military police.*
> *Do not be afraid.*
> *We are here to help you.*
> *Come out now with your hands raised.*

CHAPTER 50

4:38 AM

"**D**arn it!" Molka instantly regretted her frustrated exclamation because her radio was monitoring channel four, the command channel, which broadcast to every team radio.

And what she monitored from Bravo told her they breached the compound and worked to secure the inhabitants.

Very little from Alpha, though, other than Jaron delivering the extra machinegun ammo from their landing boat.

Her frustration stemmed from the fact during her map study preparation, she hadn't studied a direct route from the colonel's position to the compound. Because she was never supposed to have made the journey.

And without scout Jager to guide her, she got mired in another large citrus grove and lost her bearings, which meant she would have to backtrack to the landing beach and take the path from there she had studied for hours.

She began to run back that way when Savanna's voice sounded in her headset. "Molka, Captain Savanna."

She switched her radio to *Banda Pearl's* channel three and spoke into her headset. "Molka here, captain. Ignore my little yell. I'm fine."

"I actually have an urgent update on that Chinese warship."

She stopped running. "Go with update."

Savanna: "She's changed course and is heading straight to us."

"I expected that. How long will it take to get here?"

Savanna: "If she can make 30 knots, which I believe is their destroyers' full speed, she can be here in right at two hours. But she still poses no direct threat to the op, I believe."

"I believe that too. Because if we're not long gone by then, we're never leaving anyway."

CHAPTER 51

4:40 AM

Warren viewed his tactical watch and counted down 30 seconds from Kang's third and final warning call for the house inhabitants to come out unarmed with hands raised.

No compliance.

Warren said, "Glove up."

He, Jager, and Kang removed heavy-duty rubber gloves from their BDU pants' cargo pockets and pulled them on.

Luc remained crouched behind the fountain.

Warren said, "Prepare to assault on my command."

The trio moved the fire selector switches on their weapons from the safe to the 3-round burst position.

The house's front door opened to a blacked-out interior, and a male voice called out in Chinese.

Kang translated for his teammates. "It's one of the security men. He said he and the other security man and the housekeeper and cook ladies are coming out with their hands atop their heads and unarmed."

Warren nodded at Jager, and they both rose to kneeling firing positions with their weapons aimed at the door.

Warren said, "Ok, Kang, tell them to come out now."

TASK X

Kang called out instructions with the megaphone in Chinese.

A moment later, a taller, younger, muscular Asian male with very short hair emerged from the doorway wearing only a white t-shirt and white boxer shorts with his hands atop his head, moved onto the porch, and then slowly descended the metal ramp leading from the porch.

Coming behind him, a second, younger, more rotund, Asian male with a shaved head emerged from the doorway wearing only gray athletic shorts with his hands atop his head, moved onto the porch, and then slowly descended the metal ramp leading from the porch.

And behind him, two diminutive, short-haired, middle-aged Asian ladies emerged from the doorway both wearing white robes over white pajamas with their hands atop their heads, moved onto the porch and then slowly descended the metal ramp leading from the porch.

Warren stood and nodded at Jager.

Jager stood, ran up the ramp onto the porch, and took a covering position to the open door's left side.

Warren addressed Kang and pointed to a spot in front of the fountain. "Tell the men to lay face down there. Tell the ladies to sit on the fountain's edge and not be scared. We're not going to hurt them."

Kang translated the orders, and the two security men lay face down, side-by-side in front of the fountain, and the two still-shaken ladies sat on the fountain's edge to the men's left.

With Kang covering the men, Warren pulled four sets of flex cuffs from his cargo pockets and tossed them to Luc. "Cuff the men, wrists, and ankles."

"Roger that." Luc stood and secured the detainees as ordered.

Warren addressed Kang again. "Now ask them where their boss is. Alberto Ramirez. And if he has any weapons."

Kang translated to the foursome.

None answered.

Kang repeated the question.

None answered again.

But one of the women reached into her robe pocket, removed a phone, and held it out screen first to Warren.

He moved closer to view a video call in progress from the completely gray-haired and prematurely aged face of Alberto Ramirez.

Warren took the phone from the woman. "I know you speak English, Ramirez. You're under arrest for crimes against humanity. Come out with your hands atop your head."

Ramirez answered in good English with a slight Hispanic accent. "I do not know who you are. But I do know you have not come to arrest me. I will tell you where I am if you give me your word as a soldier, and as a man, you will not harm my people."

Warren answered. "You have my word as a soldier, and as a man, your people will not be harmed."

Ramirez: "I thank you for that. I am upstairs in my office. First door to the left of the stairway landing. I am seated at my desk, and I am unarmed."

Jager said, "Careful, XO. He may have a big, nasty IED waiting in there for us. Remember the ramp."

Warren addressed Ramirez again. "Why don't you just come out here."

Ramirez: "If you want me, you will have to come to me and face me." He closed his eyes and shook his head, resolute and negative. "On this, there is no negotiation."

Warren said, "Then you won't mind if we have your ladies lead us to your office upstairs?"

His eyes opened, disgusted. "And they called me immoral."

Warren said, "And they've never called me a damn fool."

"Very well. Do what you must. Now come and face me."

CHAPTER 52

4:51 AM

"Molka, Warren."

Molka: "Go, Warren."

Warren: "Compound breeched, security and staff detained, and the target has been located, verified, and secured."

Molka: "Roger that. Outstanding, XO."

Warren: "ETA?"

Molka: "I'm coming up to the front gate now."

Warren: "Acknowledged. I'm waiting on the front porch."

Before Warren even made his radio report, Molka already had a pretty good picture of what happened inside the compound from monitoring their radio chatter on the command channel. The only thing not clear was Warren's negotiation with Ramirez to surrender. And right after they captured him, the radios went silent until Warren's report.

Molka reached the compound's open front gate to find Kang inside it in a kneeling shooting position facing the outside with his goggles down. He offered her a somber nod as she ran past him.

Her boots crunched on the crushed coral, and she flipped her goggles up due to the compound's bright emergency lighting.

She cut to the right to go around the fountain, where Luc stood watching over the two prone security men and the two frightened women sitting on the fountain's edge. He, too, offered her a somber nod as she passed.

Warren waited on the porch outside the open door with a somber face.

Molka ran up the ramp to join him.

Warren said, "The target is upstairs in an office, first door to the left. Jager is watching him."

"Ok." She removed heavy-duty rubber gloves from her BDU pants' cargo pocket and pulled them on. "Prepare for fast extraction. That Chinese warship is coming our way."

"Roger that."

She entered into a dimly lit, tile-floored, open floorplan resembling, like the exterior, a Chinese version of a Latin American hacienda.

Before her lay the staircase with a wrought iron railing on its right side and a chair lift against the wall to its left side.

She high-stepped up the stairs to a carpeted landing and turned right into a hallway where Jager waited somber-faced to the left of a closed, gray-colored door. An empty wooden chair, perhaps used by Ramirez's security men, sat to the door's right.

When Molka reached him, Jager said, "We searched him and the room for weapons and explosives. Nothing found. He's sitting at his desk. And he's docile and resigned to his fate."

She said, "And the facial scan confirmed 100 percent?"

"One hundred percent. And he is also…."

She flashed a perplexed face. "Is also what?"

Jager's eyes flicked away. "Nothing. Orders?"

"Wait for me downstairs. This part is all personal."

"Roger that." He trotted down the hall and downstairs.

Molka unslung her MP5 and placed it on the chair, removed her tactical rig and also placed it on the chair, drew her Beretta from the thigh holster…

Nathan's voice sounded in her headset. "Molka, Nathan."

She switched to channel one. "Go, Nathan."

Nathan: "Drone report. Good and bad news. You were right about them sneaking out from the barracks' backdoors and windows. A 12-man armed patrol is moving along the east side

TASK X

seawall, slowly and cautiously but steadily. They're already behind Shizi's position. A second 12-man armed patrol is forming up along the west side seawall opposite the harbor. That's the bad news. The good news is the rest of the garrison is still sheltering in place."

Molka said, "But regarding those patrols, it looks like someone knows what they're doing and got 24 volunteers. They're going to sweep the perimeter and then try to envelop us."

The colonel spoke up: "Team leader, I suggest we deploy the smoke and CS grenades onto the second armed patrol forming in a spoiling attack before they can get moving."

Molka: "Make it happen."

The colonel: "I will need to call Jaron back from the beach to man his machinegun while this is done."

Molka: "Order it. Keep me advised." She switched her radio to channel two. "Bravo, armed patrols are on the east and west perimeters. Get back to the boats and extract to the ship. I'll still extract with Alpha as planned."

Warren: "Roger that. Good luck."

Kang spoke up: "I'm staying here to cover Molka. No arguments."

She didn't argue. She switched the radio back to the command channel, re-pocketed it, racked her Beretta, closed her eyes, inhaled deeply, and exhaled slowly.

I feel you here with me, my little Janetta.

She opened the door and stepped inside the softly lit office.

Filled bookcases covered the office walls and emitted an old book and leathery aroma. It reminded her of her grandfather's study on the kibbutz. As did the man seated behind the desk with his pale, haggard face and joyless dark eyes looking almost dead already.

She moved before the desk and spoke, barely holding back rage. "Alberto Ramirez?"

He frowned at the Beretta pointed down in her right hand. "You know who I am, assassin. Your people have already scanned, photographed, swabbed, and gawked at me."

With her left hand, she removed the laminated photo from her right front pocket and held it up for him to view. "This is

Janetta Kolasa. Ten years ago, you murdered her. She was only 11 years old. And tonight, she will finally get her vengeance."

His eyes moved to her face. "Then you are Molka, the older sister of Janetta Kolasa. You flew the helicopter that helped murder my son Pasquale. He was only 8 years old. And as for the vengeance you seek, murdered children can never truly be avenged, as you will soon, sadly, learn."

Molka's rage broke free, and she yelled: "Your son wasn't murdered! What happened to him was a tragic mistake we all felt horrible about and still do!"

He spoke in a calm, steady tone. "Regrets are the weakest form of rationalization."

"Stand up!"

He maintained his calm, steady tone. "You think you know what happened. But you don't know everything. It's too late now for explanations, though."

"Stand up!"

"For the first few years, I lived every day in mortal dread of your coming."

"Stand up!"

"Then I lived a few years of uneasy confusion of why you had not come yet."

"STAND UP!"

"Then, for the last few years, I have lived every day in mortal dread of you *never* coming. Because I was too cowardly to do this myself."

Warren's voice sounded in Molka's headset: "Molka, Warren."

"Go, Warren."

Warren: "The landing boats have been shot up. We just eluded the two-armed soldiers on the beach who did it. What are your orders?"

The colonel's voice in Molka's headset: "Molka, Krasnov."

"Go, colonel."

The colonel: "Our grenades scattered the westside 12-man patrol, but they quickly reformed into two-man teams and dispersed widely into the citrus groves."

Molka: "And one of those teams took out our landing boats?"

The colonel: "Unfortunately. What are your orders, team leader?"

Kang's voice in Molka's headset: "Molka, Kang."

"Go, Kang."

Kang: "A dozen armed men 150 meters from compound and closing. If we don't leave very soon, we'll be trapped here. What are your orders?"

Molka's jaw tightened. "Alpha, Bravo, hold for orders." She glared at Ramirez and yelled again: **"Stand Up!"**

He continued in a calm, steady tone over a slight smile. "From your communications, it sounds like both of us will be buried and forgotten on this lonely island tonight."

She raised her weapon, pointed it at Ramirez's forehead, and screamed:

"DAMN YOU TO HELL, YOU BASTARD!"
"STAND UP!
"LET YOUR LAST ACT BE THAT OF A MAN!"
"STAND UP AND DIE FOR MY LITTLE JANETTA!"
"STAND UP NOW!"

A small electric motor hummed, and Ramirez moved to his left from behind the desk, seated in a powered wheelchair.

His right arm was missing below the elbow.

His left hand was a shriveled, discolored stump resting atop the chair's control joystick.

And both his legs were missing above the knee.

He rotated his chair to face Molka. "I have not been able to stand up since the night you helped to murder my son. The same explosive charge that killed him did this to me. I watched him die before I passed out. Now, please give me closure and send me to see my little Pasquale again. I beg you."

CHAPTER 53

5:08 AM

Molka—with her Beretta holstered and carrying her MP5 and tactical rig—burst from the house's front door, fast-stepped down the ramp, sprinted across the compound and joined a crouching Kang just inside the gate.

Kang said, "Is it over?"

She nodded. "I'm all done here. Sitrep?"

He pointed to the grove about 80 meters to the left. "Still coming to the rescue, they think."

She put her tactical rig back on, re-slung her MP5, pulled her night vision goggles down and observed the 12-armed men, led by one with a flashlight, moving toward the compound.

"Let's get some safer cover over there." She pointed to the grove about 40 meters to their right.

They both crouch-ran to the grove and entered it.

About 10 meters into the trees, Molka stopped and took a knee. Kang took a knee beside her.

Molka said, "I need to coordinate with the teams and the ship and arrange a new extraction plan."

"Understood," Kang said. "While you do, I'll go back to the grove's edge and keep an eye on that patrol." He leaped and ran back the way they came.

Molka switched to channel three, the *Banda Pearl* channel, and spoke into her headset. "Captain Savanna, Molka."

Savanna's voice in her headset: "Go, Molka."

"We lost the boats."

Savanna: "We know. We've been monitoring your comms."

"Can you send the ship's lifeboat to the seawall behind the compound and pick us up?"

Savanna: "Negative. She's only equipped with two non-motorized survival rafts."

Molka ripped up a handful of grass. "I should've checked into that. Overlooking the little details always comes back to haunt you."

Savanna: "Can you get everyone to the new harbor? If they've dredged it for use, I can come straight in for a fast turnabout and evacuate you from the big pier."

"We can try that. What if the harbor's not dredged yet?"

Savanna: "Then she'll run aground, and we'll all become a permanent part of the ecosystem here."

"How long will it take you to get to the harbor?"

Savanna: "I can be in position in about 15 minutes."

She time-checked her watch. "Ok. Hold outside the harbor until we're ready. I'll let you know a-sap."

Savanna: "Roger that."

Time to unify the teams. She switched her radio back to the command channel. "Alpha, Bravo, switch comms to command channel. Team leaders confirm."

Pause.

The colonel's voice in her headset: "Alpha confirmed."

Warren's voice in her headset: "Bravo confirmed."

Molka: "Captain Savanna will attempt to extract us from the harbor pier. Warren, sitrep?"

Warren: "We're concealed in a grove about 50 meters from our beach landing spot. Two two-man armed teams have passed near us."

Molka: "Acknowledged. Standby. Colonel, sitrep?"

The colonel: "We are still holding our original positions, with Jaron rejoining us and taking over Nathan's machinegun while he operates the drone. I believe the bulk of the troops to still be sheltering in their barracks. However, my concern is those dispersed two-man teams in the groves to our rear."

Molka: "Mine too."

The colonel: "I suggest for the harbor extraction, Alpha redeploy to the outdoor construction material storage area located about 150 meters from the harbor pier and use it for a covering and screening position as the extraction is taking place."

"Great idea, sir. Execute that now."

The colonel: "Roger that."

Molka: "Warren, get Bravo to the construction material storage area outside the harbor."

Warren: "We're already on the way."

Kang's voice in her headset: "Molka, watch out! Watch your—"

Static, then silence.

CHAPTER 54

Molka sprung to her feet and ran toward Kang's position.

She exited a row of trees to see him less than 10 meters away with his back turned to her, helmetless, weaponless, and hands atop his head.

Standing before him was a very thin Asian male wearing a camo combat uniform with matching duty cap who pointed a QBZ-95 bullpup assault rifle at Kang with his right hand and held a two-way radio in his left.

Molka raised her MP5, aimed at Kang's captor, and yelled: "Drop your weapon!"

The man yelled at her in Chinese.

Kang yelled over his left shoulder: "Molka, behind you!"

Before she could turn, the barrel of another QBZ-95 bullpup assault rifle poked hard into her back, and the weapon's holder yelled in Chinese.

She kept her weapon aimed at the man covering Kang.

He moved the barrel against Kang's forehead and yelled at her.

She grasped the implication and placed her hands atop her helmet.

The man behind her kept the barrel pushed into her back while he removed her MP5 from around her neck and her Beretta from her thigh holster and poked her to move her forward.

She complied and stood next to Kang.

Kang said, "Sorry, Molka. The little shits snuck up behind me when I was focused on that big patrol. Then he sent his friend to sneak up on you. He yanked my helmet off before I could warn you."

Molka's captor moved around her, tossed her weapons on the grass a few steps away next to Kang's equipment, stood beside his partner, and flipped up her night vision goggles to view her face.

The men exchanged surprised glances, took a few steps back, and talked to each other.

Kang translated. "They're shocked a woman is with the pirates."

Molka said, "Ha. They think we're pirates. Well, I guess with Captain Savanna on the team, technically, we are."

The man with the radio spoke into it, received an answer, and spoke again.

Molka said, "Find out what they're going to do with us, and we'll decide our next move."

Kang said, "Understood."

While Kang listened, she observed, and with her goggles flipped up, the moonlight revealed the men's uniforms as the blue and white camo pattern of the Chinese Navy.

The man's radio conversation ended.

Kang translated. "They called their lieutenant. He told them to stay put with the pirates. He's on the way with six more men. Be here in three or four minutes."

The two men kept their weapons pointed at Molka and Kang and chatted among themselves.

Molka said, "You know what I see?"

"What?"

"Two young, nervous, confused navy techs or construction specialists not well-trained as infantry or in handling prisoners. Just being out here is their first mistake. Their second mistake is allowing us to talk in a foreign language and leaving me my radio which is on the command channel."

Kang said, "Even if the team figures out we're in trouble, they'll never get to us in time."

"I know. So we have to do this ourselves."

"And knowing you, you have a diversion in mind before we strike."

Molka said, "Keep your ears open. Shizi, Molka."

Shizi's voice in her headset: "Go, Molka. You, ok? Monitoring some odd transmissions from you."

"Please tell me you still have a spare C-4 block and a timer-detonator?"

Shizi: "I have two spares."

"Can you give me a nice, loud diversionary detonation in 60 seconds with a five-second countdown?"

Shizi: "Consider it done."

"Thank you, marine. Did you hear that, Kang?"

Kang said, "Yes. Count me down, please. I'll take the one on our left."

Molka said, "Roger that."

A moment later, with the captors still chatting, Shizi began a countdown in Molka's headset.

She repeated it for Kang.

"Five."

"Four."

"Three."

"Two."

BOOOOOOOOOOMMM!!!

Simultaneously:

The young navy men jumped and flinched like startled cats.

Then turned their heads toward the loud southeast explosion.

Their final mistake of the encounter.

Twin, black blurs launched toward them.

Kang hit his sailor's temple with a tornado kick.

Molka hit her sailor's jaw with a flying jump kick.

The navy men sank fast to the grass and took a nap.

Molka and Kang grabbed their weapons and equipment and ran side-by-side through the grove toward the harbor.

Kang said, "I love your style, Molka. And once again, we make a great team. I'm almost going to be sorry when this op is over, and I have to go back to working solo."

FREDRICK L. STAFFORD

CHAPTER 55

5:21 AM

The recon overhead images presented the construction materials storage area as non-descript, drab-colored shapes.

But upon arriving there at ground level with Kang, the non-descript drab colored shapes proved to be many bundles of rebar, many rolls of wire mesh, a pallet of bagged concrete mix covered by plastic, some scrap lumber in piles, and four head-high stacks of prefabricated, cement seawall sections separated by shoulder-width gaps mimicking a bunker with three firing holes.

A terrain feature not lost on an expert like the colonel who lay prone behind the stacks, aiming his machinegun out the left side gap. His grenade launcher and its bandolier lay to his left.

To his right, Jaron lay prone, aiming Nathan's machinegun out the right-side gap.

Kang joined the rest of Bravo—Warren, Jager, and Luc—crouched beside the bagged cement pallet a few steps behind the firing positions. And Nathan sat on the crushed coral directly behind the colonel operating his drone.

Molka did a quick head count.

All present but Shizi.

She lay prone beside the colonel and said, "Where's Shizi, sir?"

The colonel answered. "I left him behind to keep up a masking fire to let the enemy think we are all still in our original positions."

"Good tactic. Bring him here, sir, so we can call in Captain Savanna, and all leave together."

He spoke into his headset. "Shizi, Krasnov."

Shizi's voice in the headsets: "Go, colonel."

"Bravo has arrived. Please join us so you all may depart this place."

Shizi: "Roger that."

Molka spoke into her headset. "Captain Savanna, Molka."

Savanna: "Go, Molka."

"Where are you located?"

Savanna: "Circling about a kilometer outside the harbor entrance, ready to commence run on your order."

"Acknowledged. Where's that warship?"

Savanna: "Fifty nautical miles away and closing."

"Maintain your position."

Savanna: "Roger that."

Molka assessed their position.

To their front lay a 100-meter wide by 50-meter-deep open section of crushed compacted coral. And beyond that sat another citrus grove.

Behind them, the harbor and its large concrete pier to the right, hosting two big, red cargo cranes, was located about 150 meters away with another flat, open, crushed coral stretch between them.

And behind the pier sat yet another wide flat, space only much longer and wider—presumably waiting to be turned into an airstrip—which ran all the way to the seawall on the island's southwest coast.

Two orange flashes accompanied by automatic weapon fire sounds came from the grove to their position's front, and rounds churned up sand 5 meters from their cement seawall sections bunker, and a couple more impacted it with a clipping noise.

The colonel said, "It appears their rules of engagement for us are of a free-firing zone in nature."

Molka said, "I can't blame them. They didn't invite us here."

More fire came their way from the grove.

The colonel and Jaron fired short, non-lethal suppression bursts into the trees above the orange flashes.

The orange flashes abruptly ceased.

Molka spoke into her headset: "Shizi, Molka."

"Go, Molka."

"Location?"

Shizi: "Just ready to move into the grove across from your position."

"Be advised, we're taking fire from the grove from at least two weapons."

Shizi: "I heard them."

"Let me know when you're ready to move from the grove to our position. We're going to lay down suppression fire with everything we have."

Shizi: "Acknowledged."

Nathan spoke up. "I hope Shizi gets here soon so we can leave sooner rather than later. Check this out, Molka."

She moved beside him and called out what she saw on his drone camera view screen as it hovered over the new barracks. "We have dozens of men in camo uniforms carrying QBZ-95 assault rifles forming into platoon-sized units behind the new barracks."

Warren spoke up. "Them not having night vision has saved us so far. But after reports from those shooters in the grove, it's not going to take that many patrollers long to confirm we're all now concentrating here."

Jager spoke up. "And then pin us in place with their superior firepower and flank us."

Shizi's voice in the headsets: "Molka, Shizi."

"Go, Shizi."

Shizi: "I'm in position."

"Acknowledged. Stand by. Move on my order."

Shizi: "Roger that."

Molka addressed Bravo. "Warren, Jager, to the colonel's left. Kang to Jaron's right. Fire full-auto above the shooter's heads on my command."

FREDRICK L. STAFFORD

Bravo—minus Luc, who remained crouched—moved into position.

She lay prone before the center gap in the seawall sections' stacks, switched her MP5 from safe to fully automatic, took aim at the grove, and spoke into her headset, "Shizi, Molka."

Shizi: "Go, Molka."

"When we open fire, you run."

Shizi: "Roger that."

Molka ordered. "Fire!"

The two light machineguns and four MP5s fired into the trees above the last shooter's position and dropped leaves and small branches in mass quantities down upon them.

All the MP5 firers emptied their 30-round mags and swapped out to another full mag to keep firing.

After about 40 seconds of sustained fire, Shizi, at a full sprint carrying his machinegun, emerged from the dark to their right and dove into their covered position.

Molka yelled: "Cease fire!"

The shooters ceased fire.

Luc flashed a sly but somewhat nervous grin, "Now if it is convenient, I suggest we leave this place immediately."

"Agreed." Molka spoke into her headset. "Captain Savanna, Molka."

Savanna: "Go, Molka."

"Commence run. ETA?"

Savanna: "Commencing run, aye. ETA six minutes. When I clear that narrow entrance—if we don't run aground—I'm going to cut her hard to my starboard and run close along that outer seawall across from the pier, move past the pier, then cut her hard to my port, and come alongside the pier nice an easy and ready for fast loading and departure."

"Ok. We'll be there. See you on board."

Savanna: "Roger that."

Molka said, "Colonel, Nathan, how many smoke rounds do you have left?"

The colonel answered. "Six, three loaded in each launcher."

"Ok. That should be enough. Prepare to deploy them all for cover on my command, sir."

TASK X

"Yes, team leader." The colonel stood, retrieved Nathan's grenade launcher, moved back where he lay, and prepared to fire.

Nathan, still flying his camera drone, spoke up. "Molka, those platoon-sized units are now moving this way fast, at least 80 strong."

Molka addressed the team. "Alpha and Shizi get ready to run to the pier. We'll deploy smoke and put more suppression fire into that grove. When you get on the pier, lay flat. Go on my command. Understood?"

They all said affirmative.

"Shizi, leave me your weapon."

He handed her the light machinegun with a half-full 100-round ammo pouch attached.

The colonel turned his head and looked back to Jager. "Jager, before you go." He reached into his right front pocket, removed a commemorative-type coin, and tossed it to Jager.

Jager viewed the coin. "What's this?"

"It represents my former unit. I carry it for good luck. I want you to carry it for good luck from one soldier to another."

Jager nodded and pocketed the coin.

Molka moved to the open gap between the colonel and Jaron and cocked the machinegun. "Colonel, deploy smoke."

From a kneeling position, he fired three rounds from Nathan's launcher aimed at an upward angle toward the grove to their front, laid the launcher aside, picked up his launcher, and fired three more.

The rounds landed in front of the grove and shrouded it behind a 100-meter-wide, white smoke curtain.

Molka said, "Prepare to fire. Fire high, for effect."

The colonel lay his grenade launcher aside and returned to his position behind his machinegun.

Molka said, "Fire."

The colonel and Jaron fired short, high, controlled bursts.

She turned to the team. "GO!"

They all ran in a crouch toward the pier.

Molka fired two short, high, controlled bursts.

Return fire from the grove sounded from behind the smoke.

Several rounds impacted the crushed coral a few meters to their right. Another round clipped the cement seawall section the colonel lay behind.

Warren's voice in the headsets: "Molka, Warren."

Molka: "Go, Warren."

Warren: "We made it."

"Roger that." She tapped the colonel's and Nathan's shoulders. "Cease fire."

They ceased fire.

The return fire from the grove resumed.

But not from just two weapons.

More like fifteen, she guessed.

Molka said, "Hear that? The first reinforcements have arrived in that grove. Nathan, get your drone over it."

Nathan: "Roger that."

The garrison firing noise suddenly ceased, instantly replaced by…

VRRRROOOOOOMMMMMM!

A light gray, long-winged, smaller aircraft powered by a single turboprop pusher engine flew over the harbor at an altitude of about 75 meters and continued inland.

Jager's voice sounded in the headsets. "What in the hell was that?"

Warren's voice in the headsets: "Looks like a Predator drone."

The colonel said, "It is a Chinese CH model reconnaissance-combat drone armed with four AR-2 air-to-surface missiles. Undoubtedly, from the Chinese warship approaching."

Molka said, "A reconnaissance-combat drone. Did they send it for reconnaissance or combat?"

Nathan said, "I'll track it with my drone, but they've spotted us and are now probably discussing what to do about us."

The colonel: "More likely they are transmitting information about our positions to the ground forces here preparing to assault us."

Savanna's voice in the headsets: "Captain Savanna to assault teams. Entering harbor in three minutes."

Molka: "Acknowledged, captain." She addressed the men in her position. "We'll hold here to cover the others as they board."

TASK X

Nathan: "Their drone is climbing and coming back around."

A moment later, the drone, at about 200 meters altitude, flew slower circles around the harbor and over Molka's position.

Nathan: "I wish I could ram the sensor pod under its nose and take out its cameras."

Molka: "Can you?"

Nathan: "No, it's way faster. I'm just holding at the same altitude and trying to—"

Over two dozen weapons opened up from the grove, and rounds in the hundreds roiled the crushed coral around them, and others impacted and chipped away their concrete seawall sections protection.

Molka said, "You were right, colonel. That drone has pinpointed us for them."

Nathan yelled: "Missile away! Missile away! Pier is the target!"

All eyes viewed the drone's fired missile's bright orange tail flame streaking over the harbor.

Warren's yelling voice over the headset: "Cover! Behind the seawall!"

The five men on the pier leaped to their feet and sprinted across the open space behind them toward the seawall.

They would never make it in time.

The missile's tail flame disappeared.

A moment later, the powerless missile fell into the harbor's center with a long splash.

Nathan yelled: "No way! The rocket motor flamed out! Too lucky!"

The colonel said, "Probably older ordnance sitting on that ship for years."

The drone banked hard right and flew inland again.

Bravo team and Shizi had taken cover behind the seawall, and Warren spaced them at wide intervals so one missile could not kill them all.

Jaron said, "Look! It's coming back!"

The drone had swung around and reapproached the harbor.

Nathan: "I think it will fire at them again."

Molka: "But its target has dispersed. One missile, one man?"

Savanna's voice in the headsets: "Captain Savanna to assault teams. Entering harbor in 60 seconds. Prepare to board."

Nathan yelled: "Oh no! *Banda Pearl* is the target!"

Molka yelled into her headset: "Captain Savanna! Armed drone over the harbor! Missile launch imminent! Take evasive action! Take evasive action!"

The colonel shook his head and frowned. "It is too late for that now."

CHAPTER 56

The woman and men of Alpha and Bravo all watched in silent horror as the *Banda Pearl* approached the harbor entrance at nearly full speed.

No more words of warning or even quick goodbyes would be appropriate at that point. They could only wait and witness the drone's next fired missile's bright orange tail flame streak over the harbor, destroying their vessel and killing their teammates and friends.

But first, a blindingly bright white ball spewed from *Banda Pearl's* foredeck, and with a ripping roar, the ball flashed skyward and in two seconds...

BOOOOOOM!

Fireball explosion in the dark sky.

Drone destroyed.

Jager's voice on the headsets: "And what in the hell was that?"

Fiery drone remnants rained down into the harbor.

Dov's voice on the headsets: "Splash one drone! Molka, I told you the Stingers might come in handy!"

Molka: "Yes. You. Did. You're the man, Dov!"

Banda Pearl raced into the harbor.

Molka gave orders: "Warren, get your people ready to run back to the pier on my command."

Warren: "Roger that."

Savanna expertly piloted the 85-footer hard to starboard, ran her close along the outer seawall across from the pier, moved her past the pier, then cut her hard to port, and slowed drastically to come alongside the pier, nice an easy, ready for fast loading and departure.

Kang's voice on the headsets: "Hope everyone saw that once-in-a-lifetime incredible display of seamanship."

Even heavier fire opened up from the grove.

The colonel and Jaron returned suppression-effect fire.

Dozens more rounds smacked the concrete barrier.

Savanna's voice in the headsets: "Captain Savanna to assault teams. We're at the pier."

Molka ordered: "Warren, go, go, go!"

Warren: "Roger that."

The five men leaped back over the seawall and sprinted for the ship.

Molka joined the colonel and Jaron in suppression fire.

The five men made it aboard the ship.

Nathan held up his controller. "Molka, looks like they're all in the grove now!"

Molka moved beside him to view the entire island garrison forming inside the tree line. "They're getting ready to rush us."

The grove erupted with even more massive fire.

The colonel and Jaron returned suppression fire.

Uncountable rounds chewed into the concrete barrier.

The colonel flinched and winced and kept firing.

Molka addressed Nathan: "Crash that drone and get to the ship."

Nathan: "Roger that." He put the drone into a tree, the controller into his backpack, and ran for the ship.

Molka addressed Jaron: "Leave your weapon and get to the ship."

Jaron: "Roger that." He leaped up and ran for the ship.

The colonel opened fire again.

Molka dropped back into a prone firing position beside the colonel behind her machinegun and viewed six-armed garrison men being chased back into the smoke screen from the colonel's rounds, throwing up crushed coral at their feet.

He ceased fire. "That was a small probing patrol to draw our fire and establish how many weapons we have left in this position. Shortly, another probe will be sent out to confirm the first. Then the main assault will be launched to quickly overrun this position, charge forward, and destroy the ship."

Molka said, "Then let's go before any of that happens."

The colonel shook his head. "No. I am not going with you."

Savanna's voice in the headsets: "Molka, Savanna."

Molka answered. "Standby, captain. We're on the way."

Savanna: "Roger that."

She addressed the colonel again: "What do you mean?"

He rolled onto his left side and exposed a bloody bullet hole in his tactical vest over his abdomen.

Her face flashed shock. "Oh no, sir. There's a first-aid kit on the ship. Can you walk?"

"We must now speak privately." He unbuckled his helmet's chin strap, tossed the helmet aside, removed the radio from his right front pocket, and tossed it aside.

Molka understood and pressed the mute button on her headset mic.

He spoke with a firm conviction. "Team leader, a first-aid kit will not help me, and I will not survive the three-hour trip back to Palawan."

She said, "Then we'll turn ourselves into the Chinese. Maybe they have a doctor or at least a medic here."

"No, team leader. I want no medical attention to save my life, as this would only return me to my Belgian cage."

Molka offered a knowing nod. "Old wolves do not fall into a trap twice."

"Yes." He rubbed his right hand over the blood-soaked puncture. "And with this blessed wound, I cannot live long enough to be extracted. However, I can live long enough to fight and die here. On my feet. As a free man. And with a soldier's honor. This what I have always desired."

Molka's heart tumbled toward her stomach's pit. "Colonel, I'm so sorry I brought you here."

"No, I thank you for bringing me here. And it has been—" His face flipped toward the firing opening. "Their second probe is coming."

He rolled back onto his stomach and engaged their second probe as he did the first, chasing them with 7.62 rounds back into the smoke screen's safety, and faced Molka again. "You must leave now before the main attack. It has been an honor to have served with you again, team leader." He offered his right hand for shaking.

She shook his hand with reddening eyes. "Thank you, sir. It's been an honor for me too."

He pulled her hand to his lips and kissed it. "And Molka, let my last thoughts of you be those of knowing you have escaped and will go on to live a happy life." He released her hand and turned his face away. "Now go!"

Molka gently laid her hand on the colonel's back. "Goodbye, Red Wolf."

She leaped up, sprinted toward the ship, unmuted her headset mic, and said: "Captain Savanna prepare for departure."

Savanna: "Roger that."

As she covered the 150 meters, she viewed Warren, Kang, Jager, Shizi, Luc, and Nathan lined against the stern railing, watching her approach.

Dov and Jaron stood on the pier near the bow and stern, ready to cast off lines.

She ran across the pier and jumped onto the aft deck through an open gate in the side railing.

Savanna waited on the ladder at the bridge's rear door and called down to her: "Lady Molka, where's the colonel?"

She answered. "Right where he wants to be! Let's go!"

Molka moved to the stern railing with the others.

Dov and Jaron cast off the lines and jumped onto the deck.

Savanna ran back onto the bridge and buried the throttle.

The turbo diesel motor roared.

The propeller churned up white water from the stern.

The bow rose.

And the *Banda Pearl* raced for the harbor exit.

Nathan pointed inland and yelled. "There's the colonel!"

All seven at the rail bore witness through their goggles.

TASK X

The colonel rose.
He held two of the SIG LMG-68 light machineguns.
Moved to his right from behind the concrete barrier.
And stood in the open.
At least 50 armed troops emerged from the smoke screen.
Many aimed their weapons at the escaping *Banda Pearl*.
But before any fired…
The colonel raised both machineguns to his hips.
And opened fire at their feet.
They retreated in panic back into the smoke.
The colonel ran after them, still firing.
He reached the massive smoke cloud.
And then he was gone.

CHAPTER 57

5:57 AM

"That issue was never in doubt," Savanna related to the team, and Molka gathered around the *Banda Pearl's* galley table. "You see, my very able first mate, Mister Dov, instantly recognized that drone for what it was when it flew over us. And instantly deduced what it would be ordered to do and already had a spectacular answer for it, as you all witnessed."

Up on the bridge, very able first mate Mister Dov manned the controls while loyal Jaron kept watch on deck in the dawn's first light for more armed drones as the vessel cruised back to Palawan and its homeport of Ulugan Bay.

From the galley's porcelain coffee cups, Warren, Kang, Jager, Nathan, Luc, and Savanna sipped the resort's premium bourbon pilfered by Savanna and Shizi and Molka sipped from canned energy drinks as Savanna answered Luc's question about the amazing drone downing.

Due to the warm humidity, the men of the assault teams had stripped off all their gear, including their BDU shirts, lounged in their black undershirts, and Savanna changed out of his pirate garb into a black t-shirt and BDU pants.

Molka, however, remained geared up, minus her helmet, but including both her weapons.

Savanna finished his story. "I believe when the unwritten history of this never happened operation is discussed, Mister Dov's action will rank among the many heroic acts of this night as not one of us would now be on our way home." He raised his cup. "To Mister Dov!"

All raised their beverages in unison: "To Mister Dov!"

Kang spoke. "And how about an underrated hero? Our explosive specialist, Shizi here, had the forethought to bring adequate backup supplies that got us out of a tough spot in Manila and me out of one tonight." He raised his cup. "To Shizi!"

All raised their beverages in unison: "To Shizi!"

After they drank, Shizi spoke up. "I'm just going to come out and say what I think we're all thinking: when it comes to the real heroes of this night, and that is, the colonel went out like a real hardcore boss."

Luc spoke. "The fact that he also had personal reasons for sacrificing himself to cover our escape made it no less honorable in my eyes."

Savanna spoke. "Nor in my eyes."

Kang spoke. "They definitely don't make pure, unapologetic warriors like the colonel anymore. I'm glad I was with him during his last battle."

Jager spoke. "He was a soldier's soldier, to be sure. And I now don't believe he was guilty of a single thing they accused him of."

Warren spoke. "I'm not convinced that last rush by the garrison force could have stopped us from leaving if it got past the colonel. But earlier, after we lost the boats, his situational awareness, attention to detail of the terrain, and tactical prowess, to quickly established that strong covering position probably saved us from capture at the very least." He raised his cup. "To Colonel Krasnov!"

All raised their beverages in unison: "To Colonel Krasnov!"

After they drank, Jager spoke again. "I just hope they give the colonel a soldier's burial and not just toss his body over the seawall."

Molka spoke up for the first time since they left Base X. "Speaking of the colonel's body, it won't take them long to identify it, and that will lead back to Azzur and to me. But I promise you all, I'll do my best to make sure none of your names are tied to what happened there."

Kang spoke. "In my expert opinion, I don't think we have anything to worry about."

Warren grinned at him. "Please expound, intelligence specialist."

Kang continued. "The Chinese will obviously figure out we weren't a South China Sea pirates raiding party and why we came to Base X. So if they want to make an international incident of the notorious Colonel Krasnov being there, the ones who brought him there could also make an international incident of them sheltering notorious terrorist Alberto Ramirez. Which Jager has the photographic and DNA proof of to show the world, correct?"

Jager nodded. "Correct."

Kang continued. "This would be highly embarrassing for the Chinese government leadership, especially if they didn't even know their own intelligence service had put Ramirez there. But much more embarrassing, intolerably embarrassing, I would say, would be the world finding out one of their prized, super-secret bases was breached by a bunch of scruffy old men." He presented a playboy smile and raised his cup. "To the scruffy old men!"

All but Molka raised their beverages in unison: "To the scruffy old men!"

The team enjoyed a good laugh.

Molka didn't join in.

She rose from the table and moved to the ladder.

Descended to the third deck.

Moved down the passageway.

Entered the small sleeping cabin.

Closed and locked the door.

Unslung her MP5 and placed it on the bunk.

Removed her tactical rig and placed it on the bunk.

Removed her holstered Beretta and placed it on the bunk.

Sat on the bunk and removed her tac boots.

Stood and moved to the compartment's little sink.

TASK X

Washed the colonel's blood stain from her right hand.
Wetted a washcloth with cool water.
Moved back to the bunk.
Lay on her back.
Covered her forehead with the cool washcloth.
Closed her eyes.
And slept for the three-hour journey home's remainder.

But before she did any of that, she sat on the edge of the bunk for thirty minutes, holding her little Janetta's photo close to her heart while weeping uncontrollably.

CHAPTER 58

Club Utopia
3:51 PM

With the moored *Banda Pearl* behind her, Molka stood on the marina's larger dock with Dov and Jaron.

They waited as she used her laptop to make an inventory list of the surviving weapons and equipment they had repacked and stacked there in the hours since she and the team woke at 1 PM after their 8 AM arrival back from Base X.

Op over, Molka outfitted in a white polo over light blue cotton shorts and white canvas sneakers in the hot, humid afternoon. Her hair was ponytailed, and her black-framed glasses were on.

Dov and Jaron wore perspiration-wet t-shirts over jeans and work boots.

She looked up from her laptop. "Ok. That's done. You guys take our loyal little ship to the broker."

Dov said, "You sure you don't want us to stay for when Berlin's guys get here to pick this stuff up in an hour?"

Jaron said, "Yeah, we all know how shady that crew is."

"That's why I left this item off the list." She lifted her shirt hem behind her to expose the Beretta tucked into her waistband.

TASK X

"I can handle Berlin's guys. Thanks, though." She removed her phone from her front pocket and time-checked it. "The team is ready to leave for the airport. I'm going to go say goodbye to them in a moment. You're sure this Edgardo from the kitchen staff can drive the shuttle bus?"

Dov said, "Yes, he's done it many times. He's the backup to the regular driver."

She glanced at her laptop again. "Alright. And the last three things we need to do before we fly out in the morning are put the hotel conference room, my makeshift office, and the mockup for the landing beach back the way we found them."

Dov said, "We already took care of all that earlier this morning."

She squinted across the marina lagoon to see the mockup beach vanish as if it never existed and then flashed them a curious face. "Have you guys even slept?"

Dov said, "We can't sleep when there's work to be done for the boss."

Jaron said, "And we wanted you to be able to relax for the rest of the day."

Molka offered her assistants a warm smile. "Dov, Jaron, I want you to know all my perceptions about you were misconceptions, to my shame. Azzur undersold you as very competent and useful professionals. You're actually jacks-of-all trades, ready for any assignment, never complaining, tough, smart, highly capable professionals. It's been a real pleasure and a privilege to have worked with you guys, and I would do it again anytime."

Dov, with moist eyes, said, "Thank you. I'm so honored, Molka."

Jaron, with moist eyes, said, "That goes double for me, Molka."

Molka exited the hotel lobby to find the coral-pink shuttle bus parked outside under the canopied, half-moon, arrival and departure lane with its double doors opened, showing Edgardo in the driver seat.

And aside it—dressed again in their best clothes from the social mixer night—the team waited lined abreast and at attention.

She approached them with a grin. "At ease, gentlemen, Team Leader Molka has been relieved. Regular old Molka just wants to say goodbye."

They stood at ease and smiled.

She moved to the first man on the line's far left side: Shizi. "Goodbye, marine."

He said, "Aye, ma'am. Goodbye."

"Thanks for being steady as a rock."

He grinned and held out his hands, palms down and rock steady. "Thanks for believing in me, Molka."

She moved right to the next man in line: Nathan. "Goodbye, Nathan. Thanks for an amazing job."

He offered an excited face. "So, the op is over. Now you can dish details on your super-cryptic Raziela story."

She nodded. "Tell you what. I'll be home tomorrow night. Message me Saturday, and we'll do lunch, and I'll dish it all to you."

He hugged her. "That's a date, girlfriend."

She moved to the next man: Jager. "Goodbye and thanks for everything, Reinhold. It's ok if I call you Reinhold now?"

He smiled. "I wish you would call me Reinhold always." His smile faded, and he reached into his right front pocket and took out the coin the colonel gave him. "This obviously meant a lot to him. He gave it to me not for good luck last night but because he knew he was never leaving there and didn't want it to fall into the enemy's hands. At that moment, he was sure I would get out but not you. Since you did, I think he would want you to have it. I know you two had a respectful bond from previous service."

She took the coin and put it in her right front pocket. "Thanks. And yes, we did."

She moved to the next two men in line: Luc and Savanna. "I'm saying goodbye to you two together because I have the feeling you'll be spending more time together after you leave here."

TASK X

Luc smiled. "Amusing you should say that, Molka. I just told LJ I wanted to host a weekend gala party in his honor at my villa in Monaco. To which he replied...."

Savanna said, "To which I replied to Luc, I was just about to tell him I wanted to host a gala party in his honor on one of my mega yachts all weekend in Monaco Harbor."

Luc said, "So we agreed to host simultaneous gala parties honoring each other at my villa and on his mega yacht all weekend."

A sly smile creased Molka's lips, and she put a hand on each man's shoulder. "And so was born a beautiful, if not decadent and legally ambivalent, friendship."

Both men laughed.

She concluded with an earnest face. "Goodbye. And thank you, charming sweeties, for your crucial help when I needed it most."

They both gave humble nods.

Molka moved to the next man: Warren. "Thanks for being outstanding at everything, my handsome XO." She grinned again. "And tell the *kelba* the *ketzelah* says hello, and I'm ready to finish that fight as soon as she drops the baby weight."

He said, "I was waiting until the op was over to tell you this. Nadia and I know the baby's sex. We're having a girl. And we've decided to name her Janetta."

Molka's eyes reddened, and she hugged him around the neck and whispered in his ear. "Thank you, and thank Nadia for me. That's so nice. I'm so humbly grateful."

She wiped her eyes and moved to the last man in line: Kang.

Before she could speak, he said, "I won't say goodbye to you, Molka. I'll just say I'll see you later."

She flashed him a coy face. "What do you mean by—"

Her query was halted by fourteen white with blue stripes police SUVs speeding up the resort's entrance drive with their blue and red lightbars flashing. Red markings on their doors identified them as National Philippine Police.

Molka addressed the team. "They're early. They're here for the colonel. This might get a little bumpy. But we're not obligated to tell them anything. And we won't."

The team echoed in agreement.

The first two police vehicles blocked the shuttle bus front and rear, and the others spread out in the front parking area and stopped.

Instantly, all their doors opened, and at least 40 officers in green and brown camo uniforms, carrying AR-15s, and wearing ballistic helmets and vests, poured out and rushed toward the team with aimed weapons.

The team remained unflinching.

The commanding officer arrived before them and yelled in Filipino-accented English:

"Don't move!"

"Hands atop your heads!"

"Bus driver, get out and put your hands atop your head!"

Molka, the team, and the poor, terrified bus driver complied.

Individual officers then patted each of them down and confiscated Molka's Beretta.

The other officers formed three separate assault-style teams.

The commander stepped closer, scrutinized every face, and addressed the detainees. "I'm Major Quezon, National Philippine Police Special Action Force. We have an international arrest warrant for the fugitive war criminal, Krasnov. Where is he?"

Molka spoke up in anger. "COLONEL Nikolai Vasilyevich Krasnov was never convicted of any war crime, and the legitimacy of the court who issued that warrant is dubious at best."

The major addressed her in firm seriousness. "Nevertheless, it is quite legal. So, you won't mind if we look inside the bus?"

"I do mind. But out of respect for your country, I won't protest."

"My question was rhetorical." The major ordered six of his men to board the bus.

While they searched, Molka noticed a man standing beside the police SUV parked farthest away.

He featured a grayish suit, grayish hair, and a face with a grayish pallor skulking behind dark glasses.

A moment later, the six officers stepped off the bus carrying the team's luggage, laid it on the cement, opened the cases, and started to search through them.

263

TASK X

Molka smirked at the major. "Really, major? I know the colonel is considered an expert in camouflage but isn't that a little extreme?"

He addressed the detainees again. "Where is Krasnov?"

No one spoke.

He repeated. "Where is Krasnov?"

Molka answered. "He's not here and none of us know where he's currently at, and that's the honest truth."

The major continued. "We are going to thoroughly search this entire property. More officers are coming, and the K-9s too."

Molka shrugged. "Go for it. Oh, just ignore the illegal black-market weapons on the dock. They were only leased. The illegal black-market weapons dealer is coming to pick them up in a little while."

The major ignored her snark. "All of you will be coming with us back to Puerto Princesa to be extensively questioned. Expect this to take the rest of the day and perhaps all night."

Molka's anger reappeared, and intensified. "Major, this is outrageous. These men have international flights to catch this afternoon and evening and—" Her eyes flipped to the grayish man across the parking area. "Never mind, sir. I apologize. I know you're only under orders to harass us. And I know who is really in charge here who gave those orders."

She lowered her hands and strode toward the grayish man.

No one moved to stop her.

As she approached the grayish man, his body stiffened.

Fear?

Defiance?

Loathing?

All three?

She stopped a step away from him and said, "Colonel Krasnov was a guest here at my invitation. The rest of these men had nothing to do with that. You have questions about that, you question me. I'm—"

The grayish man interrupted in English with an odd Dutch, French, and German blended-type accent. "They know who you are, Molka. And they disapprove of your actions here. And they will not soon forget what you have done."

She flashed an annoyed face. "Who's they?"

"They are the world authority."

"The world authority." She smirked. "There's that omnipresent, ambiguous new term again." She folded her arms across her chest. "I've wanted to talk to the world authority for a long time to tell them they're doing an absolutely horrific job. Because from what I've witnessed, for their part, they make good people into bad people and bad people into heroes."

The grayish man responded with an entitled smugness. "While, for your part, you have prioritized the trivial personal matter of your insignificant little sister over the primacies of the world authority. And who are you to dare challenge them?"

"Who am I?" In a second's fraction, Molka spun a ferocious roundhouse kick into his left temple.

His dark glasses flew from his face

And he collapsed hard and unconscious.

She stood over him and glared down. "That's who I am. And you tell the *world authority* I haven't even begun to challenge them."

**SATURDAY
AUGUST 6TH**

CHAPTER 59

**Tel Aviv Cemetery
8:06 AM**

Molka knelt before her little sister Janetta's grave in a long, black mourning dress, wearing a small black crossbody purse and her hair down.

She had just finished telling Janetta what happened on Base X and tried not to rub her contact lenses while wiping tears as she struggled with the right final thoughts and words to go with them.

Her dilemma was deterred by her attention being diverted to a new model, black Mercedes-Benz sedan arriving in the deserted—except for her car—cemetery parking lot about 20 meters behind her.

The driver's door opened, and a tall, mid-30s Asian male exited and strode with ultra-assertiveness toward her.

He styled a tailored black suit, white shirt, thin black tie, and high-shined black leather shoes and sported a fresh haircut styled hip in a sleek side-parted pompadour with devilishly pointed sideburns.

Black wraparound sunglasses completed his coolness.

Molka stood and faced the arriving Kang.

"Hello, Molka," he said. "I told you I would see you later."

"How did you know I would be here?" She smirked. "Azzur, of course."

"He knows you very well."

She wiped away a lingering tear. "Too very well. I'm sorry again about that 12-hour detainment I got for all of us in Puerto Princesa after I kicked that bureaucratic bastard in the face. Before that, I believe the National Philippine Police were about to let us leave. They knew we would never tell them anything about the colonel."

"No apologies necessary," he said. "I've wanted to kick the bureaucratic bastards in the face my whole life. I understand he didn't want to press charges, though."

"He just didn't want his name divulged publicly. But I'm sure he and his *world authority* friends aren't done with me yet. And you called it correct, not a word officially or unofficially from China about our visit to Base X."

"As far as they're concerned," Kang said, "nothing out of the ordinary happened there that night, officially or unofficially. And that's exactly the way they hope it stays forever." He took off his sunglasses and viewed Janetta's headstone with respect. "But did you tell her yet what really happened?"

"Tell her what really happened? What do you mean?"

"That you didn't kill Ramirez."

Molka flashed him a suspicious glance. "What makes you think I didn't?"

"It's my theory."

"Based on?"

He said, "Before you got to the compound, Jager told us the condition the target was in. We all went and looked at him. Macabre curiosity, I suppose. And when you came and faced him. Ramirez probably told you he wanted to die and begged you to put him out of his misery."

"But you didn't. And not because you thought leaving him to live all carved up like that was even worse than death. It was because you have a sense of proportion and decency deeply embedded within your core that you can't fight, and must adhere to, no matter the circumstance."

She offered a slight, respectful nod. "That's quite a theory you have there. Some people would be very upset at me if that were true because of what they went through."

He shook his head. "Don't worry. I didn't share this theory with the rest of the team. And I never will."

Molka's eyes drifted off to an unfocused point in the distance. "Well, whatever happened in that office between him and me that night, you were definitely right about that too. It wouldn't be enough. And it can never be enough. Now I wonder if it's possible to ever learn to live with it?"

"I don't know, Molka. I'm still on that same journey. If you find out before I do, please let me know."

"Alright." Her eyes refocused on him, confused. "Why are you dressed so sharp and what are you doing here, anyway?"

He presented a playboy smile. "If you haven't noticed yet, I always dress sharp. And I came to take you to lunch in a nice restaurant at the airport. We have some important matters to discuss."

"I'd actually love that. But in an hour, I have a meeting with Azzur. Time for me to get back to work."

He put his sunglasses back on. "That meeting has been canceled."

"Ha. Azzur tell you that, too? You can't believe *everything* he says, you know?"

"Check your secured messages."

She removed her phone from her purse, logged into her secure messages, confirmed Kang's claim, and offered him a quizzical face. "I don't understand that. He's been pushing me to meet since the minute I got home. I still owe him one more high-priority task."

He nodded. "Your task to take care of the Raziela problem. But now the Raziela problem has also become a Pentad problem, and you've been assigned to Pentad to help take care of it."

"Have I?" she said.

"Yes, and we're going after her together."

"Are we?"

"We are," he said.

"Starting when?"

"Right now."

TASK X

"Starting where?" she said.

"First stop, Paris."

"After I say goodbye here, of course."

"Of course," he said. "And fair warning."

"About what?"

"This is an extremely dangerous mission."

"How extremely dangerous of a mission?" she said.

"The most dangerous one I've ever been assigned."

"Really?"

"Maybe the most dangerous one you've been assigned too."

"That's saying something," she said, blowing out a breath.

"Raziela's crazy-formidable to go up against."

"I agree. And just plain crazy too."

"The oddsmakers at Pentad only give us one chance in a hundred," he said.

"Which means it's more like one chance in a thousand."

"Yes, but that's not the odds of mission success."

"What is it odds of?" she said.

"Us just not getting killed on the first day."

"And today is the first day."

"Yes. And then there's this too." He removed his phone from his front pocket and pulled up a video. "This came into Pentad headquarters earlier this morning."

He started the video, and an attractive woman's smooth-skinned, high cheek-boned, large oval blue-eyed, under-side-parted, shoulder-length brown hair face appeared on screen: Raziela.

She spoke. "Good morning, Pentad. It's come to my attention you have so much faith in your very best man to come find and kill me you felt you had to get him some help. What's that tell you about the futility of your threats and schemes?"

"I know Kang and Molka will also see this, so…."

"Kang, your short but promising career with Pentad is about to come to an abrupt, brutal, final end. But before it does, you'll be on your knees begging my people to turn you over to the GBR for a more merciful death. They won't."

"And to my old project, Molka. After passing my little test in Arizona, you're probably feeling really good about yourself and less terrified of coming after me. How wonderful for you."

"But despite that; notwithstanding, and all the same, you'd never find me unless I allow you to. And after I have Kang killed and make you search maddeningly and suffer incredibly, I may allow you to find me. And then you WILL die." Raziela fabricated a cheery smile. "Oh, by the way, Alberto Ramirez is a personal friend of mine. Now, come and get me. I'm waiting."

The video ended.

Kang re-pocketed his phone. "Well, according to Raziela, the oddsmakers called it right. We're on a hopeless suicide mission." He presented another playboy smile. "Ready to go get killed with me?"

Molka's eyes blazed with a fearsome determination. "Nothing is decided until it's decided."

What Happened Next? Keep Reading!

FREDRICK L. STAFFORD

RAZIELA'S REVENGE

A PENTAD NOVEL
FEATURING PROJECT MOLKA

Available on Amazon!

Printed in Great Britain
by Amazon